Critical Daze

By

Spencer J. Quinn

Books by Spencer J. Quinn

White Like You (2017)
Charity's Blade (2020)
My Mirror Tells a Story (2020)
Solzhenitsyn and the Right (2021)
The No College Club (2022)

Critical Daze

The No College Club, Book 2

by

Spencer J. Quinn

Counter-Currents Publishing
San Francisco
2024

Editing: John Morgan
Proofing and layout: Greg Johnson
Cover image: Bonnie Whiteside
Cover design by Kevin Slaughter

Published in the United States by
Counter-Currents Publishing, Ltd.
www.counter-currents.com

Hardcover ISBN: 978-1-64264-050-2
Paperback ISBN: 978-1-64264-051-9
Ebook ISBN: 978-1-64264-052-6

Thanks to John Morgan, Richard Houck, James O'Meara, Gaddius Maximus, Sam Dickson, Nullus Abnormocracy, & Donald Kent.

Part 1

Chapter 1

Will Askew remembered the last time he tried an extracurricular activity. It was the soccer team in eighth grade. While chasing a ball during practice, he whiffed on a kick so hard he went reeling toward the sideline in the direction of a diminutive teammate named JD Craiglow. JD hadn't seen him coming. Being a particularly huge eighth grader at five feet, ten inches tall and nearly 200 pounds, Will did not want to crash into the poor kid, whom he more than doubled in weight. As he felt himself losing his footing, he saw that his only other option was to spin away from JD and land awkwardly on his right ankle.

Any other kid would have instinctively rolled his body as he hit the ground. But not Will. No one could have ever mistaken "the Willrus"—as he was known back then—for being nimble. His ankle snapped under his considerable weight—crack!—and the rest of him flopped gracelessly against Planet Earth as flopping bodies always do.

Moments later, he wondered why his coaches were insisting he stay down until the paramedics arrived. He had heard the crack—he was sure *everyone* had heard the crack—but the pain was strangely tolerable. It didn't tickle, but he seemed *insulated* from it somehow. At first he thought it was only a sprain and asked for another try at the soccer ball. But then he sat up and saw the break. He was the last person on the field to realize what had happened.

***

It was a warm and hazy Saturday afternoon in August four years later when Will went down to the nearby state university to attend the first Critical Theory Club meeting of the semester. He didn't need to arrive on time. He barely even knew what critical theory was, and so making the effort to arrive on time—or even arrive at all—would have been highly unusual for him. Unsurprisingly, he arrived late. As it turned out, so did everyone else.

Because high schoolers from the entire region had been invited, the Bernice Lefkowitz Memorial Auditorium was chosen for its central location, even though the building which housed it was still under construction. The running joke at the time was that the state's federally funded university was always under construction—or *de*-construction, as some of the older teachers at school would darkly mutter. Outside the building, orange flagging tape, safety cones, and piles of bricks were everywhere, as well as construction machinery, which Will recognized but could not name. The place was already hilly, and with uneven ground everywhere, the construction site made it seem even hillier.

He descended into a paved, semicircular plaza filled with metal tables and benches. On the left side, beyond a short flight of steps, was the auditorium entrance. With its top-heavy roof and sharp angles worked into its architecture, the building seemed designed to call attention to itself. It reminded Will of something vaguely unpleasant, but he couldn't figure out what it was.

With his senior year having just begun, he figured the Critical Theory Club would be his best opportunity to get to know Connie Craft. She had occupied his mind for years now, and that summer he had resolved to finally do something about it. Fortune favors the bold, and all that— even though he knew his chances with her were less than meager. Last May he had overheard Connie in the lunchroom talking about joining the Critical Theory Club. That's what did it for him, and nothing else.

Connie Craft was just his type: tall, smart, and pretty. She had wavy black hair, transparent blue eyes, a slender nose, and a mouth which became a defiant pout whenever she smiled. Heavyset, but not too heavyset. Like him. Almost. Will had hardly spoken a word to her in over a year, not since that dreadful week as sophomores when they had been lab partners in biology class. He had asked her out on a date while they were dissecting a frog. Twice. She ignored him both times. He was still kicking himself over that. The embarrassment hurt more than his ankle ever did. But at least she hadn't said no. This kept a glimmer of hope alive in him ever since.

Something seemed enticingly *off* about her as well. She was never quite as popular as Will thought she should have been. Every once in a while, he found her walking alone in school—or even *eating* alone. He never understood why. Why *wouldn't* such a pretty and interesting girl have friends surrounding her at all times?

Of course, he knew something was off about himself as well. Very off. He had a weight problem. He wasn't terribly popular and had few interests aside from video games and comic books. He didn't distinguish himself academically, or in anything, really. He couldn't even kick a soccer ball. So if Connie was even a tiny bit as flawed as he was, who could blame him for nurturing hope?

He was the first to arrive. Had the meeting time been changed? Was he going to be the only one there? Looking around the auditorium, he wondered why they hadn't selected some place smaller. Surely, no more than 20 people were going to show—at least according to the club's online roster. They weren't going to need dozens of rows. They weren't going to need the stage, podium, or giant-sized movie screen behind it. They certainly weren't going to need the large projection booth jutting out over the back seats like an awning.

He took a seat six rows from the stage and tried to relax. Could he enjoy this then? Could he simply let his mind wander as he usually did during class? Unlikely. Connie would be there soon. His mind was hopping on hot coals considering all the possibilities.

He chuckled, reminding himself that this meeting was completely beside the point for him. *Who cares about critical theory?* He understood it had something to do with white people being nice to other races—which he guessed was fair, given all the history he'd learned in school. Television, movies, comics, and the internet all told the same story, so he never really questioned it. He'd also been getting doses of it from his father Andrew for as long as he could remember. Andrew would use the terms "anti-racism," "political correctness," and "social justice" almost interchangeably. It was strange because he seemed to imply that these were things Will *didn't* already believe in, and that if he turned his back on his son even for one minute, racism would start spilling out of him like tar from a pit. It felt almost like *scolding*. Critical theory seemed only to formalize it somehow.

Will's biggest problem with critical theory, however, was not that it was wrong, but that it was *boring*. So were the people who talked about it all the time—including his father. He already knew how to be a good person: obey the law, be honest and respectful, be kind to your family and friends, and help people in need. What else was there? He never understood how grownups could teach whole courses and write whole books and talk *incessantly* about things he had known by heart since he was eight.

The door opened with a dull thud. He felt his chest expand as he both anticipated and dreaded her entrance. One of the advantages of being so big was that it was hard for him to appear startled. He simply could not move his body quickly enough to register alarm like a normal person. This made him seem cool and unflappable, and was probably the source of whatever middling popularity he could scrape together at school. But as he turned and saw Connie sitting down two rows and seven seats away from him all alone, he was feeling quite flappable indeed.

Failing to make eye contact with her, Will asked and

then *demanded* of himself all the reasons why he shouldn't start a conversation with this girl. Wasn't this their senior year? Wasn't she most likely going to some elite East Coast university after graduating? Would he ever even see her again after that?

He watched her out of the corner of his eye as she crossed her legs and tapped rapidly into her cellphone. Her hair was tied in a fuzzy, disheveled bun, and silver earrings dangled alongside her face. She wore a short-sleeved, one-piece yellow dress with a striped collar. The pleats of her skirt creased along her thighs and exposed her knees just above a pair of tall leather boots.

Will noticed how mature Connie's taste in clothing had become since he'd last seen her. She reminded him of his mother Melissa, who also had a passion for fashion, which Will always admired. Connie obviously had not come here to be ignored. So why should he? Following a hunch, he entered "critical theory" into a search engine on his cellphone and then clicked the local news links until he found what he was looking for.

"So, did you go to that protest last week?" he asked, still scrolling through an article.

Connie stopped tapping on her phone and looked up. "What?"

"You know, where they were protesting the critical theory ban over in Covington."

"Oh, that!" she said, brightening. "No. I didn't go. I heard about it though."

"About a hundred students walked out of class and showed up at a school board meeting with signs and megaphones."

"Wow! I heard the high school voted to ban it. People were very upset."

"Yeah," Will said, now having read most of the article and hoping to impress her. "The people banning it are on some political action committee with some wealthy donors. They're part of a big church, too."

"No way!" she exclaimed, now giving him her full attention. "What happened at the protest?"

Will was stunned. A rapt audience from Connie was the last thing he had expected. Not stammering was proving difficult since eye contact with her was preventing him from consulting his phone.

"Uhh . . ." he began, forcing himself to remember the story. "The school's black student union was there. Latino and Asian groups too. A couple teachers joined in. Their signs said 'Protect our education' and 'History is supposed to be uncomfortable.' They talked about slavery and segregation and white supremacy and—"

"Ohmigod," Connie muttered as she uncrossed her legs and dropped her phone into her backpack. She was still zipping it shut as she sidled past seats to get closer to Will. She plopped down next to him and leaned in so close she nearly poked into his personal space— something a girl had never done before. Will could not speak for the excitement.

"Tell me more! Tell me more!" she urged, eyes flashing with anticipation. Will noticed excessive makeup caking her already-pretty face.

He was about to dredge up whatever else he could remember from the story when he felt her hand slide softly onto his forearm. He knew it was an innocent gesture; there was nothing suggestive about it. But what it *did* suggest beyond a doubt was that Connie Craft did not consider the Willrus to be an untouchable leper. This, for him, was a triumph. He suddenly worried that she might notice the goosebumps which were popping up on his skin like pimples.

Then she said something which would change his life forever: "Were you there?"

Will's mouth fell open. He blinked until her face became a fluttering blur. Was she a real person anymore?

Was any of this even happening? How could he possibly answer her question? Covington was over an hour away. He wouldn't have gone to that event even if he were interested in critical theory.

To lie would be wrong, he knew. Deliberately deceiving people went against his nature and everything he had been taught since childhood. But he also knew that by lying and saying he *had* attended that protest, he would keep this girl's hand on his arm. *This* he desperately wanted. A girl had never touched him on the arm like that before, and it made him feel lighter by a hundred pounds. For the first time in his life he could imagine what it felt like to be normal and complete.

He stopped blinking and understood sadly that these wonderful feelings would be destroyed only by the truth.

He said nothing. All he could do was helplessly prolong this exquisite moment and pray that it never end. Was he indeed lying? Was he deceiving her with his silence? He didn't have time to explore such thorny questions because as soon as he raised them in his mind, the doors flung open and the auditorium began filling with people.

The Critical Theory Club meeting was about to begin.

Chapter 2

Nearly 40 people entered the auditorium, almost at once. Only after Connie pulled her hand away did Will register his surprise. She leapt up to join her friends who were filling the second row. She didn't once look back, despite having whispered "bye-bye" before darting off. Did she feel he was actually *worth* saying good-bye to, or was she merely being polite? Befuddled, he could only enjoy the memory of Connie Craft actually having been *close* enough to him to whisper anything.

He shifted in his seat, afraid the meeting was going to be a long one. The faculty liaison to the Critical Theory Club was Madeline Johnston, a short, slender, middle-aged woman with blonde hair streaked with gray and dark-rimmed glasses which seemed wider than her face. Not the worst teacher Will ever had. She'd given him a B-minus in his freshman world history class, which even he felt was a bit generous. She was approachable and perfectly nice, but *dull*—a bit condescending as well.

Will got as comfortable as he could and zoned out while Miss Johnston kicked off the meeting. She welcomed new members and discussed previous meetings, summer events, book recommendations, and an upcoming statewide scholarship competition. Entrants had to submit material about critical theory in one of three categories—essay, art, or video—by the first Saturday in December. Finalists would present their material two weeks later in the very auditorium in which they were sitting. Winners in each category would be announced in January and awarded a $10,000 university scholarship. This produced an excited murmur among the students.

Will cared about none of this, of course. He had grades and test scores decent enough to get into State, and his parents had the money to send him there. He had never planned for anything beyond that. As for Connie, he had broken the ice with her, which had been his goal all along. Moving forward, he could ditch Critical Theory and chat her up in the halls the next time he saw her. If she liked him it wouldn't matter if he joined this stupid club or not.

Miss Johnston then yielded the stage to a female student Will had never seen before. He quickly realized, however, that she wasn't a student—at least not a *high school* student. She was too confident, too well-dressed. Her nose was too long and her skin too splotchy for her to be pretty in a traditional sense. Yet she was oddly attractive. She was shapely and fit, and her brown hair fell in pleasing waves over both shoulders. Her smile showed just the right amount of teeth despite her strong jaw. She also wore a dress similar to Connie's, yet somehow more elegant, Will thought. Was Connie *copying* this woman? Most striking were her dark brown eyes, which had a near-religious quality as they flashed about while she spoke. Will had to resist the urge to be mesmerized. Her name was Nadine Alterman and she was a Cultural Studies doctoral student at State. She would be teaching a critical theory class at his high school that semester. Her voice was almost as deep as a man's.

"As a white person," she began, "critical theory has been my path to enlightenment. I'm glad to see so many people here since critical theory is leading the way forward to social change and a better future. We must recognize that racism is everywhere. We benefit from institutionalized white supremacy whether we realize it or not. This was how it was during slavery and segregation, just as it is today with subtler, more deceitful forms of racism. This is why all forms of white identity are toxic. White identity oppresses people of color, especially African Americans.

"This is why we have to abandon outdated notions such as colorblindness and meritocracy. These are loopholes that allow white identity to flourish. Whenever a

conservative claims he is not racist because he treats everyone the same or evaluates people on merit, *don't believe
him*. He is simply perpetuating the racial inequality which
led to centuries of torture, rape, and slavery. Remember,
we bring our histories with us wherever we go.

"Now, white supremacists might find this racist—racist
against whites, if you can imagine such a thing. But that's
the irony! To call critical theory racist *is in itself racist!*"

At this, Will's eyes began to glaze. The infinite loops of
logic this Alterman woman was leading him down quickly
exhausted him. There was nothing in her speech he could
grab on to, nothing anchoring it to reality which could
serve as a starting point for an argument apart from the
cliché that whites should be nice to other races. From
what he could tell as a fairly astute consumer of media,
whites were doing a pretty good job of that already—that
is, whenever he still found white people in the media at
all.

Having lost interest in Nadine Alterman, Will put his
phone on mute and logged into a martial arts video game
he'd been playing a lot recently. This one involved com-
batants with breathtaking gymnastic ability delivering po-
tent strikes against each other in a dystopic urban environment. His fat fingers made the fighting difficult, but he
managed to get up from a couple knockdowns and score
one of his own with a right high kick to his opponent's
head. Will laughed to himself, imagining ever trying a kick
like that in real life. The soccer ball incident sprang to
mind.

He perked up. From the audience reaction, he surmised that Nadine Alterman had just told a joke.

"See what I did just now?" she said, her hand on her
chest. "This is subconscious racism in action! *My* subconscious racism, which I have to be on guard against at all
times! Don't laugh!" Nadine was moving about the stage
and engaging the mostly female audience. They followed

her every word with open mouths, as if hungry for more. She stopped and clapped her hands once. "What did I just do?" she asked. Will felt the tension in the room rise and then release once the group realized the question had been rhetorical. "When I said that we need to abandon our racial identity, I was assuming in my white conformist mind that everyone here is white. We must overcome this mindset! Centuries of white normativity have made most whites oblivious to the very *existence* of people of color, to say nothing of the burden of racism we force them to carry!"

A collective "ooh" came from the audience. Nadine smiled her pretty smile and slowly nodded. "That's right. And speaking of persons of color, we have one here."

Will recoiled. He scanned the room and saw only white students. Like most American high schools, his was racially diverse—almost to the point of whites being a clear minority. But not so in the Critical Theory Club. Here it was as if decades of immigration and integration had never happened. Where was this person of color?

"Connie?" Nadine said, holding out her hand to her. Connie stood and waved to everyone in the room, beaming like a celebrity. Over half the audience applauded, which puzzled Will. Why *applaud* someone just because she's not white?

"Connie, I was impressed when Miss Johnston told me about you and your Native American heritage," Nadine continued. "I would like to say how welcome you are and how glad we are that you've joined us today! Would you like to tell us about yourself?" More applause from the crowd seconded this sentiment, but Will was too perplexed to join them. Connie had moved to town from Vermont over five years ago. This was the first he had heard of her being Native American.

Connie grinned self-consciously and cleared her throat. "Yes! Thank you!" she began, recognizing the audience but then focusing mostly on Nadine. Her cheeks were turning pink, and her speech, Will noted, was much choppier than usual.

"I'm Connie Craft. Uh, my father was a pureblood Choctaw Native American who my mother met during a Columbus Day protest in Denver, like, 20 years ago." She cleared her throat again. "I usually don't like to talk about my, uh, heritage because of social pressures and stuff. But this past summer, my mom and I decided it was time to, you know, stand up for who we are."

More applause, led ostentatiously by Nadine.

"So, anyways, I'm glad there's such a great turnout," Connie continued, now gazing into the audience. She did a double-take on Will. "I think critical theory is crucial for the development of young citizens. As a person of color I know how important it is to be compassionate about, uh, racial minorities. History, as Professor Alterman said, is always with us. And history is not supposed to be comfortable." She then adopted a more confident tone and began wagging her finger. "History is supposed to be *un*comfortable! Just last week, students were saying this at a protest in Covington where the high school voted to ban critical theory!"

A loud gasp from the crowd. Students whispered vicious things to each other as Nadine folded her arms and nodded righteously. Connie then looked expectantly, almost mischievously, at Will. He did *not* like that look in her eyes. "And we have somebody here today who was, like, actually there and saw the whole thing!" she announced. Will's stomach began to tighten as he anticipated what she was about to say. Still, he clung to a stubborn disbelief that any of this was really happening. How could it be? A moment earlier he had been in his cozy seat playing video games and reflecting on his successful conversation with Connie Craft. And now—

"Will!" she called. "Everyone, this is Will Askew!" All

heads turned to him. She stretched her arm out to him like an invitation. "Can you tell us about what happened at Covington High School, Will?"

With blood rushing into his cheeks, Will squirmed so much on the inside that he suspected even his big frame couldn't hide it. He felt his heart race and his fingers tingle and his lungs struggle under the weight of his thick torso—a feeling he always hated. Sweat began to leak beneath his arms, making body odor something else he had to worry about. With so many faces fixed on him like spotlights, he eyed the door covetously, but knew that the auditorium's tightly-packed rows would make a smooth getaway impossible. He felt his phone in his hand, on mute and with the game still playing. It could be of no help to him now. All he could do was tell the truth. "Ah, well, um, no," he stammered. "I'm sorry. Uh—"

"Oh! I thought you said—"

"No, I didn't—I didn't go," Will blurted, clearing his throat. "I didn't go to the protest! I just—I just found that article on my phone so I could impress you . . . with my knowledge."

Tittering from the audience told him that he had just committed a grotesque social blunder. Embarrassment flooded into his mind like sewage. Impress her? With his knowledge? What knowledge? How to make a complete fool of himself? Was he back in biology class all of a sudden, having the nerve to ask a girl like Connie out? Twice? Way to go, *Willrus*.

Sounds from his video game made him jump in his seat. Aghast, he realized that one of his fat fingers must have inadvertently slid over his phone's volume button and unmuted it, sending grunts, screams, and action movie music crashing through the auditorium. The shock caused him to nearly fumble his phone. For a frantic moment, he was reduced to trying to catch his bobbling device with both hands. With what was left of his dignity at stake—and with everyone in the room now laughing at him—Will suddenly grew angry and determined. He had *not* come here for this. His embarrassment was going to end now.

His phone was proving difficult to catch since it was thin and smooth and lacked a case. But after a few bounces he tapped it into the air above his head like a volleyball. This gave him time to anticipate where it was going to fall. He reached out and caught it with one hand.

Hoping that this little victory would cancel out the string of defeats which had preceded it, Will fell back into his seat, relieved. He knew it wouldn't, but enjoyed the moment regardless. Then he realized that his video game was still blasting sounds of hand-to-hand combat throughout the room.

***

The meeting dragged on another half hour, during which Will wished he could tuck his head into his chest like a turtle. After it ended, he walked outside and held out his arms to allow the warm breeze to engulf his body through his shirtsleeves. He stood there for a few moments as all the others walked past him, paying him no mind as usual. It helped not think about what had just happened. Instead, he was looking forward to stopping at a fast-food restaurant and defying his diet once again. Before he reached his car, however, he heard Connie calling his name.

He turned to the right as she was passing him on his left. He laughed as he spun around to finally see her. She was breathing heavily, and touched his shoulder as she composed herself. "I'm so sorry I put you on the spot, Will!" she said. "I made a mistake! I thought you said you went to that protest, but then I remembered that you never said that, so—"

"It's okay," Will said, not letting her hand on his shoulder make him any happier than he deserved to be. "It was the most exciting part of the meeting, anyway."

She stood to her full height—about five feet, nine inches, to Will's six feet, three—and took her hand off his shoulder. Her wispy bangs were falling over one eye and not the other. "Anyways, I'm happy you're in the Critical Theory Club. Will I see you at the next meeting?"

Will smiled and wished he had the strength to say what he really felt. "Sure," he said.

"Good! I'm hoping we can both enter that scholarship competition. It'll look good on our resumés even if we don't win. Maybe we could help each other with our essays. Would that be okay?"

He tensed up trying to navigate the twists and turns of this bewildering proposition. While he was keen on never hearing another word about critical theory, he was even keener on going out with Connie Craft. Between the two options there really was no comparison. He shrugged and smiled and said what he dearly hoped would be the magic word: "Okay."

She smiled back and was about to respond when she peered past him and put her hand to her mouth to stifle a squeak of excitement. "It's Pete! My boyfriend!" she said. "I'm supposed to meet him!" She then dashed off. She stopped, however, and rushed back to give Will a tight hug. "Thank you," she whispered, before running off once again.

As he watched Connie leap into the arms of Peter Dorr, the star quarterback for the high school football team and one of the most popular kids in school, Will felt her lingering warmth on his shirt and mourned what he feared would never be his.

Chapter 3

The thick, pulpy pages stained his fingers. The colors were faded, and the spaces around the panels had been yellowed with time. "Everything is so *hand-drawn,*" Will said as he leafed through the old comic book. He hovered over the advertisements and limited offers and fan letters and mail order forms, and wondered how all of this at one time could have been *normal.* Smooth, sonorous murmurs reverberated from his mother Melissa's music room upstairs, where she was giving a cello lesson to one of her elementary school students. Nearly drowning it out was the thumping and scraping coming from the kitchen directly above, where Will's father Andrew was making dinner.

Will returned to his comic and was transfixed by its majesty—the muscles on the men, the shapeliness of the women. Beneath the masks were either square jaws or pretty faces, and the stories were all action and intrigue compared to digitally-rendered modern comics, with their puzzling preoccupations with homosexuality, racial diversity, and political messaging. And so many of the characters were white. It all seemed so *innocent.*

"Dude, these are awesome!" JD exclaimed as he dropped one comic and reached for another from the jumbled pile on the floor of Will's basement bedroom. "I didn't know your dad was into comics!"

"I didn't either," Will said. "He saw me reading some last week and pulled his collection out of storage. These are, like, 50 years old!"

JD Craiglow sat comfortably on the floor with his back against Will's bookshelf, expressing profane approval as he flipped through his comic. He wore ratty jeans and a T-shirt promoting an obscure music group Will had never heard of. Long brown hair fell over insolent eyes and a thin, scruffy, acne-scarred face. "And much better than the stuff you read," he declared as he tossed his book back onto the pile and stretched out his legs.

"Ya think?"

"Sure! Comics these days stink. I'm an artist, so I can say."

"You're an artist," Will repeated skeptically.

"Well, video artist."

"How come you never let me see any of your videos?"

"Because they're not ready yet. I'm still getting better."

"I'll bet."

"Dude, when I get out of college, I'm going to be an independent filmmaker," JD insisted. "I got, like, a million ideas, and no way any of 'em are mainstream."

Will sighed and hoped JD would get tired of the subject.

"Anyway, how hard could it be?" JD went on obliviously. "Movies are so bad these days *anything* that's any good is bound to sell. And comics are worse. Comics today are anti-American, anti-male, anti-everything! It used to be about fighting bad guys with explosions and cool tech and origin stories. Now they're all psychoanalyzing about gay stuff or white privilege or whatever. They're actually making the bad guys look good!"

Seated at his desk, and secretly envying his small, slender friend for being able to lie on the floor so easily, Will narrowed his eyes. "It's not as bad as all that."

JD slapped his knees. "Come on. Every other new hero these days is black. And if he's an old hero, they replace him with a black."

"Okay, I admit that's pretty bad. But the rest? You make it seem like it's a conspiracy or something."

"It is!"

"You sure?"

"Dude! I'm always sure." JD grabbed a comic from the pile and waved it at Will. "It ain't like it used to be! And it's not like I have anything against black people. I'm not racist or anything."

"I know you're not."

"But why focus on them? It can't be by accident. There has to be a political purpose behind it. Especially when both major comic companies are doing it."

"Maybe they just wanna sell comics?"

"Well, they're not doing a very good job of that, are they?"

Will was growing tired of the conversation. He liked JD and appreciated his candor. He also felt a little sorry for him since he was so roundly disliked at school. Will was probably the only friend JD ever had. But JD was loud and he couldn't take hints. He also relished clamping down on topics like a bulldog. Everything always ended up being a debate with him. Will was fishing around for something else to talk about, when JD broached the subject he was hoping he wouldn't.

"I think Connie Craft is making you soft in the head with all this critical theory stuff," he taunted.

Will couldn't tell if he was being playful or not. "Stop it."

"She totally is! Is she the reason why you're into all that racial stuff in comics these days? Are you trying to show off how *woke* you are?"

Will turned, preferring to look at his bedroom wall rather than his friend. He knew JD wasn't finished. JD was *never* finished.

"*Oh, Will! Can you write my essay for me?*" JD drawled, fanning himself with his comic like a Southern belle. "*Meanwhile, I'll do some 'research' in the library with Pete Dorr. Maybe when we come up for air I'll give you a peck on the cheek. And then we can be friends!*"

Will rolled his eyes. "Look, we're just helping each other out."

"I'm sure."

"Hey, at least I'm getting *some* female attention. Unlike you!"

"Whatever," JD scoffed unpleasantly as he glanced at his comic book. "What are you writing about, anyway?"

Will pursed his lips in thought. "For the scholarship competition? Not sure. Connie said she wants to focus on historical racism, like the Tulsa, Oklahoma riot of the 1920s. And then there's the origins of critical theory."

JD forgot his comic and looked sharply at Will. "I know something about that, you know."

"About what?"

"The origins of critical theory."

"Really?"

"Yeah. My grandfather's brother. My Uncle Gus. He was a professor. Like, in the 1950s."

"Of critical theory? That long ago?"

"I think so," JD said, scratching the back of his neck. "I told my dad last week that you were getting into critical theory. And he was like, 'You know, my uncle Gus knows all about that.' And I was like, 'Really?' And he looked at me like I was an idiot and said, 'He went to Columbia after the war.'"

"Colombia? South America? What does that have to do—"

JD snorted and then laughed obnoxiously. "No. Co-lumbia the Ivy League university in New York City. You dork."

"Excuse me. You're the one with intimate knowledge of Ivy League universities in New York City. Who's the dork here?"

"*What*-ever," JD said dismissively. "Anyway, if you want, I'll call Uncle Gus. He could tell us stories about the early days of critical theory."

"That would be great. I'm sure we could use that. Thanks!"

"Hey, no problem. Anything I can—Waitaminute! Is this *her* project or yours?"

"Mine."

"You're actually gonna write an essay on the origins of critical theory?"

"Probably not. I'm really not all that into it. If I do anything, it'll be a comic since there's an art category, and I used to be good at art. I picked up three critical theory books from the library the other day, and I'm planning on starting them this weekend after I do research for Connie."

"You're doing research for Connie?"

"Yeah. On the Tulsa riot."

"And is she gonna do research for you?"

"Uhh . . ."

"Dude, what makes you think she'll help you as much as you're helping her?"

Will turned red. It was a fair question, and since he couldn't answer it without embarrassing himself, he kept quiet. His friend, as usual, was cutting to the heart of the matter. Will's partnership with Connie was hardly two weeks old, and he already felt he was shouldering most of the burden. He was well aware that he did not have the strength to say no to Connie Craft.

JD held out a hand like a peace offering. "I just don't want you to get hurt, Will. She's using you, and you're too nice to see it."

Distraught but grateful, Will wondered how JD could switch so quickly from his usual annoying self to an almost likeable person. JD's unquestioning loyalty also set him on edge. Could he be as loyal to JD in return?

Rustling papers and friendly murmurs from above. The cello music had stopped. The lesson must have just ended. JD pointed to the ceiling. "You said your mom gets done at five-thirty, right?"

"Yeah."

"Gotta go," he said as he bounced to his feet, his casual athleticism causing Will to shake his head wistfully. "We have guests tonight. Promised my mom I'd be home in time. Mind if I borrow this?" JD waved a rolled-up comic at Will.

"Go ahead," Will said, hoping his father wouldn't notice the book's absence from his collection. Knowing him, he probably would.

After leading his friend up the stairwell and into the narrow hallway, they stopped by the front door as Melissa and Andrew—but mostly Andrew—were paying their respects to Mrs. Wu and her talented grandson Edison. Will quickly grew bored of the conversation. From her strained expression, it seemed Melissa had as well.

"I just want to say that of all of my wife's students, your grandson is the most talented and hardworking!" Andrew gushed, with his salmon-pink shirtsleeves rolled up to his elbows. "I am very impressed! Very impressed!" Trim and muscular, he had the piercing eyes and square jaw of a superhero, but his thinning brown hair formed a growing spot of scalp on the top of his head. Deep dimples formed creases on his wax-paper cheeks. On his apron were two words: "COOL DAD."

From her crooked teeth, short hair, and drab clothing, Will could tell that Mrs. Wu was a recent immigrant from China. She nodded deferentially to her host and uttered a mishmash of broken English, while her grandson fidgeted beside her next to his cello.

Andrew pointed at him. "This kid is gonna go places! I'm gonna keep my eye on him. Or my *ear* on him, if you know what I mean." As Andrew began laughing at his own joke, Mrs. Wu took the cue and started chortling obliviously. The entire display made Will want to squirm until he felt an unwelcome jab in his ribs. JD was calling his attention to something on the wall. At first, Will thought it was his mother's quotation art, etched on wooden slats, which read, "Hate has no home here." Instead, it was the framed photograph of Andrew in a blue martial arts gi launching a kick toward the camera, a picture he shared widely on social media. Front and center was the under-side of his bare left foot—a ridiculous image made worse by JD's tactless efforts not to snicker at it. Luckily, the forced hilarity of Andrew and Mrs. Wu drowned him out until that mercifully died off as well.

Andrew clapped his hands together. "Welp! It was wonderful seeing you again . . . Shoo-Sha? Show-Shoo? How do you pronounce your name again? I'm sorry."

From her prattling response Will gathered her name was pronounced "Shaw-Sha." He imagined it being spelled unhelpfully with many X's and I's.

"Shaw-Sha! Got it! I apologize and promise to do better next time."

Mrs. Wu must have misinterpreted this as another joke and began laughing stridently until she stopped short, re-alizing her mistake. As if to make up for the uncomforta-ble silence, Andrew took a bow. "Okay! I would like you to know how welcome you are here! I look forward to seeing you and your grandson next week!"

Will saw his mother's relief the moment Mrs. Wu and Edison were ushered out the door. No longer needing to smile, she leaned against the door and enjoyed a deep breath. She was wearing a green and white loose-fit tunic top over khaki shorts. Her frazzled dark blonde hair fell chaotically past her shoulders. Her eyes were puffier than they used to be, and she was filling out in her hips and thighs. But her clear skin, small nose, and delicate freckled features made her seem a lot younger than her 42 years.

Observing his parents side by side, Will wondered how he could even be related to his father. Andrew was so ac-tive and athletic, while he and his mother were nothing like that. And they both gained weight so easily. Melissa excused herself and rushed up the stairs, probably to use the bathroom. JD nudged Will in the arm.

"Dad, I'd like you to meet my friend," Will said. "This is JD Craiglow."

Andrew was slipping past them in the hall when he shook JD's outstretched hand.

"Nice to meet you, sir," JD said.

"Hey," Andrew said, glancing down and then back up again. "You're welcome to borrow that comic you've got rolled up. But I'll need it back, okay?"

Will winced, remembering how his father had warned him never to roll up his comics.

"Of course!" JD said, startled.

Andrew smiled. "Good man! And I'd invite you to dinner, but we only have enough pot roast for the three of us! Don't let the door hit ya where the Lord split ya!" He disappeared into the kitchen laughing at his own joke once again.

JD pretended to sigh melodramatically as he opened the front door. "Why didn't he say how welcome *I* was?"

Will shrugged. "Dude, as long as I'm here, you're welcome."

"Thanks!" JD laughed as he stepped outside, and then handed the comic to Will. "Here, take it. I don't want it that bad."

"Sorry he said that to you. He can be that way sometimes."

"No problem," JD said as he trotted toward his car in the driveway. He pointed back at Will. "And dude! Don't let Connie take advantage of you. You're better than that!"

After Will closed the door, Andrew called him from the kitchen. He sounded vexed. Will looked longingly up the stairs and wondered what was taking his mother so long. Things were always less awkward with Andrew when his mother was around. He gritted his teeth and trudged into the kitchen, flattening the comic against his chest. Andrew, who was energetically sautéing vegetables over the stove, called again before realizing that his son was already standing in the doorway.

"I'm sorry JD rolled up your comic, Dad," Will said. "He

gave it back."

"I don't care about the comic, Will," Andrew said, banging the pan loudly onto the stove. He turned and looked accusingly at his son. "So, tell me. Are you a racist?"

Will caught his breath the moment he understood his father was being serious. He closed his mouth, not wanting to appear more stunned than he really was.

"I asked you a question."

"I know. Uh, no. No!"

"Good," Andrew said, nodding aggressively. "Is that the truth?"

Will's mouth fell open, and this time he didn't think to close it. He didn't know what to say. His relationship with Andrew had been getting tense lately, but never before had his father accused him of *lying*. Andrew stepped closer. "I went downstairs to ask you if you wanted cauliflower in your veggies when I overheard you disparaging black people with your friend." Andrew shrugged. "Sounded racist. So, I'll ask again. Are you racist?"

It finally occurred to Will to start resenting his father for eavesdropping. Did he not have basic privacy rights in his own home? With his father now standing in front of him, expecting an answer, Will could see how angry— almost hostile—he was becoming. Despite being three inches taller and perhaps 80 pounds heavier than his father, Will knew he'd be no match for him in a fight. Andrew Askew was a black belt in taekwondo and in great shape. Suddenly, kicking for photographs in a gi didn't seem so ridiculous. Not for the first time, Will yearned to leave the house and never come back.

"All right, that's enough, you two!" Melissa said as she stepped between them. Will hadn't even heard her approaching. She placed her palm on Will's chest, but focused all her attention on Andrew. "I'm sure Will didn't mean anything by it, Andrew."

"Okay," Andrew said as he turned back toward the stove. "But it sounded bad, Melissa. It sounded bad."

Melissa took her hand off her son's chest and went over to Andrew to reassure him. In that moment, Will slipped out of the kitchen and was about to pass through the front door before either parent realized he was gone.

Chapter 4

Will had nearly reached his car when his mother burst out of the house. "Will! Where are you going?" she demanded, eyes squinting in the declining sunlight. He kept walking and then turned to face her, leaning against his decade-old sedan. She approached him, seemingly more concerned than angry, which was what he had expected. What he hadn't expected was a gentle punch in the chest.

"Why are you leaving?" she asked.

"What are you talking about? Dad hates me."

"He doesn't hate you," she said, now stroking his chest as if to take back the punch.

Will aimed an ironic look at his mother. "Seriously?"

"Yes! Don't be ridiculous."

"He was eavesdropping on me, Mom. And then he went into his tyrant routine again, interrogating me and getting in my face."

Melissa pulled her hand away, looking in all directions to make sure no neighbors were in earshot. "He's only trying to protect you," she whispered. "You know how we feel about racism in this house."

Will made as if he were about to pull his own hair. "That's not the point!"

She pursed her lips for a moment and then nodded. "You're right. He shouldn't have listened in on your conversation. I'll ask him to apologize."

"You shouldn't have to, Mom. He should do it on his own."

"I'm sure he wants to."

He didn't believe her, but appreciated the sentiment anyway. "Or better yet, maybe he shouldn't have eavesdropped on me at all."

Melissa began rubbing his shoulder. "There's something you need to know," she said ominously.

The dire tone of her voice startled him. "What?"

"We were going to tell you, but your father kept putting it off."

"What!" he insisted.

"And you have a right to know."

She sounded worried, which made Will worry as well. "Are you getting divorced?"

She took a step back and folded her arms. "No."

"Is someone sick? Is someone going to die?"

"No. Nothing like that."

"Then what?"

Melissa looked at him gloomily. "Two weeks ago, your father lost his job at the library."

Will saw the tears welling up but not quite spilling out of his mother's eyes, understanding that this news was indeed as devastating as it sounded. "What happened?"

Melissa gestured as if at a loss for words. "According to your father, it was somehow political. It may have gone up to the Governor's office. I don't know. But he was forced to resign."

Will felt his upper lip curl in outrage. "What happened?"

"They gave him a good severance. But he lost his pension."

"*What happened?*"

Melissa threw up her hands. "I'm not sure! Your father's not giving me details. But—"

"But what?"

"Well, the mother of one of my students works in the Governor's office. A few days ago she shared a rumor with me. Remember Latesha Leonard?"

Will recalled his time working in the library as a freshman. The image of an overweight, light-skinned, middle-aged black woman slowly emerged in his mind. Large glasses, dreadlocked hairdo, loud blouses, and heavy perfume. She was exceedingly nice and always called him "baby." He squinted uncertainly at his mother. "Wasn't she the one who let those homeless people sleep in the northwest branch? One of them died from an overdose. And the other took a knife and—"

Melissa shut her eyes and held up a trembling hand. "Yes. Don't go there. Yes."

"Okay. And . . . ?"

Melissa took a moment to respond. "She had been bucking for a management position for a long time, and your father kept not recommending her because . . . . Well, you know . . ."

Will *did* know. Having overheard much of the scuttle-butt at the time, Latesha Leonard was simply not qualified to manage a library, her 30 years' experience notwith-standing. Having worked with her for a summer, he often wondered what she *would* have been qualified for. As a lackadaisical high school student, even he had a greater working knowledge of literature than she did.

"Then a few months ago she filed a racial discrimina-tion complaint against your father," Melissa explained. "And she convinced many of her colleagues to back her up, or file their own."

"You mean her black colleagues, right?"

"Don't go there!"

"Okay! Okay!" It took a moment for the gravity of this new normal to sink in for Will. "But I don't understand. Dad's the least racist person in the world."

"I know! It's crazy."

"How can they take all this seriously?"

"They have to. Because of the racial politics in this state, they have to. According to the rumor—and I think the ru-mor is correct—the Lieutenant Governor himself sat your father down and gave him a choice. Either fight it and pay the tremendous legal costs himself, and likely lose. Or qui-etly resign with a generous severance package."

Melissa's tears finally came, and her hands and fore-arms were not enough to contain them. She reached into her pocket for a wad of tissues and dried her streaming face. "I knew these would come in handy sooner or later," she joked.

A question then occurred to Will. He had the feeling he shouldn't ask it, but went ahead anyway. "Mom, the Lieutenant Governor is black, isn't he?"

Melissa flinched. "That has nothing to do with anything!" she insisted with a bleary redness in her eyes. "Don't think like that!"

"All right. I'm sorry!"

"This is why we don't allow racist talk in the house, Will! You never know when it will come back to haunt you. And it doesn't matter if you're innocent!"

Again, she looked in all directions to make sure no neighbors were nearby. Will could sense his mother's fear, and for the first time it felt like *his* fear, too. Is this what it meant to grow up? If so, he did not like it one bit. "I get it. I get it," he said, trying to soothe her. He took her hand in his.

Melissa sniffed and wiped her eyes again with the saturated wad of tissue. "I'm telling you this because you said you wanted to go to State. I don't know if we can afford that now, Will. You know I've lost several students recently. The cello is not exactly the most popular—"

"No, I understand."

"We would have to go deeper into debt or jeopardize our retirement. I'm sorry!"

"It's okay."

"The local community college is not a bad option, really. Maybe if things change after a couple years, you could transfer?"

Will felt himself deflate with disappointment. He clenched his fist and made like he was about to smash his car window in slow motion. He pulled back at the last moment.

"You know your dad's situation, Will," Melissa said.

"His two daughters *also* want to go to college now. He has to pay for them, too."

"They're in their twenties."

She shook her fists in frustration. "I know! But he signed an agreement. He's legally obligated. And I can't complain because I married a divorcée. I knew what I was getting into. That's why we never had any children—" She shot a look at her son and touched his hand. "—after you."

"So what's dad been doing these past two weeks?"

"He's picking up morning and afternoon shifts at the museum," she said, dabbing her eyes. "They like him there. He's usually done by three."

"So *that's* why he's been doing so much cooking lately. He's had the time."

"Yes. And to save money. We can't afford takeout like we used to."

"Is he not going back to library work?"

"Well, he's had some offers, but they're all too far away or too junior for him to consider. We'll get by. He's even talking to a lawyer about suing the state. But lawyers are so expensive, and we have no one to help us."

Will's eyes widened as an idea occurred to him. "What if I get a scholarship?"

"What?"

"What if I get a scholarship?" he repeated, now wanting to get the words out faster than he could speak them. He couldn't remember ever feeling this way before. He grabbed his mother urgently by the wrist. "Say, a $10,000 scholarship. Could I go to State then?"

Melissa pretended to flinch. "Sure. I guess. A scholarship? Really?"

"Yeah! I'd have to pick up my grades a little. But I have the test scores. I could do it."

"I've never heard you talk this way before." She laughed and touched his forehead. "Are you feeling all right?"

"I feel fine."

"How will you get a scholarship?"

He looked into the pink sky above their nondescript, two-story house. The only home Will had ever known had a beige brick façade, dark brown shutters, and an orange front door. Its long porch stretched nearly the length of the house, and its prominent brick chimney took up almost all of one side. Tall, rough-cut shrubbery girded its base like evergreen armor. It was getting late, and Will was getting hungry. For a moment he fretted over his tense relationship with his father and whether he would have the discipline to keep to his diet that evening. There was already so much for him to worry about. Should he tell his mother the truth? He still wasn't sure if he was going to enter the scholarship competition, let alone get any closer to Connie Craft. "Do you know about critical theory, Mom?" he asked.

"Critical *race* theory? Yeah. CRT."

"Well, I kind of—there was—there's gonna be . . ."

"Gonna be what?"

"A multimedia scholarship competition. Students submit essays, art, or videos about CRT."

"And the winners get a scholarship?"

"Yeah. Deadline is early December. I was gonna tell you."

Melissa's face lit up. "That is so exciting! Are you going to submit an essay, or—"

"I'm thinking about artwork. Maybe a comic. They accept graphic art up to five pages."

"Great! You have talent in art. I don't know why you don't do it more often."

"Mom, it's been years since I've done any art. I'm not *that* good."

"I think you are."

"Well, thank you. I'm working with someone on it. I'm helping them on their essay, and they're gonna help me with my comic—once I get started." Will squinted in embarrassment, suspecting that his use of the pronoun "they" sounded dubious.

"Who is it? Is it your friend JD?"

"Heh. No. It's, ah—"

"Who is he?"

"Uh, well—"

"Do I know him?"

Will took a deep breath. "It's a her," he admitted.

Melissa pulled back and gasped with her hands over her mouth.

Will waved his hand dismissively. "No, Mom. It's not like that. Stoppit! She has a boyfriend. She's not interested in me."

"Okay, okay!" she said. "But still! A girl?"

"Mom!"

"I'm just excited for you!"

"Well, keep it down, please!" Will said, looking around. Fortunately, the neighborhood remained empty except for them.

"Oh, all right! If you say so," Melissa teased, tugging him tenderly by the arm. "But yes, this could be a big opportunity for you! You know, your father knows a lot about CRT. And he loves comics. I'm sure he'd be happy—"

Will cringed. The last thing he wanted to do was bring his father into it. "I don't know, Mom."

"I know things are a bit strained between you two right now. Maybe this could help?"

"Okay, I'll give it a shot."

"What's her name?"

Will sighed. "I'd rather not talk about it."

"Not even to tell me her name?"

Will sighed again and looked away. It was always so *embarrassing* whenever his mother overreacted to developments in his personal life. Still, with JD being so dismissive of his relationship with Connie, he had no one else to turn to. "Her name is Connie Craft," he said.

"Okay. I don't know her. Do I?"

"No." Will confirmed it in his mind. No, he had never told his parents about his disastrous attempt at asking Connie out over that dead frog during his sophomore year.

"Is she nice?" Melissa asked, pulling her hand back. "Is she pretty?"

Will grunted in frustration. "It doesn't matter if she's pretty, Mom! We're not dating!"

"I was just asking."

"She is half Indian, though." Will had not planned on saying it, but for some reason he did.

"Oh!"

"Yeah."

"Indian dot? Or Indian feather?"

Will chuckled at the distinction and felt a cool respect for his mother for making it. "Feather. Choctaw, I think."

"That's so interesting!"

"Yeah. She's really into CRT. She's the one who got me into it."

Melissa thought for a moment. "Will, are you *really* into CRT? I've never heard you talk about it. And it doesn't seem to be up your alley."

Will had no idea how to respond. The truth was that he *wasn't* into critical theory, and wasn't hopeful that he would ever be into it. He was only into Connie Craft, and wasn't exactly hopeful about her either. So why was he considering entering this scholarship competition to begin with? Was it only for the money? Will suspected there was no shame in that. But there *was* shame in pretending to be interested in something he disliked and didn't respect. He simply could not bear to live a lie. At that moment, however, another depressing thought occurred to him: he might have to live a lie—even just a little bit and for a short amount of time—if he wanted a chance to go to a good college.

Chapter 5

Will knocked gently on the door. He didn't know how this Alterman woman would react to being disturbed during her afternoon office hours. He wasn't taking her class, but he was fairly certain she'd remember him. How many kids fumble their phones in front of everyone during Critical Theory Club meetings? People were still talking about that.

"Come in," she said.

When you're six feet, three inches tall and 278 pounds, you don't slip through doors. Every entrance is a grand entrance. Sitting at her desk before her laptop, Nadine looked up to where she expected to find the face of the person entering her neat and tidy office—and then looked up a bit further to find Will. She shrunk back just a little as women often did when finding themselves alone in his hulking presence. But then she sat up tall and asserted herself.

"Well, hello!" she said.

"Hi, Professor Alterman," Will said amiably. "Do you have a few minutes? I have a couple questions, if you don't mind."

"No, of course!" she said, smiling politely. "Sit down, please."

"Thanks," Will said, thinking he might need to first engage this woman in small talk and pleasantries, but was too keen on not getting flustered for any of that.

"What can I do for you?"

"Well, I'm considering entering that critical theory scholarship competition—"

"Great," she said curtly.

Will noted that Nadine hadn't even asked for his name. He cleared his throat as he cautiously sat down on an old swivel chair, which he hoped would carry his weight. He breathed easily when he felt that it could.

"Um, I have a few questions about it if you have a couple—"

"Questions about the competition?" she interrupted. "Or about critical race theory in general?"

As she waited for a response, Will noticed for the first time how much her wide, strong jaw resembled a man's. He began to sense masculine vibes from her as well. Her light, flowery blouse, silver necklace, and earrings offset this somewhat. So did her long brown hair, which was held in place by a white headband. But she had strong, veiny hands and long fingers with tightly trimmed nails. Her stern, all-business demeanor suggested he had no time to lose before she would start losing patience with him.

"Both, actually," he said as he reached into his backpack. He placed a notebook and three critical theory library books onto her desk. "I've read the books you recommend on the club website. I took notes and have some questions that might help with my submission."

Nadine hardly glanced at the books. "You're friends with Connie Craft, right?"

"Yeah," he said, nodding with pride. "We're helping each other with research." He waited for doubt to register in Nadine's expression, but it never did. Maybe it wasn't so strange that a guy like him could be friends with a girl like Connie?

"I haven't seen you at the club meetings," Nadine said, her tone a little friendlier than before.

Will shifted his weight and realized too late how squeaky his chair was. "Um, well, I'm not a joiner, much. But I don't have to be a member of the Critical Theory Club to enter the—"

"No! No, you don't."

"Good."

Nadine leaned forward on her elbows, intertwined her fingers, and rested her chin on them. "Well, ask away," she said, not impolitely.

Both encouraged and hopeful, Will took a deep breath. He figured he'd start with the easier question. "Well, among the list of topics on the club website, there's 'history of race relations in the United States.' We're thinking about covering the Tulsa Race Riot from 1921."

Nadine clapped twice. "Oh, that's a wonderful idea! The centenary was just two years ago." Will took a moment to reacquaint himself with the word "centenary." He stopped when Nadine raised a finger. "But we should call it the 'Tulsa Race Massacre,' because that's what it was."

Will nodded solemnly.

"It was an atrocity. A pogrom. Do you know what a pogrom is?"

"I do," Will said, recalling how often the term came up in his classes.

"Up to 300 innocents were murdered by racist whites," she told him hotly. "And no one was ever prosecuted. This is a prime example of the evil of white supremacy and how its legacy lingers on with us today."

Will nodded again, hoping to steer Nadine away from the topic since he found her growing excitement bordering on hostile. "Okay, and as for my second question—"

Nadine held up a hand to stop him. "But you understand that knowledge of our past is the key to controlling our future, don't you?"

"Yes, of course."

"Good."

Will cleared his throat and shifted in his seat again, glad to be moving on. "What I don't understand about critical theory is why colorblindness is a bad thing. I've always been taught that in order to fight racism, we're supposed to look past—"

Nadine nodded vigorously before interrupting him again. "Yes, colorblindness looks nice on paper. But white people are too racially biased for it to work in reality." As she lifted her hand to gesture, Will caught a glimpse of something multi-colored under her sleeve. A tattoo. It wasn't small.

"I don't understand. If a person is colorblind, how can they be racially—"

"Because colorblindness is a subterfuge."

"A what?"

"A ruse. A lie."

"I don't under—"

Nadine thumped her hand on her desk and interrupted him once again. "Look at it like this. You're a racist—"

Will did a double take. "Me?" He sounded much more alarmed than he had meant to.

She closed her eyes and grunted impatiently. "I'm speaking rhetorically. You understand what that means, don't you?"

He nodded, not wanting to respond to such a condescending question.

"Good," she continued. "So you're a racist. You hate black people. You think they're inferior to you. You want to oppress them and rule over them, just like your ancestors did a century ago."

Will was astonished. Such thoughts had never occurred to him. He didn't even *know* anyone who had ever confessed thoughts like that. He felt himself frown as he waited to see where this woman was going with this.

"Of course, today you can't just say things you once could. So instead, you pretend to be colorblind so you can apply so-called standards against blacks and people of color that at first blush seem objective, but are really racist. That way, colorblindness helps you achieve white supremacist goals."

Will tried to speak and failed. He shook his head and focused on the photographs and posters on her wall. Most were of well-known female world leaders or media personalities, but the ones that weren't drew his attention the most. One was of a well-dressed black man with gray hair waving his fist before a large crowd. Some revolutionary African, he guessed. Next to it was an old black-and-white image of two uniformed men seated on either side of an old man in shirtsleeves. With frizzy white hair jutting from either side of his bald head, he looked like a clown but seemed to be discussing something very serious, like a war.

"It's not explicit white supremacy," Nadine continued. "It's subconscious. Colorblindness conditions people of all races into a white supremacist mindset. It allows them to practice covert racism. Does that make sense?"

He extended his arm, careful not to knock over her large coffee mug near the edge of the desk. "Well, how do you know the standards aren't objective? I mean, math and standardized tests—"

"Because those things dehumanize people of color by not taking environment into consideration," Nadine responded. "Oppression and poverty and a host of other reasons are why people of color score poorly on those exams. They are not objective. They perpetuate the discredited and offensive racist belief that whites are intellectually superior to people of color when really it is their superior environment, their history of oppressing others, and their white privilege that accounts for the vast majority of their success."

These words flowed suspiciously well together, Will thought. Had Nadine read them somewhere? He remembered her saying something similar during her talk at the Critical Theory Club.

"But then why are so many of the best students in school Asian?" he asked. It was a question he'd been asking himself for a long time.

Nadine smiled and raised her finger. "Now, that is a white supremacist question."

Baffled, he hunched forward and drooped a little to his

left. "How can a question be—"

"I'm saying this out of concern, Peter," she warned. "I don't mean to frighten you, but you could get in trouble talking like that."

Will fell back in his chair in dumfounded silence, no longer caring about the squeak. *Nadine Alterman thinks I'm Pete Dorr,* he realized. But how? Why? He gathered that this riddle had many possible answers, all of which involved Connie and were beyond his grasp at that moment. A sick feeling in the pit of his stomach, however, caused him to shake off his astonishment. He had to consider the subtle threat this teacher had just conveyed. *Is Nadine Alterman calling me a white supremacist? What does she mean by 'get in trouble'? Get in trouble for what? And how could asking a question about Asian superiority possibly be white supremacist?*

"Your question could be construed as white supremacist because it employs a form of logic which is an artifact of Enlightenment rationalism," she explained. "And this, as we all know, is steeped in a European tradition that has been historically violent to people of color and produces an exclusive, race-based hierarchy of knowledge. Does that make sense?"

Will said nothing, and wasn't even sure if Nadine had noticed.

"And to answer your question, Asians overperform because if you study history you'll see that Asians have not suffered nearly as much as American blacks. Really, the Trans-Atlantic Slave Trade, slavery, segregation, Jim Crow laws, and the poverty and genocide blacks have had to face have no comparison in history. Thus, their performance on these racist exams cannot be expected to equal that of whites . . . or Asians."

Will was coming around to himself, finally. He felt determined and secure in his own innocence. Asking honest questions cannot possibly be racist, and nothing this woman could say was going to change that. Still leaning back in his chair, he asked almost defiantly, "Well, if whites are not supposed to be colorblind . . . what *are* we supposed to be?"

"Good question," she said. After placing her fingers on her forehead, she spread them into the air. "You have to expand your mind. Enlighten yourself."

"Okay."

"You have to become skilled in deconstructing your race consciousness to become aware of the hidden ways racism causes uneven power dynamics. That's what critical theory is all about. Abnegating your white privilege."

"*My* white privilege?" he asked, unsure if she was still speaking rhetorically, and even less sure of what this privilege actually was.

"Yes. *Your* white privilege. You must understand how white supremacy destroys the identity and culture of minority groups. It strips them of authenticity by pressuring them to conform to a Eurocentric world which only looks to oppress and control. You have to renounce everything about yourself that contributes to unwanted racial disparities. And you can't do that by being colorblind. You have to be color aware."

Having suffered through three tedious books on critical theory, Will was now familiar enough with the basic ideas to predict much of what Nadine was going to say. But to him it had all the structure of a bowl of spaghetti. He couldn't tell where one idea ended and another began.

"Color aware," he repeated.

"Yes."

"But weren't the white slaveowners color aware?" he asked. "Weren't the Jim Crow people *also* color aware?"

Nadine's eyes widened as she let out a tiny gasp. She then shrunk back, covering her mouth with her hand. Her chair squeaked more loudly than his. "That is definitely a white supremacist question," she said. She dropped her hands onto her lap and glared at him. "I must ask you to leave right now."

A burst of fear caused Will's fingers to tingle and his heart to race. Such a sudden and unwelcome change—his body was just not used to it. "What?"

"I'm sorry, but I'm very busy. You have to leave."

Will extended his arms to demonstrate his good intentions. "But I'm saying these are bad things! Slavery, racism, Jim Crow. All bad. But if you tell white people not to be colorblind, they may go back to that. That's my big problem with critical theory!"

Nadine cleared her throat as she sat up as tall as she could. "Connie has said nothing but nice things about you, Peter," she said. "She thinks very highly of you. And I can see that you are a very well-spoken and intelligent young man. I trust that soon you will see the error of your ways, and that from now on you will make decisions that will not jeopardize your future in college and beyond."

The way Nadine tightened her lips and folded her hands indicated without any doubt that the meeting had concluded. She gazed at him with wounded eyes until he stood. He felt a powerful urge to apologize. The last thing he wanted was to hurt her. Feeling guilty and ashamed, he collected his things and began silently composing an apology as he stepped toward the door. Her parting shot, however, rendered any apology completely moot.

"There is a white supremacist group in Virginia called the No College Club that thinks it can promote racial hatred and entice people like yourself to forego university training," she warned. "They have been debanked, banned from all major social media platforms, and are currently being sued out of existence. You don't want to be like them."

"Thank you," he muttered as he stepped through her door, perplexed and angry. A moment earlier he had regretted hurting *her* feelings. And now she had hurt *his* feelings by bringing up this No College Club and threatening to ruin his entire future. She had also accused him of having white privilege, yet *he* was the one being forced to tread lightly in order to stay out of trouble. How could that possibly be privilege? Moreover, Nadine Alterman was white—like him. How could she even talk to him like that?

Moments later, as he passed through the school's front entrance and faced the warm orange glare of the afternoon sun, a strange dread suddenly possessed him. What was he going to do if he couldn't go to college? Several students passed him as they entered and exited the building. Big as he was, no one seemed to notice him. Up ahead, students were filing into school buses, which were parked along the curb like cars in a yellow locomotive. Beyond them was the parking lot, where Will's car awaited. But he was in no hurry to go home. Instead, he headed toward an empty bench which sat apart from the buses and behind some trees. He desperately wanted to sit and let his enormous body adjust to the stress and worry he was now feeling. He needed to ponder his situation—for all the good it would do him.

As soon as he sat down, he spotted someone walking toward him between the trees. It was Connie. She was crying.

Chapter 6

Thrill gave way to unease as Will considered the possibilities. Why was Connie coming to him? Had she changed her mind about the scholarship competition? Did she no longer want to work with him? "Hey," he said as she approached.

"Can I sit here?" she asked timidly. Up close, he noticed her puffy face and the stray strands of her ponytailed hair fluttering in the breeze. She wore a pink windbreaker with black trim over faded blue jeans and white tennis shoes. Her sad-sack expression made Will's heart leap with empathy.

"Sure!" He was about to stand out of politeness, but she sat down before he could.

"You don't mind that I'm—"

"No! No, of course not. What's wrong?"

Connie sniffed. "I just wanna say I'm sorry."

Will frowned in surprise. "For what?"

"I don't want you to think I was manipulating you or anything."

"You mean about helping you with your critical theory essay?"

She sniffed again. "Yeah."

"Are you okay?"

"Yeah."

"Are you crying?"

"No."

"Then what's wrong?"

After several false starts she said, "I'm just such a bad person." It was hardly more than a whisper, and Will wasn't sure he had heard her correctly. As she was now unmistakably sobbing, he couldn't ask her to repeat herself. He looked around. Fortunately, nearly all the buses had left, and no one could easily see them in their isolated spot.

"No!" he insisted. "Don't think that way. It's okay. I don't feel manipulated."

Connie wiped her eyes with her sleeve and took a deep breath, regaining control of herself. "I totally manipulated you, dude."

"What?"

"I mean, I knew you didn't go to that protest in Covington, and I called you out anyway. In front of everyone."

"That was two months ago."

"So?"

"Okay, why did you do that?"

"I don't know," she said, and then sighed wearily. "Or maybe I do. I don't know. Maybe I thought you were a big fat liar like me. I thought maybe you would make up some cool story that would impress everyone. And then it would be, like, our little secret. You know?"

Without even realizing it, Will let out a strident chuckle.

"What's so funny?" she asked, sounding hurt.

He felt confident enough to keep chuckling. "Because I had a similar idea."

She chuckled as well. "Maybe I'm not such a bad person after all."

He frowned. "I don't know if you should be holding me up as a standard for—"

"Why not?"

"Because!" he said, waving his hand. "We're so different. You've got so much going for you, and I have nothing. You're popular. You're gorgeous. You're—"

"Okay, Will. You can stop now."

"I mean it."

"*I* mean it!"

"I don't under—"

"Look, Will," she cut in testily. "I'm letting you off the hook, okay? You don't have to help me with my essay."

"But I want to," he said without thinking.

"Why? Because you're so into critical theory?"

"Uhh . . ."

"See? That's what I'm talking about. You're *not* all that into it. You've shown up to only one meeting. You're not taking the class. You said last week you still weren't sure if you were even gonna submit anything. And it's not like I'm offering to help you. So it's wrong for me to rope you into helping me. I feel guilty about that."

Will remembered how JD had warned him about her. "You could help me," he said, finally committing himself to this scholarship competition—which, after his meeting with Nadine Alterman, he was now dreading. Sadness came over him in waves. There was no going back now unless he wanted to undo whatever progress he had already made with this mysterious girl.

"How can I help you?" she asked.

"If I submit anything it will be a comic. Like, a mini-graphic novel. You can give me feedback on the script. On the dialogue. You can tell me if it's any good. You know."

Connie thought for a moment, and then nodded. "I can totally do that. If that would be okay."

"Yeah. I'm thinking about doing it on the origins of CRT."

"Okay."

"And I just had a meeting with Alterman. She liked your idea about the Tulsa Race Riot. I'm sorry I haven't researched it yet. I'll get started this evening."

"Stop apologizing, Will. I should be apologizing to you."

"I don't see why."

"I do."

Will tried to smile. "Look, Connie, I'm flattered you even wanna work with me. I don't know how to play these social games. So I'll just be honest with you. I like you. I like talking to you. So I don't mind working with you. I also respect the fact that you have a boyfriend. And that's that."

Connie waited a moment before letting out a slow chortle.

"What's so funny?" he asked.

"You are such a doofus," she teased.

He playfully raised an eyebrow. "What's *that* supposed to mean?"

Urgent, crunching footsteps interrupted them. They looked up and saw JD aggressively approaching. He was in denim shorts, work boots, and a T-shirt featuring a be-spectacled dinosaur reading a book. His unbuttoned red-and-black flannel shirt fluttered in the breeze. "I don't think you're making the bus there, Con," he said. "It just left."

Will and Connie looked at each other. "What?" they asked simultaneously.

JD took his seat next to Connie on the bench, forcing her to scooch awkwardly toward Will, who had little room left as it was. "So where is everyone, Connie?" JD asked. "Usually around this time you're surrounded by all your fawning groupies."

Offended, Connie leaned away from JD as if he had something contagious. "Get *away* from me!"

"I saw you getting in a tiff with one of 'em this after-noon. I forget which one. All you popular girls look alike to me."

Will held up a hand. "All right, that's enough."

JD dropped his elbows onto his knees and looked past Connie to Will. "Seriously, dude, this one isn't nearly as popular as she seems. Everyone knows she's a big faker."

Connie took a hissing breath through her teeth and shoved the diminutive JD off the bench. The force she mustered surprised all three of them as JD landed hard on the ground. "What is *wrong* with you?" she asked hotly as she stood up.

"What's wrong with *me*?" JD asked as he got to his feet and brushed himself off.

"Yeah! Nobody likes you. You have no social graces."

"Yeah, but I don't go around shoving people!"

"I don't go around insulting people!"

"At least I tell the truth!"

Livid, Connie placed her arms akimbo and looked down at JD, her cheeks turning a bright pink. "What do you know about the truth?" she challenged. "You runt!"

The insult seemed to have no effect on JD other than to encourage him. "I know you're manipulating my friend here into doing your stupid critical theory project."

Connie leaned in close to him, emphasizing her four-inch height advantage. "*I apologized for that!*"

For once, JD had nothing to say. Will diplomatically wedged himself between them, but focused his attention on JD. "Dude, I appreciate your honesty and your friendship. But Connie is my friend too. You can't talk to her that way."

"But—"

"And she did apologize. I agreed to team up with her by own volition. So no more about that, all right?"

All JD could do was purse his lips and nod in frustration.

"Come on, Will," Connie said. "Can you give me a ride home? We can talk about your meeting with Professor Alterman."

As she started walking toward the parking lot, confident that Will would follow, JD took her by the shoulder and stopped her. She whirled back around. "*Don't touch me!*" she snarled.

JD was neither intimidated nor impressed. "Connie, I was rude to you a moment ago because I'm so roundly disliked at school that I've given up trying to be popular with anyone. I'm such a lowlife I didn't think *anything* I could say would hurt you. Okay, so I was wrong. I did hurt you. I didn't mean to. I actually feel bad about it now. So, I'm sorry. I won't ever be mean to you again." He smiled mischievously. "Unless of course you deserve it."

Connie's jaw fell open in shock. She turned to Will, who started hooting with laughter. "You think this is funny?" she demanded.

"Well, yeah. Kinda," Will said, trying to hold it in.

She glared at him and was about to respond when JD intervened. "Connie, before you say anything, you're gonna want to hear me out. Both of you." They looked to JD and waited. "Guess what" he said through a thin smile.

Connie and Will said nothing, continuing to wait.

"Come on, guys. When someone says 'Guess what,' you're supposed to say 'What.'"

Connie crossed her arms, while Will shifted his weight. "Okay, what" he said.

"Why is it that I have to teach you guys about social etiquette?" JD asked.

Connie groaned in annoyance. "You're enjoying this, aren't you?"

"Enjoying what?"

"Stringing us along! Making us say, 'what,' when you say 'guess what.' Making us hang on your every word when you could just tell us in plain English what you mean! It's so stupid!"

"It's not—"

"And you call *me* a faker? Who's manipulating who?"

JD held up a finger and smiled. "Actually, it's 'whom.' You should have said 'Who's manipulating whom.'"

As Connie stared at JD in disbelief, Will stepped between them again and put his hand on his friend's shoulder. "JD, get to the point."

"Fine. Remember when I told you about my Uncle Gus, Will?"

"Yeah?"

"And about how you said you wanted to do something on the origins of CRT for this scholarship competition?"

"Yeah, so?"

"Well, Uncle Gus is, like, 90. He doesn't have a cell-phone and he never picks up his landline. I had to write him a letter. Like, with a pen and paper and an envelope and a stamp—"

"We *know* what a letter is, JD," Connie said irritably.

"Anyway, my mom just texted me this afternoon. He finally wrote me back! He says we can come by this Saturday. He lives right outside of Indianapolis. Less than three hours away."

Will and Connie exchanged a look of surprise.

"Not only that, he says he's got tons of books and articles on critical theory from its early days. Stuff you're not gonna find the on the internet!"

Connie tilted her head, unimpressed. "So?"

"So?" JD repeated incredulously. "We have an expert. He can help us on this project and give us information that no one else can! Unless they're *also* related to Uncle Gus. See?"

Connie squinted at him, interested but still skeptical. "What's this 'we'? You're going to submit something, too?"

"Yeah, why not? State has a great film school. I interned there this past summer. I'd like to apply, but my mom is a divorced mother of three, and my younger brother has special needs. It'll be real tough going to State without a scholarship."

"But I thought you weren't into CRT," Will objected.

"And you are?"

Will shifted his eyes uncertainly to Connie, who was now focusing fully on JD. "Go on," she said.

"We won't even be competing with each other," JD said. "That's the beauty of it. We're in different categories. I'll do a video. Will can do a comic. And you, Connie, can write an essay. And with Uncle Gus helping us, the chances of one of us winning are pretty good. Don't you think?"

Will frowned in confusion. "But how do you know your Uncle Gus's information isn't out of date?"

"It isn't if you wanna focus on the origins of CRT, you doofus!" JD answered.

Will blushed. Why did JD call him that? Had he heard Connie call him that earlier?

"Do you think he might know something about the Tulsa Race Riot?" Connie asked.

"Yeah! I asked him about that too because Will mentioned it. He says he has magazine and newspaper articles from back when it happened."

Connie raised her hands to her mouth. "Oh, my God! I think this can work."

"I know, right?" JD said, beaming.

"Wow!" she said, seeming to reevaluate JD.

"Yeah!"

"So Saturday, you say?" she asked him almost deferentially.

Sweat seemed to pop like sparks from Will's forehead as he wondered jealously if Connie had ever been that deferential to him.

"Yeah," JD said. "Uncle Gus said it was fine. I can drive. I'll text you the details on Friday."

"That's great! Thank you!" Connie said. "Tell your uncle we say thanks to him too!" She nudged Will in the ribs. "You're gonna come with us, right?"

"Yeah, sure!" Will said, trying to sound more enthused than he really was. What did she mean by asking him *that*? As if *he* would be accompanying *them*?

JD raised his hand solemnly. "But on one condition."

Connie's lips tightened as her shoulders sunk in dread. "What?"

"You apologize," he demanded. "When I was mean to you, I apologized. And you were mean to me. You called me a runt. Apologize for that!"

Connie stared at him, hissing in outrage.

"Apologize right now," JD insisted triumphantly. "Or no deal."

Chapter 7

Will snuck out of his house before sunrise that Saturday. It shouldn't have felt like sneaking, but it did. On the surface, all was well. Both his parents had wholeheartedly approved of the scholarship competition and had allowed him to visit JD's uncle. The night before, Andrew offered Will a forthright apology and also admitted that he had been wrong about JD. Following this, he lectured Will for nearly half an hour about why young white men must internalize critical theory. Will had heard it all before. Having read three books on the subject, he knew more about it than his father did. Nonetheless, he kept quiet, all the while wanting to say what he really thought. He knew that Andrew Askew would not listen to anything negative about critical theory, despite whatever his son was going through. That morning, he closed the front door as quietly as he could and jogged through the chilly air to the street where JD's bright red car awaited. He felt like a thief, but had stolen nothing.

"Go, go," he said to JD as he climbed in. JD had thoughtfully slid the front seat back to give Will's big body as much room as possible. Even in the car's semi-darkness, Will could see his friend's insolent eyes. That he was clean shaven for once only made his angry acne scars seem even angrier. Again, JD was wearing a flannel shirt, one Will had never seen before. How many flannel shirts did he own?

"Your book," JD said, darting his eyes to the backseat as he steered out of Will's neighborhood. "Thanks for lending it to me."

Will glanced back and saw one of his critical theory library books—this one written by a young black author. He had found it repetitive and preachy. Oddly, it was hostile not so much toward whites such as himself and JD, who were skeptical of his message, but toward whites like his mother, who earnestly tried to be colorblind. He eyed it with distaste before turning away. "What did you think?" he asked.

"Eh," JD shrugged. "I don't know. I don't think white people have the kind of power he says they do."

"What do you mean?"

"The book pretty much blames whites for everything that's wrong with blacks," he began. "It's a copout. I mean, oppression can't make a person bomb a math test. If that were the case, everyone would. But they don't. And look at how the blacks behave today, with all the crime and violence, and mostly against each other. Is that our fault? Then throw in affirmative action and welfare and all the nice things we do for them. I'm sorry, but nothing that guy said made me care."

Will found this comforting, since it resembled his own viewpoint. "Yeah. And I didn't like how he kept describing blacks as victims of white privilege. If whites have privilege, why couldn't they stop him from writing a book that pretty much trashes white people?"

"Yeah. Whites get punished all the time for being 'racist.' Like that pro-white college group you told me about."

"The No College Club?"

"Oh my God. They just lost their *third* credit card processor, Will. They can barely raise money, and they're getting sued all the time. Where's their white privilege?"

"Yeah. And what about this scholarship competition and the ten thousand dollars we could win? This is happening in seven states, dude. The entire fund is a quarter million dollars. Where's all that money coming from if blacks are such victims?"

"Well, I don't care as long as some of it comes to me," JD said. "Alterman is on the judging committee, you know."

"Yeah."

"There's only, like, two blacks out of seven."

"Eight, I think."

"That's why I think I have a chance, especially if Uncle Gus can deliver fireworks. And you know what?"

"What?"

"It's times like this when I really wish I was part Indian—or, Native American—like Connie."

Will shot a disappointed look at his friend. "I don't know, dude. That doesn't seem right. You are who you are."

JD shrugged. "Just being honest. But hopefully it won't even matter. This past week I've been making this awesome video about CRT."

"Oh, yeah?"

"I have so much talent when it comes to filmmaking, dude. The ideas just keep coming and coming. I am going to be, like, the greatest filmmaker ever. I just know it."

"Really?"

"And I'm banking on the fact that my video will be so awesome the committee will have to give me that scholarship. It won't matter that I'm white, straight, and male."

"Well, I don't know about that second part," Will joked.

"Ha!"

"That has yet to be proven."

"Shut *up!*" JD said, laughing.

"Can I see the video?"

"It's not done yet. I have eight minutes so far. I laid down a bunch of narration last night."

"But you can still show it to me."

"Nope. I'm a perfectionist. No one'll see it till after the deadline."

"Okay, whatever," Will said, trying not to sound skeptical.

JD glanced at him sharply as he turned into Connie's neighborhood. "You know the Lefkowitz Auditorium where you had your Critical Theory Club meeting?"

"Yeah. That's where the finalists will present to the judging committee in December."

"Well, that's part of State's film school building. It was added fairly recently. The building itself is being expanded, which is why it's constantly under construction."

"Yeah, so?"

"Do you remember that huge projection booth that sticks out over the back seats?"

"Yeah, I remember."

"Last summer I practically spent every day in that room."

"During your internship?"

"Yeah. Only ten high school students across the state made the cut. They really liked my application reel. That's what they told me."

"Oh, wow. I didn't know that."

JD slowed down and came to a stop in front of Connie's house. "So don't doubt me," he said defensively, as he unstrapped himself. "I will be vindicated by history, I promise."

Will nodded sadly, concerned that he might have hurt his friend. "Okay. I'm really sorry, JD."

"Dude, don't worry about it. It's bad enough my whole family doubts me. And my teachers, and everyone else in school. They all think I'm a loudmouthed shrimp. It would be nice if my only friend didn't feel that way too."

Chastened, Will shook his head. "I never felt that way, JD. I swear."

JD smiled encouragingly at Will as he climbed out of the car.

The morning was still chilly, but warming rapidly. Streaks of sunlight were coloring the thick, coniferous tree line forming the horizon beyond Connie's house. Hers was an older two-story colonial atop a small hill with a tiny portico and two shutterless bedroom windows peeking out beneath a gabled roof like sleepy eyes. In the diffuse morning light, the home was a drab white, and Will doubted it would become less drab as the day brightened. As he and JD walked up the thin, cracked driveway they were struck by the sleek, shiny sportscar parked outside the detached single-car garage. It was purple and built for speed. Next to it was a drab gray sedan, but neither JD nor Will spent much time looking at that. The purple car's license plate read "CONNIEC."

"Those things run for around 50 grand new," JD said. "But this one's like 10 years old, so—"

"How do you know that?" Will asked.

"My dad's into cars. Hey, bigger question: How come we never see Connie drive this thing? She's always taking the bus, and she's a senior like us."

"I don't know."

"She's gotta have her license by now."

"Like I said, I don't know."

"And where the heck is she?" JD asked, consulting his phone. "This is the right address. She said she'd meet us outside. We're even a little late."

Will didn't know the answer to that as well, and so remained silent. Crisp, fallen leaves crumbled under their sneakers as they walked toward the door.

"Why don't you text her?" JD asked.

"Why don't *you* text her?" Will answered.

"You're closer to her than I am."

"I am not."

"You are too!"

"Dude. I'm not dating her."

"Yeah, but you want to."

Will clenched his fists in exasperation. "That's got nothing to do with—" he began, and then stopped, realizing his mistake.

"Ah! So you *do* wanna date her!" JD crowed triumphantly. "Romeo finally admits it!"

Mortified, Will looked around to make sure no one had

heard this indiscreet pronouncement. Cheeks burning with embarrassment, he tried to grab JD to playfully shake him, but JD easily evaded his clumsy grasp. Will's irritation spiked and then dissipated as he vicariously enjoyed his friend's amusement. After a moment he felt his best course of action would be neither to affirm nor deny.

"Why don't you ring the doorbell?" JD suggested.

"What? And wake up her mom? It's seven-thirty. No."

"Then. Text. Her."

Sighing hoarsely, Will grabbed his phone from his pocket and began texting. No response. They waited nearly five minutes, their banter growing more awkward by the second. A couple cars drove past, making both boys self-conscious about appearing like loiterers at such an odd hour. The day was rapidly brightening, and Will began to sweat beneath his windbreaker as the temperature continued to rise.

Moments later, JD raised his hands in defeat. "Well, I feel like a chump."

"You're not a chump," Will said.

"Really, Will?" JD asked sarcastically. "Come on, let's go. She's not coming."

"But wait—"

"What? No text, no call?"

"But—"

JD started back down the driveway. "Dude! She's not coming. Come on."

Will looked pensively to the house. He had been looking forward to spending time in a car with Connie Craft, and not just because she was an attractive girl who could help him with the scholarship competition. There was something about her he almost desperately wanted to *understand*. Something *was* off about her. He was certain of that now. And if it was as bewildering for her as it was for him, perhaps he could connect with her? Perhaps he could show her that life didn't have to be so lonely? Perhaps he could even prove to her—and to himself—that he deserved to love her?

JD stopped and turned to Will. "It's for the best," he said, comfortingly.

Will looked at him critically. "What's that supposed to mean?"

"Connie's not all there," JD said, pointing to his head. "She says one thing and does another. You should get over her."

A flash of anger consumed Will for a moment, during which he thought of all the mean, petty things he could say in response to a social reject like JD. He held himself back, however, and the anger subsided as it always did. That JD might have told the truth once again made it fade away a little more easily. Will nodded, ready to concede the point and head back to the car.

"Will!"

His heart stopped as he turned and saw Connie standing in the doorway in a white bathrobe. With disheveled hair, she seemed taller than usual. She stepped onto her tiny porch, leaning on the front door handle as if to keep from falling. Her pallid face and half-shut eyes startled Will into silence.

"I'm sorry, I can't go," she rasped painfully.

Shock quickly gave way to concern as Will rushed toward her. "Connie!"

"I'm sick," she muttered through bloodshot eyes.

"Oh, no!" he said as he met her at the doorstep. "Are you all right?"

"Yeah, I'll be fine. I just got this headache and can barely move. I think I have the flu. I'm sorry, Will. I really wanted to go with you guys."

Will smiled, relieved that it was only the flu. "It's okay. Don't worry about it."

"My phone died. That's why—"

"Please, Connie—"

"No, I'm sorry," she pleaded. "I know I'm letting you down, Will. Please forgive me!"

"Connie, it's okay," Will said, feeling embarrassed. He wished she would also apologize to JD. She was letting him down as well.

"I need to make it up to you. I feel terrible."

"Make it up to me by going back to bed and getting better."

Connie sniffed, hesitated, and then touched him tenderly on the chest. "I got in a big fight with Pete last night," she said. "I think we're done. I don't know." As her shoulders began to heave in anguish, she placed her arms around a flabbergasted Will and rested her forehead on his shoulder. Will had never been embraced by a girl before, and was afraid to embrace her back and reveal how fast his heart was racing. The idea that Connie Craft might now be available thrilled him. Would it be selfish for him to see this as an opportunity? If so, did he deserve it?

Before Will could decide how to react, she pulled away. She kissed her fingers and placed them on his lips. "Take good notes for me, Doofus," she said with a tired smile before slowly closing the door and disappearing inside.

Chapter 8

As they drove out of Connie's neighborhood, Will's hands began to tremble. She touched him! She hugged him! She all but kissed him! He bit his lip in a vain attempt to grapple with his emotions. Because of the ample flab engulfing his body, nervous tension was something he usually felt rather than showed. Now he was practically shaking in his seat.

"You all right?" JD asked. "Do I need to call 911 and get you on a stretcher?"

"I'm fine," Will said. "I just need some time to let it sink in."

"To let what sink in?"

Will looked at his friend quizzically and decided not to answer. JD had been suspiciously quiet since they left Connie's house. Will expected him to either share in his excitement or smother him with wet blankets like he usually did. Either would have been welcome. But since Will was getting neither, he let his mind wander over the hum of the automobile and the occasional notification from JD's cellphone, which was leading them to Uncle Gus's house two-and-a-half hours away. As the minutes flew by, and the forested suburban scenery gave way to the spacious countryside of the nearby state highway, the churning emptiness in his gut made him long for the comfort of food. But the comfort of reclining in his seat and thinking about Connie helped him overcome it. The straightness of the highway, the flatness of the terrain, and the car's monotonous rumbling gently lowered him into a state of bliss. The overcast sky made it easy for him to keep his eyes closed. He had been up late the night before fretting over this trip—unnecessarily, as it turned out. As all the sleep he had missed came to collect its due, Will was perfectly happy to pay up in full.

When he awoke, the sun was blazing. He adjusted his

seat and sat up to see cornfields buzzing by on either side of the car, broken up by farmhouses, billboards, and the occasional copse.

"Rise and shine, sunshine," JD said. "We're about 20 minutes out." He was now in a white T-shirt promoting yet another obscure musical group. Somehow he had removed his flannel while Will had been sleeping.

"Hot dog," Will yawned.

"You know, you kept calling out Connie's name in your sleep."

Will laughed. "I did not!"

"You were dreaming about her, weren't ya?"

"What if I was?"

JD pulled off the highway onto the exit leading to Uncle Gus's hometown. "Dude. I'm telling you. She's trouble."

"Not this again."

"Seriously. I don't think she's sick," JD said between instructions from his cellphone. He ran a yellow light and zipped through a rundown section of town. Whitewashed brick warehouses strewn with graffiti filled their lefthand view while chain-linked fences and broken-down structures dominated their right. This soon gave way to a commercial district, with dollar and liquor stores appearing frequently. Hulking brick buildings with checkered windows and zigzagging fire escapes loomed in the distance. Will spotted several rusted yet operational storefronts with signs mostly in Spanish. Quite a few older cars were parked on the side of the road.

"How do you know she's not sick?" Will asked, trying not to stare as they passed several black men loitering outside a convenience store. He counted three cars getting gas and was comforted to see that one of the drivers was white.

"Was she coughing or sneezing? Did she have a stuffy nose?"

"JD, you can be sick and not—"

"She said she had the flu. Aren't those flu symptoms?"

"She said she *thought* she had the flu."

"Even so! What was she doing blubbering all over you? *Here, let me touch your lips with my fingers and give you all my germs. Oh, that's so romantic!* If she's really sick, Will, she'll have you shivering under a blanket for two days."

Will shot a calculating glare at his friend and figured he could take what he had coming to him. "Oh, you're just jealous."

JD did a doubletake and guffawed into the steering wheel. "Dude, I admit Connie's hot. But I'm a Chihuahua, and she's a Great Dane. We operate in totally different ecosystems. And all that CRT stuff she swallows whole is a real turnoff. Plus, she could probably kick my butt. Why would she want to *slum* it with me?"

Will had heard such self-pitying proclamations from his friend many times before and was no longer moved by them. "Okay, then, doctor, what's wrong with her?" he asked sarcastically. "I saw her up close. I don't think she was faking."

They crossed railroad tracks, and then took a sharp right turn into a neighborhood less welcoming than the one they had just left. Overgrown tree limbs grasped each other above the street like gnarled fingers. Oblong apartment buildings formed unkempt, grassy alleys between them. Windows were either boarded up or blocked by air conditioning units. Dark roofs and brown siding gave the neighborhood a depressing lack of visual interest. Plants and foliage were everywhere, but almost none of it was *green*.

"I don't think she's faking, either," JD said.

"Then what's wrong with her?"

JD closed his mouth, suddenly reluctant to answer.

"Come on. Tell me," Will prodded.

"She was hungover, okay?" JD said almost regretfully.

"What? No!"

"Yeah."

"I don't think so."

"Will, you don't drink, and your family doesn't drink. How would you know?"

Will grimaced like he always did whenever JD cut straight to the heart of the matter, which was frustratingly often. "What makes you think she was hungover?"

"Because before the divorce my dad used to come home drunk every once in a while, okay?" JD said defensively. "I know what a hangover looks like. Plus, it makes sense."

"How?"

"She has a beautiful car and never drives it. She's, like, the only senior at school still taking the bus."

"So?"

"So? Put two and two together, Will. Her mom doesn't let her drive!"

"Because she has an alcohol problem," Will said, resigning himself to his friend's inescapable logic. Still, he was reluctant to accept it.

"Right!"

"You don't know that, JD," Will said, even though he knew he didn't sound very convincing. He was grateful that his friend didn't seem interested in continuing the discussion. But why? This was the first time JD had ever mentioned his father and alcohol. Was everything okay with his family? Will felt a pang of shame for not knowing.

After passing a cemetery and an intersection, the neighborhood began to improve. Old one-story homes appeared prefabricated in their box-like smallness. Each had wide, gabled roofs forming triangles of siding above living room windows and front doors. Some had detached garages; others had carports. All had driveways and modest yet well-kept yards. Shrubbery and trees appeared often, standing trim and erect—unlike the gangling vegetation from before.

Uncle Gus's house resembled the others, and was likewise just as well kept. A single comfortable-looking rocking chair occupied the structure's front patio. The house stood next to a large thicket of trees on one side and an empty grass lot on the other. Across the street was the overgrown lawn of a dilapidated church. Tall grass was sprouting through the cracks of its long, paved parking lot.

The boys pulled into Uncle Gus's worn-out gravel driveway. After resting a moment, they exited the car and noticed a handsome extension behind the house which took up nearly half of its meager backyard. Its several windows had dark-brown shutters, and its beige vinyl siding matched the rest of the home. Thick metallic doors extended at an angle from the structure's base. Beyond the detached garage were more trees, between which Will could see cars cruising through the adjacent neighborhood.

Will followed JD up the steps and into the large, screened-in porch, which stretched parallel to the driveway. He hoped that Uncle Gus would appear as soon as JD pressed the doorbell. That hope began to fade when JD pressed it a second time. By the third, Will was beginning to doubt that Uncle Gus would appear at all. Embarrassment set in as the boys were once again forced to wait outside someone's home that morning. This time, however, they didn't make chitchat. For all they knew, Uncle Gus was dead or in the hospital. Fortunately, JD had the good sense to knock, and within a few seconds they could hear slow, shuffling sounds coming toward them from inside.

A jowly old man with baggy eyes, a lumpy nose, and a rash on the left side of his scruffy face opened the door. He was short, made shorter by his posture, and the wisps of gray hair on his scalp seemed as if they could be blown off by the wind. But his eyes were sharp, if tired, and the sturdy shoulders on either side of his thick torso defied his age. He wore a white undershirt beneath a brown cardigan, blue sweat shorts, leather slippers, and white tube socks with red stripes, which were pulled up almost to his knees. Eyeglasses hung from a chain around his neck.

"Uncle Gus!" JD exclaimed.

Uncle Gus's thin mouth curved into a smile as he reached out a few inches to shake JD's hand. "Hey there, JD," he wheezed.

"This is my friend Will, Uncle Gus. We really appreciate you taking the time to—"

Confused, Uncle Gus looked from JD to Will and then back to JD. "Didn't ya say ya'd have a girl with ya?"

"Connie couldn't make it. She's sick."

"Sick!" Uncle Gus exclaimed with a weary chuckle. "I'm sick too. At 90, every day you're sick with somethin'."

Will and ID glanced at each other and laughed politely.

Uncle Gus squeezed JD warmly by the forearm. "Ah, what're you kids doin' standin' out here? C'mon in."

The boys followed Uncle Gus inside through the musty air of a thin passageway. Jackets and sweaters hung on hooks to their left. Beneath them were a jumble of old shoes and boots. Will presumed the dusty shutters on the window to their right hadn't been touched in years. The kitchen seemed functional and well-kept, but mean and outdated. A white imitation tile floor reflected light from the bare fluorescent bulb on the ceiling. Garish wallpaper flashed geometric shapes in red and green. As for the appliances, Will had never seen any like them except as curiosities on the internet—a white refrigerator resembling a giant marshmallow, a stovetop with coiled burners, a tall blender with yellowed mechanical buttons, and a coffee maker with an analog timer. He looked and couldn't find a microwave.

"Sorry I didn't respond to your last letter, JD," Uncle Gus said as he led them through the kitchen. The boys had to slow their normal pace not to bump into their host.

"That's okay, Uncle Gus."

"So, I've seen this CRT business. It's what you wanna talk about, right? I know all about it."

Beyond the kitchen was the dining room, where fake tile gave way to fake hardwood, and the wallpaper gave way to cheap wood paneling. A plastic folding table served as a dinner table, with one comfortable-looking leather-bound chair at its head. Metal folding chairs occupied the three remaining places. Will's nose told him what awaited on the table before his eyes could—two large pizza boxes, one stacked upon the other. Recently delivered. At least one was pepperoni. Hungry as he was, Will had to hold back, ashamed to admit that he could devour both pizzas in 15 minutes if he wanted. But with Connie now seeming to show real interest in him, he wondered if he should start counting calories. Would slimming down increase his chances with her? He smiled, realizing he hadn't felt that kind of hope in a long time.

"Oh, pizza!" JD exclaimed. "Thanks, Uncle Gus."

"Yeah. Help yourselves," Uncle Gus urged as he eased into his leather chair with a groan. "Put your bags down. You must be hungry." He opened one of the boxes for JD, who took a paper plate from the edge of the table and began helping himself. Will cringed with hunger. The pizza had sausage and hamburger on it as well.

"I got nothin' to give ya to drink 'cept tap water. I hope that's okay," Uncle Gus said, pointing to a plastic pitcher and some glasses on the table.

"S'fine. T'anks," JD mumbled through a mouthful of food. "You gonna sit, Will?"

The question pulled Will from the quicksand of his hunger. "Uh . . ." he began, now stalling for time. He both wanted and did not want to eat that pizza. He hadn't had anything since a bowl of cereal, half a muffin, and a banana before leaving home that morning.

"What? Ya don't like pizza?" Uncle Gus asked.

"I do," Will said. "It's just that—" He took a step back, knowing that if he were to sit down and start eating, he wouldn't stop. He needed an excuse more quickly than his clumsy brain could come up with one. "I have to go to the bathroom," he blurted finally. After being directed by Uncle Gus, he slipped through the living room and a short hall, and entered the bathroom.

Once inside, he leaned against the door and contemplated his predicament. Was he that weak? Could the mere sight and smell of a couple pizzas rattle him so easily? Couldn't he just have lunch like a civilized human being without being a destroyer of worlds? He clenched his fists and suffered a few minutes before resolving that he should at least *try* to win Connie over. He should at least *try* to lose weight, something his mother was always nagging him to do, and would be good for him regardless. His stomach growled, seemingly in protest. It was a *persuasive* protest—persuasive enough to convince him to have two slices, and no more. In order for his diet to work—and for him to have a prayer with Connie Craft—he would have to do without. He had no choice.

Will reemerged into the living room moments later and noticed how welcoming it seemed. The couch appeared to be an antique, but comfortable nonetheless. A beige blanket lay neatly folded upon an old leather recliner. Will was not surprised by the absence of a television, but was surprised by the three tall bookshelves standing against the wall between the dining room and the front door. One of them blocked part of a large window. They didn't hold books. They held *note*books. Perhaps a thousand of them, he estimated.

Back at the table, JD and Uncle Gus were engaged in a heated discussion. Uncle Gus was adamantly refusing to take part in their project. He insisted that everything they were taught about critical race theory was a lie.

Chapter 9

JD flung up his hands as he swallowed his bite of pizza. "I don't get it!"

"What don't ya get?" Uncle Gus asked patiently.

"You make critical theory sound so complicated."

"They *make* it complicated."

"Why?"

"Critical theory's a cult. Ya gotta understand what they're sayin'—or pretend to—before they let ya in."

"But who, Uncle Gus?" JD asked. "Who is 'they'?"

Uncle Gus waved his hand contemptuously. "These people. I *knew* them! I studied with them. I was there when they published in the '50s."

"But w*ho* are you talking about?" Will asked, his half-eaten slice of pizza completely forgotten in his hand.

Uncle Gus groaned. "The architects of critical theory. They didn't call it that back then. Their whole thing—I guess ya can call it *schtick*—is critique, psychoanalysis, social change. But really it's just tribalism. They say they're about freedom, but once they get power—heh heh—they don't care so much about freedom. At least not for guys like you n' me."

"So you can't critique the critiquers?" Will asked, thinking cynically of Nadine Alterman.

Uncle Gus chuckled. "If ya do, watch out."

"But I still don't know what critical theory back then has to do—"

"All right, I'll lay it out for ya." Uncle Gus wheezed, and then thumped himself twice in the chest. "You kids hearda Karl Marx, right? Marxism? Communism?"

"Yeah," both boys said.

"What was it? Supposedly, it scientifically analyzed economics and history, right? And it came up with laws that predicted the collapse of capitalism and the workers revolting and getting class consciousness and whatnot.

But what they really wanted—not the true believers, but the radicals who pushed this stuff—was to come up with some authoritative rubric to destroy . . . kings, tsars, aristocracies, nations. And kill whoever got in their way. They wanted to replace old power with new, with them in charge. It was all about power, y'see.

"Then it fell apart. Nothin' they predicted came true. A little over a hundred years ago, somethin' happened. Somethin' big that threw a monkey wrench into everything. Any guesses on what that was?"

Will put down his pizza and considered all the history he remembered from that time period. *The Roaring Twenties? The Great Depression? Jim Crow? The Tulsa riot?*

"World War I," JD said without a pause.

Will turned to him, astonished at how quickly he had responded.

"Bingo," Uncle Gus said. "Instead of the working class rising up against the capitalists, most working people were just normal folks. They went to church, loved their country, raised families, followed tradition. And when their leaders told them to, they slaughtered each other."

"Jeez," Will said, not knowing what else to say.

"So the Marxists went back to the drawing board and came up with critical theory. They still wanted to destroy. They still wanted power. They still pretended to be scientific. But now they looked somewhere else." He tapped his temple. "They looked in here, y'see."

Will began a slow, gratifying nod. "You're talking about psychology," he said. It wasn't a question, because somehow he knew.

Uncle Gus assented with a grunt, and then began rambling, causing both boys to lean in closer to listen. ". . . theories of 'hegemony' and 'reification' . . . no *a priori* values they cared to tell us about . . . good parenting causes authoritarian impulses . . . repression of primitive urges . . . but guess where the Depression *wasn't* so bad . . . couldn't stop talking about sex . . . fascism, fascism, everything led to fascism . . . pathologizing what was natural and healthy—"

"I'm sorry, Uncle Gus," JD interrupted. "We can't understand what you're saying."

Uncle Gus sagged in his seat. "Sorry, JD. I'm just an old man."

"It's okay. Do you need anything? A glass of water? We don't have to—"

"Nah, I'm all right," he said, running his tongue delicately along his lips and catching his breath. He gripped the wispy hair on his head and closed his eyes without squinting. Will was about to ask if he should call 911 when Uncle Gus finally became alert.

"Basically, critical theory wants to destroy everything that made Western society great. Ya gotta have discipline to do great things, see? Ya gotta be eugenic and not dysgenic. It's not always fun, but that's how it is. That's why ya have religion, tradition. That's why people formed groups based on kin and ethnicity. That's what made Europe so strong. But these people invented a body of thought that made all that seem oppressive and criminal, and the people who followed it were intolerant or ignorant. The only way out was to turn your back on it all."

"But if these things made us great, why did they want to destroy them?" Will asked.

Uncle Gus convulsed in a brief, noiseless laugh. "They're neurotic. They're clannish. They felt threatened, so they gained power over us by controlling how we think. And they have this presumption of innocence. They forget when *they* do evil things that kill millions. But when there's backlash—Oh!" Uncle Gus flopped his hand onto the table. "Ya never hear the end of it."

JD squinted at him skeptically. "Uncle Gus, are you still talking about the people who started critical theory?"

The old man smiled and thought for a moment.

"Among others, yeah."

"But what does this have to do with critical *race* theory?" Will asked.

"Oh, that! A less erudite version of the same thing. I took a glance at it a couple years ago. That's about all it was worth."

"How are they different?"

Uncle Gus tilted his head and squinted at the ceiling. "Well, I guess in my day they still cared a little about class. They studied economics and epistemology. They still, y'know, drew from guys like Hegel, Nietzsche, Kant." He smiled as Will stared at him blankly. "Not the answer you were lookin' for, was it?"

Will hesitated, afraid that answering such a frank question would be rude.

"Well, now their target is white people, and it don't matter if you're rich or poor," Uncle Gus went on. "It's almost like Christianity. Being white is an original sin. Ya have to, y'know—" He waved his fist from shoulder to shoulder as if lashing himself.

The boys looked at each other, confused. Will turned to Uncle Gus and gathered his courage. "But we did do some bad things, didn't we?" he asked. "I did some research about segregation and racism. I mean, I'm not sold on critical race theory. But they have a point about this, don't they? When I read about it, sometimes I feel ashamed."

Uncle Gus shrunk away from Will, almost in slow motion. "Why?" he asked.

Will stole a glance at JD, who was smiling expectantly, and continued. "I read about how in Tulsa, Oklahoma a hundred years ago whites killed 300 blacks and burned their whole neighborhood. How can I—I don't—I mean, I'm not sure—"

"What do you kids know about Reconstruction?" Uncle Gus interrupted, not even looking at his guests.

Will and JD looked at each other. "What's that?" they asked.

The old man fidgeted in discomfort. "Ya gotta study it. I can recommend a couple books. For a few years after the Civil War, free blacks were given a lotta power in the South. They were corrupt and ignorant. It was a mess. And they started committing a lotta crime, y'see, 'specially against *us*. Murder and ravishing, as they called it back then, happened a lot."

"Ravishing?" Will asked. "What's that?"

"Ya gotta cellphone, son?"

"Uh-huh."

"Look it up. A verb. As in, 'to ravish.'"

After realizing that Uncle Gus was serious, Will obliged. He noted the definition in the online dictionary and understood. He placed his phone back in his pocket, embarrassed for not having known.

"We were upset about all the crime," Uncle Gus went on. "Especially when the victims were women. Anyway, most of the people they strung up were guilty of what they were accused of—black, white, Mexican, whatever."

JD sat back in his seat. "Are you justifying lynching, Uncle Gus?"

The old man shook his head. "No. Mob justice is murder, too."

"Then what are you saying?"

Uncle Gus leaned toward them, sliding his hand along the table. "Lynching was bad, sure, *but what it was reacting to was worse.*"

Everything suddenly crystalized for Will. It felt as if he were finally aligning himself with history—*his* history. Why did his ancestors behave in certain ways? Why did they so often do things that are considered abhorrent or blameworthy today? Was it because of hate or racism? Or were they, as Uncle Gus was saying, reacting to things that were *worse*? Things that Nadine Alterman would never dare mention? Will almost laughed. Everything made sense for him now—Alterman's threats, his father's bullying, his mother's fear, all of it. Even critical theory began to make sense. It was so empty and vapid because it was never meant to uncover the truth like other academic studies. It never needed that kind of rigor. It was simply about power—empowering blacks over whites. That's all it ever was. Will slumped in his chair, too stunned to think, both relieved and frightened at the same time.

JD was still unconvinced. "But 300 people, Uncle Gus. Come on."

"Well, we all know how *some* people like to embellish. They wanna sell books and stir up trouble so they take 150 and make it 300. I don't know. I wasn't there. But I know I can't trust 'em."

JD threw his hand in the air. "But still!"

"I gotta couple newspaper articles from back then somewhere. None of 'em say anythin' about 300."

"Even if it's just 150, though. It's still bad."

Uncle Gus smiled. "Lemme ask ya, what's the date today?"

The boys looked at each other. "November fourth," Will said.

"And how many of us have the blacks killed so far this year?"

JD shook his head sharply, as if he didn't understand the question.

"By 'us' you mean white people?" Will asked.

"That's right. White Americans."

"I don't know," JD responded.

"Why not?" Uncle Gus asked. "A minute ago ya cared about numbers. Now ya don't?"

"But that's different."

"Only if some victims matter more than others."

Flabbergasted, JD stared silently at Uncle Gus.

"How many of us *have* they killed?" Will asked.

Uncle Gus shot a dread look at Will. "476. As of last month. It's probably a little north of that by now."

"Wow," Will exclaimed.

"That ain't a guess or an estimate, son. It's all confirmed. It happens every year. Must be over 20,000 of us been murdered by blacks in the past, what, 50 years? And we kill a much smaller number of them, despite still bein' the majority. So far this year it's around 80. So who's killin' who?"

"But Uncle Gus, we have no way of knowing this," JD said. "No one reports on it."

"Ya sure about that?"

Again, the boys looked at each other. Will suddenly wondered if the No College Club kept track of information like this.

"Mainstream news won't," Uncle Gus said. "But some people do. They lose their bank accounts and get kicked off the internet—all by the same people who invented critical theory years ago, funny enough." The old man grimaced in contempt. "Ehh! They ain't honest. They pretend to be Americans, but they always do what's best for *them!* But when we do what's best for us, they call us Nazis."

Will nodded without realizing he was nodding. "I got that impression from CRT. If we acted the way blacks act, they'd call us racist."

Uncle Gus nodded back. "Them, too."

After a moment, Will noticed that getting so worked up must have finally tired Uncle Gus out. He tilted forward and blew out a deep breath. His eyes became glassy and he winced several times. If his elbows hadn't already been propping him up, Will feared the old man might have fallen forward onto the table. To Will's relief, Uncle Gus soon recovered and even smiled puckishly at his guests. Will looked over at JD who was slouching in his chair and staring pensively at the ceiling.

"There goes our critical theory project," Will said, taking a stab at levity as he finished his slice of pizza. He might not have sounded serious, but he was. He resolved then and there not to submit anything to that scholarship competition, despite needing the money and liking Connie Craft. He no longer wanted to pretend he had faith in critical theory. It would have been too—he searched for the correct word—corrupting? Degrading? Humiliating? He was surprised at how happy this decision made him feel.

"How do you know all this stuff, Uncle Gus?" JD asked.

All the air seemed to leak out of the old man as he slumped back in his chair. "My library," he said softly, not looking at his guests. "It's in the basement. My wife put it there years ago before she died since she didn't want her guests seein' my books and asking questions. But I can't climb stairs anymore, y'see. I haven't been down there in years."

"That's too bad," JD said. After some silent prodding from Will, he asked, "But we could go down there and bring it up for you, couldn't we?"

"Ah!" Uncle Gus said, seeming to like the idea. "Yeah, ya could. Sure. I gotta pretty big library. Anyways, I'm gonna sit here a while, while you kids check it out. I'm kinda tired. The basement's just past the bathroom on the left."

The boys made chitchat with Uncle Gus as they ate some more pizza, and then headed for the basement. The light switch at the top of the stairs didn't work. Their cellphones illuminated a concrete floor below through a haze of cobwebs and dust. After carefully navigating a creaky wooden staircase with no risers and a metal beam for a banister, JD and Will understood that Uncle Gus's library could not possibly be in his basement. The single bulb on the ceiling, controlled by a chain, revealed a cramped, windowless space, which housed an out-of-order washing machine, a bicycle with no wheels, an antique treadle-powered sewing machine, and a pile of old board games rotting in their cardboard boxes. In the corner was an old hot water heater and a gray rusted furnace. Three of the walls were cinderblock, and the fourth was unpainted sheetrock. Disappointed, they poked about the basement for nearly a minute before giving up.

"Hey, Will," JD whispered as they reentered the hall. "I think I know why the old man keeps track of crime statistics."

Will looked to make sure Uncle Gus wasn't in earshot. "Why?"

"Did you see some of the neighborhoods we drove through to get here?"

"Yeah."

"I wasn't gonna say anything."

"Me neither."

JD pointed in Uncle Gus's direction with his thumb. "I bet he's worried. He moved here in, like, the '60s, and I know that local crime has gotten pretty bad since then."

Will nodded sympathetically as he put his arm around his friend and led him back to the dining room, where they found their host sound asleep in his chair. They chuckled softly as they watched him snore.

"You know, he once said the funniest thing," JD said. "I didn't remember until just now."

"What?"

"He's a strange guy, Uncle Gus. He and my grandfather had a brother. Lyle. He was between them in age. As a kid, Gus was real close to him. But when World War II started, my grandfather enlisted and talked Lyle into enlisting, too, even though he was underage. They fudged his birth certificate or something. My dad's a little sketchy on the details."

"What happened to Lyle?" Will asked, dreading the worst.

"He was killed. Somewhere in France. And Uncle Gus never forgave my grandfather for it. Gus became, like, the black sheep of the family. I hardly ever saw him growing up."

"You said he said something funny?"

"Oh, yeah. He once told me we lost World War II."

"Who did?"

"We did."

"Who? America? What are you talking about? We won the war."

JD nodded solemnly. "That's what I said. And he said America won the war, all right. But *we* lost it."

Looking closely at his friend, Will was about to ask what he meant by "we"—but stopped himself because he already knew.

A piercing bang from outside caused both boys to jump. It sounded almost like a firecracker, but was too loud and powerful for that. Several blasts followed, which woke Uncle Gus with a gasp. It was the unmistakable sound of a firearm. The boys looked at each other in horror as they heard footsteps outside. Whoever was firing it was rapidly approaching.

Chapter 10

Will and JD rushed to the window. Peeling back the curtain and keeping low, they heard more footsteps outside and some shouting. Two more gunshots made them both flinch. Will felt his hands tingle and his breathing escalate as he understood that this was indeed real. He looked to JD and saw the disbelief and fear in his friend's eyes.

"They're at it again!" Uncle Gus lamented, slapping the table. "These people!"

Squinting, Will spotted a black man in a red and black football jersey running toward Uncle Gus's house along the driveway of the abandoned church across the street. He wore gray sweatpants and an orange bandana around his head. He turned to fire twice more at unseen assailants but his weapon failed to shoot, seemingly having run out of ammunition. He uselessly pulled the trigger once more and then bolted forward, carrying the pistol low in his right hand.

Both boys backed away from the window whispering profanities as Uncle Gus met them in the middle of living room. He was saying something, instructing them to go back into the basement where it would be safe. Will was dimly aware of JD rushing down the hall and of Uncle Gus calling his name, but he kept his eyes fixed on the gunman, trying to anticipate where he would go once he reached the road. Would he turn left or right? Or would he head straight *across* the road and into Uncle Gus's front yard?

Will felt anger welling up inside of him. His eyes glared, and his fists clenched, and his teeth were set as if preparing for a fight. By recklessly firing a lethal weapon in a residential neighborhood, this gunman, Will knew, was an interloper—not merely upon another person's property, but upon civilization itself. He was a burden and a threat. As these facts asserted themselves in Will's mind, he began to taste contempt and disgust, two feelings he had never experienced before. Was this the outrage the white residents of Tulsa felt a century ago when they learned of yet another possible assault by a black upon a white?

Once he saw that the gunman was about to charge directly across the street, still clutching his emptied weapon, Will felt the need to act. He rushed into the dining room and then through the kitchen and passageway until he reached the porch. Either the gunman would veer right and out of Will's life forever, or he would veer left onto Uncle Gus's driveway, where he would soon be heard scampering on the gravel.

Understanding that that dreadful possibility was about to happen, Will slipped through the screen door and gingerly took the porch steps down onto the grass. There he waited, hidden by the porch and unseen by the fast approaching gunman. He understood that in the coming encounter he might die, but was too livid to care. He imagined he was about to protect his family or Connie. If he had to go, what better way to go than that? In the final seconds before contact, Will felt himself grow calm, determined, and confident. For the first time in his life, he saw his placement in the world with ruthless clarity.

When he sensed that the gunman was less than five feet away, Will swung out his right foot and swept him off his feet with one powerful trip. He felt the impact on his ankle, which reminded him of how he had broken it years before. But he didn't have time to feel pain. The man went sprawling forward and landed on his face, skidding painfully on the gravel. Without as much as a thought, Will leaped onto the man's back, intending to hold him down until the police arrived. He had overshot his mark, however, and the man—who was of below-average height, but wiry and strong—started wriggling beneath him. Will adjusted by centering himself onto the man's back and driving him downwards until he flattened out. For once, Will was grateful for his tremendous size and weight. He pinned the man's right hand—his gun hand—onto the ground with both hands. The man punched at him blindly with his free hand and then attempted to roll his way out from under him. Will wouldn't let him, forcing him flat to the ground every time he got to his knees. But with both hands on the man's wrist he knew he couldn't do that forever. He soon realized that this struggle was turning into a stamina competition, and if he gave out first, he would likely be bludgeoned by the butt of that gun. Not being in any kind of athletic shape, Will soon began to tire. And the blasts of panic he was feeling were only making it worse.

From the way the gunman was hissing and wheezing, Will sensed that he was tiring as well. Soon the man made a final effort to free himself and posted one foot on the ground. This forced Will to clasp him around the waist with his left hand and drive him laterally onto his back. This solved one problem but introduced a worse one—the man's right hand now had more freedom, which meant he could more easily club Will in the face with his weapon. But Will called on a reserve of strength he didn't even know he had and kept the man's wrist pinned to the ground long enough for him to lay himself across his chest and grab hold of it with both hands once again.

This burst of energy would be his last. Will quickly understood that he no longer had the strength or endurance to remain on top of the still-struggling gunman. And with no police sirens blaring in the distance, he was beginning to wonder if he would survive the encounter at all. Within seconds the man rolled to his knees and stood, and there was nothing Will could do to stop him.

Will stepped back and awaited his fate. Would the man charge him and beat him to death with his fists? Would he reload his weapon and shoot him? Would he brain him with the butt of that pistol? For a moment, the two had a good look at each other. The man had a scruffy face and wide protruding cheek bones. His bandana had fallen off in the struggle, revealing a chaotic bush of short dreadlocks. His wide black eyes and thick eyebrows resembled a child's. Will expected a malicious or resentful stare, or something that would have reminded him of the gruesome experience they had just shared. Instead, the man simply looked past Will as if he hadn't even noticed him. Nothing. He gave Will nothing. Will found this deeply unsettling and took a moment to understand *why*. This man had no regard for human life at all. He didn't even love his own life enough to *hate* Will. Going to prison would be nothing for him—because life, for him, was nothing. At once, an apocalyptic vision gripped Will. What would civilization be like if people like this were in the majority? Would there even *be* a civilization at all?

Sirens in the distance. Finally. Will groaned in relief, but did not relax until the gunman took off at a labored sprint toward the small forest behind Uncle Gus's garage. Then the man did something baffling. He stopped and jogged back. Will retreated several steps before seeing that the man had returned only to retrieve his bandana. He casually picked it up and once again took off running without a backwards glance, quickly disappearing among the trees.

After a moment, Will felt himself begin to reel toward the backyard. Someone was shouting at him. It was JD. He was calling to him from the porch. In the last slow motion moments before passing out, Will saw the extension behind the house and again noticed the metallic doors extending from it. They looked like the outside entrance to a basement, he realized. But how could that be? He had been in the basement. It had no outside entrance.

As he mused upon this mystery, Will felt himself

swoon. He expected to hear a loud thump as his body struck the ground, but it never came.

***

When Will awoke, his ankle hurt. He knew that much. JD was there, clasping him by the shoulders. "Oh, my God, dude!" he exulted. "You're a beast! You're a stud! You're a boss! You're a—you're a—you're a—"

Will held up his hand as he sat up. "Enough! It's no big deal."

"*What possessed you to do that?*"

Will shrugged coming up with an answer. "I'm fat! I figured I could just lay on him. I'm the Willrus, remember?"

"But he had a gun!"

"Come on," he said as he rubbed his ankle. "It wasn't loaded."

"But still!"

The police sirens finally cut off in the distance, which was a great relief for Will. "I wonder if they arrested that guy."

"Maybe," JD said as he helped Will to his feet. "I heard a commotion on the other side of the woods after he disappeared. I guess we can go on the internet and find out. You all right?"

"Yeah, I'm fine," Will said, suddenly famished. He imagined himself back in Uncle Gus's dining room, devouring what was left of the pizza. His eyes lit up when he felt how sensitive his ankle was. He was able to head back toward the house without a limp. But a dull pain lingered.

JD pointed at Will as he walked backwards in front of him. "Dude! I can't wait to tell *everyone* at school! What a story this is gonna be, am I right?"

"Please don't tell anyone, JD."

"I'm just sad I didn't get video on my cellphone! It would've gone viral!"

Will placed his hand on his friend's shoulder. "Just don't."

"Why not?"

Will considered what he was about to say. "My father lectures me all the time on how black people are oppressed, okay? My mother gives money to groups that bail blacks out of jail. If my parents find out that I apprehended an African-American man on the run, they'd disown me."

"Really?"

Will started up the porch steps. "No, not really. But it wouldn't be good. Promise you won't tell anyone, okay?"

JD held up his right hand, deflated but compliant. "Okay, I promise."

"Thanks," Will said as he entered the porch, now intent upon speaking to Uncle Gus. He stopped when he saw the old man standing by the door, shaking his head gravely and leaning on the door handle like a cane. Will shamefully considered how all this excitement could have affected his nonagenarian host.

"Ya stupid kid," Uncle Gus said. "Why d'ya do that?"

"Uh . . ."

"Even if they catch him, they're just gonna let him out again. And in what? Four months? I know how they do things around here. Attempted murder gets talked down to a misdemeanor, and then these animals don't get prosecuted. The blacks run the town now. This is what ya get."

"I thought you of all people would approve of what Will just did, Uncle Gus," JD objected.

"Sure. If it would do any good!" Uncle Gus said, now brimming with anger. His tight grip on the handle was causing the door to shake on its hinges.

Feeling acute guilt, Will put one hand on his chest and the other in the air. "Uncle Gus, I am extremely sorry for what I did. I did not mean to disturb you. And if there is anything I can do to make it up to you, please let me know. But in the meantime, I might have some good news for you."

"What?"

"JD and I didn't find your library when we went down into your basement."

"How is that good news?"

"Because now I think I know where your library might be."

***

The key Uncle Gus had provided them slipped easily into the old padlock securing the metallic doors. When Will had reminded him of an external entrance to the basement, Uncle Gus's tired eyes widened. He suddenly remembered that in the 1960s during the Cold War he had partitioned his basement into a large fallout shelter to protect his family from a possible nuclear attack. This was most likely where he had placed his library. It took Uncle Gus much searching in his bedroom before finding the keys.

The doors creaked open and revealed four steps which led down to a solid white door with two deadbolt locks. Thrilled nearly to the point of hyperventilation, the boys slipped the keys into their locks and found that the door easily swung open. It revealed a dark, dusty space filled with shelves, cobwebs, and shadows. Will noticed a chain hanging from the ceiling and pulled it. The sudden fluorescent brightness caused both boys to cover their eyes. Where were they? In a supermarket?

The underground room was much larger than Will had imagined and contained three tall shelves filled with foodstuffs, water jugs, and canned goods. Will ran his finger atop a dusty can of kidney beans. Its expiration date was January 31, 1994. "Going on 30 years," he whispered.

"Will!" JD called. "Look at this!"

Behind the third shelving unit, which held all manner of tool and machinery, was a walled-off and spacious living area. Two bunk beds stood against one wall, and a full-sized bed against another, each neatly made with a plethora of blankets and pillows. Between them were numerous mats on the floor, a closet filled with boxes, coats, and clothing, and a small bathroom. To their left was a makeshift kitchen, which contained a table and chairs, a sink and counter, a single cabinet, two small refrigerators, and, to Will's surprise, a microwave oven. Hanging on the wall opposite were a shotgun, two rifles, and several pistols. Stacked beneath them were numerous cardboard boxes of ammunition.

"Jackpot!" JD cried.

In a small, curtained chamber beyond the kitchen, JD had found stacks and stacks of books, papers, and magazines. There must have been over a thousand, all told. The boys coughed on the dust in the air as they investigated the treasure. There were how-to books and nuclear war survival books. There were books on hunting and camping. There were classic works by Homer, Shakespeare, and other famous authors. There were quite a few history and philosophy books as well. All were in English, and most were at least familiar. But some Will found eerily curious—as if they were suppressed voices from the previous century calling out to him. Titles such as *The Dispossessed Majority, Suicide of the West, Camp of the Saints,* and *The Forced War* whispered hints of dissidence from their summaries on faded dustjackets.

The magazines were even more curious. Will had heard of none of them: *Instauration, The Spotlight, Mankind Quarterly, The Washington Observer,* and many others. As he flipped through them he saw frank discussions on forbidden topics. He couldn't believe that there had once been an age when people discussed race, gender, history, politics, and religion from a standpoint which was openly and confidently . . . *white*. Will felt a twisting angst in his gut, wishing he had months rather than minutes to delve into this massive trove of forgotten literature.

Chapter 11

Will's visit with Uncle Gus had inspired and invigorated him. He felt lighter, and was indeed lighter the following morning, having lost nearly five pounds in all the excitement. Over the weekend, he had controlled his cravings so well that even his father noticed. He had borrowed a book and several old magazines from Uncle Gus and spent most of Sunday alone in his room reading them. There was so much ground to cover—so many taboos to dissect, revive, and embrace. Immigration. The Civil Rights Movement. The Second World War. The Civil War. The *Russian* Civil War. The Soviet gulags. Race. Crime. Psychometrics. Genetics. *Eugenics*. How had he not known about any of this? There was so much his teachers and his parents had never shared with him—he was almost resentful for it. But not quite. He was still young. He knew he had time.

Finally free from the onerous obligations of that scholarship competition—and with his friendship with JD now stronger than ever—Will placed his remaining hopes on Connie Craft. Would she have any reason to talk to him now? Would she understand and appreciate his reasons for abandoning critical theory? Were things soon to be finished between them? And if forced to choose between her and his newfound awareness, would he really be willing to say goodbye to her forever?

On Mondays and Wednesdays Will spent most of his time at his high school's north campus, where the science and math courses were taught. After his art history class in the morning, he and a number of other students walked, biked, or drove the quarter mile to the facility, which belonged to the state university system and had its own cafeteria. This meant that if Will wanted to, he could leave main campus at 9:55 am and not return for the rest of the day. That Monday, however, he came back after his afternoon classes in hopes of finding Connie.

Just as he was approaching the school building along its main drive, he saw her coming out with a pair of friends—popular girls who tended to avoid him as much as he avoided them. Both were tall, pretty, and slender. Did Connie wish to be more like them? Her thick frame and the slight side-to-side motions she made when she walked struck Will as out of place when compared to these girls. She appeared smart and well-coordinated in her ruffled smock dress, black boots, and many bracelets. The audacious waves in her hair were certainly a centerpiece of attention. Still, she seemed to lack the natural elegance of her friends in their beige capri slacks, pulled-back hair, and designer blouses. They waved amicably to Connie as they headed off to the student parking lot. Connie waved back and started off toward the buses, toward Will. Her face brightened as she noticed him, and they both hurried along the sidewalk to meet each other.

"Hey, Doofus," she said, punching him playfully on the shoulder. "Why didn't you call me back?" His look of consternation drew her concern. "What's wrong?"

"First, how are you feeling?" he asked.

Connie pursed her lips, taking a moment to understand what he meant. "Fine! I'm fine. I don't know, I must have just had a head cold when I saw you. I hear it's going around. I was feeling better last night when I called. Why didn't you call me back? Don't dodge the question, now."

Will laughed nervously as he tried to reconcile JD's hangover theory with the girl who was standing right in front of him. If correct, it meant that Connie had lied to him on Saturday morning and was lying to him once again. Could that be? As crucial as this question was to his peace of mind, he had little time to ponder it since Connie had deftly turned the tables on him.

"Ah, well, I'm sorry about that," he began. "You see, during our visit with JD's Uncle Gus, we learned that—"

She squinted in the slanting sunlight and guided him a few steps away to a nearby tree where she could see him better. "Oh, yeah! How did that go? Did you learn anything cool?"

"Um, yeah, actually," he said, mustering whatever authority he had by clapping his hands against his thighs. "We learned that CRT is not real."

"What?"

"It's just about power, Connie. Critical race theory is about blacks gaining power over whites without . . . having to earn it. There's no truth behind it. Whites were no worse than anybody else in the past. It's totally unfair to pick on us. CRT is straight-up anti-white racism. I don't think I'm gonna submit anything to that scholarship competition. I'm sorry, but I don't think it would be right for me to help you on it, either, since I don't believe in it. But I hope we can still be—"

Connie raised her hands to her mouth in shock. "I can't believe you just said that," she whispered.

Will feared the worst. He had such kind thoughts for this lovely and unusual girl that he didn't want to offend or repel her in any way. He still dreamed he could be with her, if only as a confidante or friend. But his newfound antipathy for critical theory and all that it stood for went far deeper than this.

"It's true, Connie," he said. "I wouldn't lie to you."

"And I would lie to you?" she asked defensively. "Is that what you're saying?"

"No, I—"

"What else did he say?"

"Who?"

She placed her hands on her hips, now angry. "JD's uncle! What else did he say? Did you talk to him about the Tulsa riot like you said? Did he approve of it? Did he say the blacks got what they deserved?"

"No! But he did say that blacks committed a lot of

crime back then—sort of like how they do now—especially murder and ravaging white women—"

"Oh, my God!" she exclaimed, stepping back.

"What? He didn't justify the riot, Connie. But at that time in history whites were getting tired of being victims of violent crime. And it's true! Ever the since Civil War, free blacks committed a disproportionate—"

Connie gasped, pulling at her hair. Her look of indignation contorted her face almost beyond recognition. "You support slavery!" she shouted, stepping back further. "How *dare* you!"

"What? No, I don't!" Will exclaimed. He realized that this was going beyond his relationship with Connie and into territory both murky and dangerous. He was suddenly *afraid* of Connie, but didn't have the time or the perspective to figure out why.

"Yes, you do!" she declared, now nearly hyperventilating.

"Connie, no. Please, don't be like that," he urged, stepping forward to comfort her.

She slapped his hand away. "Don't touch me!" she shrieked. After taking a moment to control herself, she folded her arms and looked at him vindictively. "You know, they used to say the same things about my people."

"Your people?"

"Yes! Native Americans. They used to say the same things about Native Americans."

"Say what things?"

She walked up to him fearlessly, fists clenched. "You are so stupid!"

Will stopped breathing for a moment as he registered the insult. He was too shocked to feel the pain Connie had meant for him to feel.

"They said the same lies about Indians," she went on. "About how all we do is commit crimes and rape women and get drunk! Are you saying *my* people deserve genocide?"

Will was too stupefied to answer. *Genocide?* Not only had that *not* occurred to him, it had *never* occurred to him. Why would he want to wish genocide on anyone? There were too many things happening at once, and none of them made sense. The insults, the accusations, the hostility—all from a girl he really liked.

Connie nodded grimly, taking Will's silence for an answer. "I knew it. You're a white supremacist!"

As she shoved past him, Will spun around and tried to follow her. But her look of glowering rage stopped him. Her lower jaw stuck out and her blue eyes glistened in malice. He had never seen her like this before.

"Racist!" she screeched, stamping her foot. "Nazi! *Racist!*" After glaring at Will a moment longer, she turned and ran off to the line of buses waiting in the school parking lot.

Breathing heavily, Will tried to process what had just happened. His conversation with Connie had gone far worse than he had anticipated. At that moment he was feeling entirely numb, but knew it wouldn't last. He knew that soon he would be emotionally crushed. Connie was forcing him to fit the newer, more confident version of himself back into the lonely old shell of his past. It would be a tight, depressing squeeze. But he figured he could manage. He closed his eyes and consoled himself, knowing that as bad has he was going to feel, working on that critical theory project would have made him feel much, much worse.

Will opened his eyes and suddenly wasn't so sure. All around him were his classmates, walking past him as if in slow-motion. Either they were staring at him blankly like spellbound rubberneckers, or were tapping furiously on their cellphones, ravenous for drama and gossip. It then occurred to him that his bitter row with Connie had been very public. How much of their conversation had anyone heard? He had to assume at least some of it. He did not know if his reputation at school could survive this kind of slander—especially from a mixed-race girl who identified more as American Indian than white. Connie Craft had just called him a racist in front of—he glanced about, counting—15 or 20 people. Within minutes, everyone in the school would know.

What would this mean for him? He was fairly certain no one had heard anything *he* had said. Connie had pulled him off the sidewalk, which had given them some privacy, and he hadn't been loud. Had anyone taken video? His heart throbbed as he concluded that yes, someone might have taken video. Will clamped his mouth shut tightly until his jaw began to ache as he replayed their entire dialogue in his mind. Had he said anything that could get him in trouble? Perhaps. He was fairly certain that Nadine Alterman would judge him unfairly. But she was just one woman. How much power did she really have?

A more important question occurred to him: Had he said anything that he regretted or wished he could take back? He pondered this for a moment. No, he hadn't. He had said nothing he couldn't prove or at least back up with sources. After he and JD had retrieved Uncle Gus's library from his fallout shelter that Saturday, the old man showed them several convincing ones.

Will looked again at his classmates. Most had moved on, but some—maybe a third of them—hadn't. *These* classmates had abandoned all pretense of going about their business, and were now just standing there, looking back at him, eyes sullen and fierce. He counted four girls and three boys, all black, Arab, or Hispanic, and all a grade or two lower than he. He shuddered, feeling a painful emptiness in the pit of his stomach. He understood that to him these people were outsiders, strangers. Now that he had been accused of the cardinal sin of racism, he could never rely upon them for anything. Their hostile glares told Will that they felt the exact same way about him.

Chapter 12

The remainder of the school year was not the calamity Will had anticipated. No one had taken video of his argument with Connie, and he didn't get expelled or even called into the principal's office. Nothing about it appeared on social media as far as he or JD could tell. He did notice, however, a chill gradually setting in all around him. Connie and her clique of friends studiously ignored him, of course. Students he had been friendly with no longer had time for him. Kids wouldn't return his texts, his smiles, or even his glances. His already meager number of followers on social media plummeted. Teachers, too, seemed colder and more businesslike whenever they were obliged to interact with him.

As jarring as this was, Will quickly grew accustomed to it. With some self-effacing irony, he noticed how vying with JD to become school *persona non grata* was not terribly different from how he had been treated before. In some ways this new status marked an improvement because now he had no ambition whatsoever to be liked by anyone. By drastically lowering his social expectations, Will discovered that these new expectations were impossible not to meet. Nevertheless, the downside emerged just as quickly. His grades suffered. Without a scholarship he wasn't going to State even if he had the grades and the inclination. So why study and get straight-As when passing grades were all he needed for community college? That is, if he had the inclination to go even there. Will also started gaining weight again. With Connie no longer in his life, what motivation did he have to look his best? Most of all, he began to appreciate how precarious his situation really was. The literature Uncle Gus had exposed him to thrilled him when he was alone in his bedroom with the door locked. But in everyday life—with black and brown students eyeing him suspiciously and with no white student other than JD willing to even talk to him—Will couldn't bear to think about it. He was not grown up enough. It seemed all too real.

Thus began Will's cozy slide into mediocrity. Both parents fretted over him, of course, with Melissa fussing most about his diet, and Andrew carping constantly about his grades. His father was especially disappointed with his change of heart over the scholarship competition. Despite Andrew's many efforts to plumb his reason, Will knew better than to ever tell him the truth.

To make up for this, Will's friendship with JD intensified. The two were inseparable at school and saw each other nearly every weekend that autumn. Companionship buffered much of the isolation they both experienced and somehow added to their social status. JD remained as annoying as ever, always saying things he shouldn't say. With his pariah status now all but enshrined among the shiny trophies in glass cases in the school's spacious front lobby, Will began to see this more as a virtue than a defect. But he always refused to discuss controversial topics with JD unless they were alone.

"No. IQ is real," JD said as he stretched out on the floor with his back against the bookshelf—his favorite spot in Will's bedroom. He wore his usual flannel and denim uniform, only his shirt was fleece-lined and hooded, which made it double for a coat. "They've linked it to things in your brain. Things they can measure in millimeters. That seals the deal as far as I'm concerned."

It was a Friday night, just over a week before Christmas. The boys had completed their final exams that morning, and had just returned from an extended celebratory outing in the nearby city. "Oh, come on, JD," Will replied, seated at his desk in cargo shorts and a T-shirt. He crossed his legs and tenderly massaged his ankle, which ached after hours of walking. "You're saying that education has nothing to do with intelligence?"

"Not according to the stuff Uncle Gus is having me read."

"I don't believe it."

"But they have neurological brain imaging now!"

"Keep it down, JD," Will implored. Although the door to his room was shut, he glanced apprehensively to the ceiling. Both of his parents were home. He could hear his mother in the kitchen cleaning up, and he last saw his father moments earlier on the phone in his office with the door ajar.

"They can practically look inside your head and tell how smart you are," JD continued. "If that doesn't destroy the egalitarian narrative, I don't know what does."

"The what?"

"Racial egalitarianism!" JD expounded, thinking that raising his voice would clarify matters. "It's a lie! They say that races have equal intelligence, but they don't!"

"Keep it *down!*" Will warned, gritting his teeth. Although he respected his friend's intellect, JD's habitual disregard for social conventions was a constant source of worry and embarrassment for him.

JD scooted forward until he was sitting Indian-style close to Will. "Look, the average IQ is 100, right?" he whispered, "All our testing says blacks are a standard deviation below that."

Will took a moment to make sure his parents hadn't heard anything. "What's a standard deviation?"

"I don't know. I think it refers to, like, 15 points. Blacks have an IQ of 85."

"All of 'em?"

"No, on *average*. The Hispanic IQ is a little higher. Then whites, and then Asians on top. That's how it's always been, and it doesn't really matter how educated you are. This is what they call 'race-realism.'"

"Dude. How can you talk like that? My God."

JD smirked. "Do you have an actual argument, Will? Or

are you just going to sit there clutching your pearls?"

Will's face contorted as if he had just tasted a lemon. "What?"

"Look, it's the truth. It's a painful thing for people to hear. That's why they suppress it."

"But how can education *not* make someone smarter?"

"Scientists say we've never been able to make people smarter."

"But you're smarter than you were three months ago, JD. Just listen to yourself."

"Just because a person *knows* more doesn't mean he's smarter. Intelligence is about, like, being able to analyze and reason, and being quick about it, and remembering things."

Will let his foot fall to the carpet and then leaned forward, placing his elbows on his knees. "I don't know, dude. Aren't they saying that IQ has been rising by something like three points every decade? I mean, the average IQ is probably 130 by now."

"No, IQ is a ratio," JD explained. "The Q in IQ stands for quotient."

"So?"

"That means the average IQ will *always* be 100 no matter how differently people perform on tests. And while *scores* have changed over time, the gaps between the races have not."

Will shook his head. "I don't understand."

"That's because you're a doofus," JD said, smiling.

Will sat up. "Don't call me that," he said sternly.

"What?"

"I said don't call me that, JD."

"Are you serious?"

"Yes."

"Okay, I won't call you that."

"Thank you." Will remained silent as blood flushed into his cheeks. His break with Connie was over a month old, but it still hurt. The last thing he could bear at that moment was JD reminding him of it, even in jest.

JD leaned back to take a second look at his friend. "I didn't mean to hurt your feelings, Will. But I tease you all the time. Usually you just soak it up."

Three sharp knocks on the door caught their attention. "Tease me all you want," Will said under his breath. "Just don't call me *that*, okay?"

"Okay. Sure. Sorry," JD said as he stood to face Will's parents as they stepped into the bedroom. They made quite the odd couple, Will noticed, with Andrew still dressed for work in black slacks, burgundy shirt, and blue tie, and his mother in paint-stained overalls and a pink headband. From the grim looks on their faces, Will could tell something wasn't right.

"Hey, guys. What's up?" he asked.

"Hey, Will," Andrew responded halfheartedly.

Melissa was about to speak, but hesitated. She looked to Andrew, who gave her a reluctant smile and took another step forward—toward JD. He put his hands together almost as if to pray. "JD, I'm sorry, but I have to ask you to leave."

Will bolted to his feet, understanding that his father was indeed serious. Had he been eavesdropping again? He didn't see how since his office was on the other side of the house. "What! Why?" he demanded.

Melissa tugged on Andrew's sleeve, but he ignored her. "Will, this is not the time to discuss it," he said patiently.

"Yes, it is! I wanna know!"

"No, we will discuss it later."

"It's okay, Will," JD said stoically. "Let me get my shoes on."

"No, JD!" Will insisted, stepping forward to meet Andrew in the middle of the room. Having recently grappled with a hardened black criminal, Will felt less intimidated by his father than he had in the past. "What's this all about, Dad?"

Melissa tried to intervene, but Andrew held her back with his left arm. "You really wanna have this out right now?" he responded.

"Yeah!"

JD sat on the bed as he put on his shoes. "Guys, really, don't do this. I can leave."

Will pointed to his friend. "You're my friend and you're not going anywhere!" He then turned to his father, nodding expectantly. "If he goes, I go."

Mouths open in shock, his parents looked to each other, not knowing how to respond to their son's burst of resolve. Melissa reached out to him in a conciliatory manner. "It's for the best, Will."

"Why?"

Andrew flashed a look of anger at Will. "Because 30 minutes ago, I received a phone call from JD's mom." He turned to JD. "She noticed that you and Will abandoned that scholarship competition only after visiting your uncle. She figured it wasn't a coincidence, and when she looked in your room she found some of the old magazines he lent you. I'd never heard of them, but when I looked them up on the internet I discovered that they were underground, lunatic fringe, white supremacist publications that would be rightly censored today!"

"I swear, Mr. Askew, I didn't know any of that when we went there," JD said. "I hadn't spoken to my granduncle in, like, two years."

"But this racist uncle of yours is the reason why you two decided not to apply for that scholarship. Correct?"

JD said nothing rather than admit the awkward truth.

"Regardless," Andrew went on, "I hope you understand that we do not allow racist talk in this house."

JD stood and looked shrewdly at Andrew, his face an insolent, enigmatic mask.

Will folded his arms in solidarity with his friend. He

knew that his father's characterization of Uncle Gus was unfair. Everything the old man had said during their visit was clear, measured, and could be backed up with evidence. Will had also read some of those underground publications his father had so thoughtlessly disparaged, and none seemed "white supremacist" to him—unless merely having a white perspective makes a person "supremacist."

"I'll be going now," JD announced as he stepped past Will's parents. "See you later, Will."

"No, I'll give you a ride."

"It's okay. I'll call a cab."

"No!" Will insisted, squeezing past his parents as well. "I drove you here, and I'll drive you back. It's not fair to make you pay for your own ride."

"Don't stay out late," Andrew warned as both boys started up the stairs.

Will turned and faced his father. "JD is my friend, Dad," he said hotly. "Not only that, he's my *only* friend. Exactly how lonely and unhappy do you want me to be?"

Deflated and embarrassed by such a question, Andrew could only shake his head regretfully and look away. Fighting back tears, Melissa reached out and took Will by the hand. "We only want what's best for you, Will."

"I know you do, Mom," Will responded cryptically as he released his mother's hand and followed JD up the stairs.

Neither friend said anything as they exited through the front door. Christmas lights from the home's seven front-facing windows lit the way for them along the driveway to Will's car.

"I am so sorry that happened, JD," Will said as they were strapping themselves in.

"It's okay," JD said. "I'm more worried about my privacy rights. I keep those old newsletters in my filing cabinet. My mom must have rifled through it."

"I guess we should expect this sort of thing from now on, even from our own families. You think you'll get in trouble?"

"Oh, yeah. My mom is a public school teacher, Will. She'd lose her career *and* her pension if she were caught being racist. She is *terrified* of black people. You have no idea."

Will chuckled, thinking of his own mother. "I believe I do."

JD laughed as well. "I've done so much reading this past month. And I've exchanged letters with Uncle Gus."

"Really?"

"I don't know what to say, Will. But I think I'm turning into a thought criminal. And I'm a little scared."

"Of what?"

"Of myself? If that makes any sense."

"What do you mean?"

"I'm not sure I can trust myself with all this information."

Will took a moment to process this and came up empty. "I don't understand."

"Look at it like this," JD began. "Being universally despised in high school is kinda funny because after a certain point, things *can't* get any worse. But I don't think it's gonna be so funny when you're a grownup, when things can *always* get worse. If I keep up with this racial awareness stuff, that's what's gonna happen to me. That's what happened to Uncle Gus. He was a professor in the 1950s. Did you know that? He spoke out against—I don't even know what to call it. Anti-*white*-ism? And they ruined him for it."

"Who did?"

"I don't know! He hasn't told me. But he keeps saying 'they.' *They* have all the power. *They* are behind everything. *They* are out to get him. It makes him sound crazy! But then he gives me pages and pages of clear, informative, logical stuff. I don't know what to think—except that he might be right, even though sometimes I wish he wasn't! And if people start hating me, like they hated Uncle Gus, then I'm afraid I'm gonna start hating them back."

"Don't say that, JD."

"Knowing me, I'll probably say or do something stupid, and then my goose will be cooked. And I won't even have family to stand by me."

Will took a deep breath and extended his hand to JD. "Friends forever?"

JD turned to Will in disbelief, and then smiled on one side of his face. "You mean it?"

"Absolutely," Will said. "I don't know if you or Uncle Gus have sold me on everything. But I do agree that white people are in trouble. And if we don't start acting as a group, we're not gonna make it."

JD took Will's massive hand in his and shook it. "Okay, dude. Friends forever."

Will's cellphone beeped and startled them both. He had to shift his weight awkwardly before retrieving it from his shorts pocket. It was a text from Connie. She was in trouble and asking him to call.

Chapter 13

"Don't do it, Will," JD warned, waving his hands like a referee. "She's trouble. I'm telling you."

Will stared at his cellphone as he waited for Connie to pick up. He knew he lacked the strength to resist. He just had to call her.

She picked up after a few rings. "Hey, Doofus," she said in a soft, husky voice. "Can you forgive me?"

JD grinned, hearing everything. "So *that's* why you don't want me to call you that."

"Connie, what's up?" Will asked, turning away from his friend.

She sniffed. "I'm sorry I was mean to you."

"It's okay."

JD sniggered obnoxiously. "Mean to you? She ruined your reputation, dude."

Will waved his hand violently at JD to shush him.

"Who's that with you?" she asked.

"No one," Will said, glaring at JD. "I'm in my car."

"Well, can you come get me?"

"Come get—? What? What happened?"

Connie sighed so deeply it sounded like a moan. "You know the finalists present their essays to the scholarship committee tomorrow, right?"

Will thought for a moment and remembered. "That's right! You're a finalist?"

"Yeah."

"Congratulations!"

Connie cleared her throat weakly. "Zack and I went to a party to celebrate, and . . . . I drank a little too much, and—"

"Who?"

"Zack Thomas. My boyfriend. Maybe ex-boyfriend now. I don't know."

"What about Pete Dorr?"

Connie's ironic laugh turned into a sob. "I haven't seen Pete in, like—Will! I got drunk, okay? I can't drive! Zack and I got in a fight, and he left. I'm all alone!"

"Oh, no."

"Can you come pick me up, please? I need someone to be with me."

"Tell her to call a cab!" JD whispered fiercely. "Tell her to call a cab!"

Will waved him off. "Okay. Want me to take you home?"

Connie grunted melodramatically. "No! I can't show my face at home like this. I need a couple hours to sober up!"

"Where are you?"

"I don't know! Brick townhouse. A few blocks from the university."

"The university?"

"I'm at a college party."

"But what—"

"I'll text you my location once I get off the phone! And hurry! I don't feel so good!"

Will's eyes lit up with concern as he heard Connie descend into a full-throated sob. "Okay! Okay! I'll be there in 30 minutes! Connie? Are you there? Speak to me!"

"Thank you, Doofus," she said before hanging up.

Will looked at JD in the darkness of the car. "I gotta go," he said helplessly.

JD rolled his eyes and grinned. "Dude, she is playing you like a Stradivarius."

***

After dropping JD off at home, Will had no trouble finding the house Connie described, an old, three-story, brick townhome two miles from campus. It was a crisp, peaceful, cloudless night. The sparse traffic along the highway and local roads made it easy for him to navigate using his cellphone. Parking proved a chore, though, since

he had to forego a couple spots on the street which required parallel parking. His car was not equipped with a
rear-facing camera, and his girth made it difficult to twist
around to see behind him. He parked two blocks away in a
bank parking lot and jogged to the house, his ankle aching
every step of the way.

He climbed the porch steps and knocked on the door,
winded and heart racing. Just as he bent forward to rest
his hands on his knees, he heard the door squeak. Looking
up, he saw a short, chunky white girl with unnaturally orange hair in a striped dress shirt and ill-fitting jeans. Will
stood and squinted to take in the tattoo of a menacing
pink-and-black cobra on her neck. Beside her was a slender Chinese girl in a green T-shirt and a flower-print skirt.
She wore a crewcut and nose ring. Behind them both was
a tall and shockingly slender, light-skinned black man in a
gray T-shirt bearing a complex design of interlocking
swords and skeletons. He reached past them to lean
against the door jamb. His fingernails were painted purple. The instant he saw them, Will felt as if he were in a
foreign country. All his instincts told him to grab Connie
and get out of there as soon as possible.

"Yes?" the white girl said.

Will took a moment to control his breathing. "I'm here
for Connie."

"Who?" the girls asked, looking at each other.

"Connie Craft. High school girl."

The Chinese girl rolled her eyes and pointed inside,
smiling. "She's in the basement."

The white girl pretended to gag as she walked back inside the house. "Take her, please."

The black man snickered as he pushed the screen door
open. Will held his breath before stepping inside as if
afraid the air would be noxious. The man stepped back to
give Will room. He was almost as tall as Will, but perhaps
half as heavy. The living area was much thinner than

Will's living room at home. A frayed brown futon and an old leather recliner sat to his right. A cheap, unsteady-looking foosball table took up the corner to his left. In front of an unused fireplace were several bicycles. Will recognized the smell of beer, but did not recognize the heavy, smokey smell permeating the house. He had smelled cigarette smoke numerous times in his life, and it wasn't that.

Young people milled about, aloof and indifferent, with mellow pop music playing from another room. Piercings, tattoos, and eclectic clothing were the norm for both sexes. No one looked at him as they socialized, but everyone got out of his way as he walked past. A commotion down the hall to his right startled him. After a moment, he heard Connie thumping up the stairs.

"Get your hands offa me!" she shrieked.

Connie stumbled through a door and leaned against the wall, inadvertently tearing a poster which was thumb-tacked to it. Will had not seen her up close in nearly three weeks, and was astonished at how she had changed. She wore a black hoodie, black boots, and ripped jeans. The right side of her face was smeared with tears and black mascara. Her lack of makeup exposed acne on both cheeks. She had gained some weight as well.

Two girls followed her into the hall, staring at her malevolently. Will recognized them both as having graduated from their high school the year before. Until that moment, he had always assumed that they were Connie's friends. "Your ride's here," one of them said, glancing at Will.

Connie steadied herself and pointed at the pair. "I know what you did. I know what you *did!*"

Will took her gently by the shoulders and tried to steer her away. At first, she arched out of his grasp, but relaxed when she saw it was him. Her eyes were unsteady and she was breathing heavily. She looked almost like a different girl, someone Will could barely recognize.

"We didn't do anything, Connie," one of the girls said.

Connie gasped and pointed her finger at them. "You are so insecure! Both of you!"

As the girls scoffed and bickered with Connie, Will coaxed her through the living room. Step by step, she retreated, all the while spewing an expletive-filled tirade. She then took a stand by the front door where the entire party regarded her more with amusement than alarm. The two girls from their high school stood front and center, taking Connie's abuse.

"I am prettier than you!" Connie proclaimed, practically falling into Will's arms. "I'm more popular than either of you! And you're jealous! That's why you were going after Zack, wasn't it?"

One girl gave Connie a heavy-lidded sneer and held up her hand. "I can't even," she said as she turned away. The other folded her arms and confronted her. "That's what you said to my sister about Pete Dorr, Connie. That's what you said to me last year about Ryan Roberts. What is it with you?"

Now fully enraged, Connie lunged straight for the girl, forcing Will to nearly pick her up off her feet. "All right, time to go," he urged as he pushed open the screen door with his free hand. In the corner of his eye, he noticed someone approach. It was the girl with the cobra tattoo. This time she was recording them on her cellphone.

"Oh, don't leave!" she cried sarcastically. "We're having such a great time!"

Connie was still screaming profanities as Will yanked her through the door. Her momentum would have caused her to fall down the porch steps if he hadn't caught her.

"Oh, honey, your life is over," Cobra Tattoo laughed. "I have a streaming channel of people doing drunk, stupid stuff. You're going viral!"

Connie seemed to understand, and let out a savage cry as she tried to pounce on her tormenter, but it was hopeless. She lost her balance and pitched forward, crashing loudly against the porch steps. She squeaked in pain, and Will knew right away she wasn't faking. The partygoers were now crowding by the door to take in the spectacle. They laughed and gossiped as they egged her on. By this point, Connie seemed to have accepted defeat and allowed Will to lead her down the steps and away.

Moments later, Will looked back and saw the girl with the cobra tattoo following them on the sidewalk, still recording. "Got nothing to say now?" she taunted. "Cat got your tongue?"

Will stopped and turned. His imposing stature and cool, hostile glare convinced her to stop as well. She lowered her cellphone but kept recording. He got a good look at her, one that he would never forget. He found her face attractive, but less so the longer he looked at it. Her eyes seemed almost circular, and her eyebrows arched like falling cats. He couldn't be sure in the dim street light, but her heavy jaw appeared littered with fine stubble. She seemed to be smirking on one side of her face. This was how she naturally looked. And that tattoo—it was placed just so on her neck to be easily seen from near and far.

"What are *you* lookin' at?" she said to Will, as several partygoers walked up behind her.

Will in fact *didn't* know what he was looking at, but was too polite to say. "You're cruel," he said to her curtly. He hoped one day she would understand.

As he led Connie away, she lurched forward and made a gurgling sound. "Will! I'm gonna be sick!"

He grabbed her tightly around the shoulders as he picked up the pace. From the way she was squirming between dry heaves he knew they wouldn't make it to the next intersection, let alone to his car a block and a half away. Not wanting to make another scene, Will steered her between townhomes to their left, intending to lead her to a blue recycling bin by a tall wood-slat fence. But they weren't quick enough. In the middle of the gravel driveway, and beside a dented sedan covered in political bumper stickers, Connie dropped to her knees and threw up.

Throughout the ordeal, Will knelt beside her and comforted her. He heard the crowd following them along the sidewalk, but didn't care. Connie was speaking to him. He didn't want to miss a word.

"I can't do it, Will!" she cried. "I can't!"

"Can't do what, Connie?"

"My scholarship presentation! It's at noon tomorrow. I'm gonna be too hungover to give it!"

"No, you'll make it."

"You saw what I'm like when I'm hungover! That morning on my porch with your stupid friend, remember?"

"He's not stupid, Connie," he said, realizing unhappily that JD had been right about her all along.

"But I can't do anything hungover! Can you do it please?"

"Do what?"

"My presentation. Tomorrow morning. Please!" Connie tried to set herself upright, but groaned in nausea before throwing up again. "I'll send you the link to my paper and slides," she offered, wiping her chin on her sleeve. "All you have to do is show up and read it. Wear a tie or something. I'll email the committee chair—Chaunté someone—and say I'm ill and that you're standing in for me. Alterman knows you. She'll understand."

"But Connie, why can't—"

"Please, Will?" she begged, taking his right hand in both of hers. "My mom and, like, all my friends, are expecting me to get this scholarship! Alterman herself told me I'm a shoo-in!"

Will noticed several partygoers watching from the sidewalk, but was too distracted by what Connie had just said to pay close attention. "Wait, what?"

Connie finally sat up on her knees. "Nadine told me in secret that they already picked the three winners. Me and two people of color from Covington. All we have left are our presentations."

Will took a moment to process this. "You mean the scholarship competition is rigged?"

"What? No! We submitted our projects two weeks ago! The committee made their decisions early. That's all."

"Have they announced the winners?"

"No, but that's beside the—"

"So people will give presentations tomorrow even though the outcome is already decided?"

Connie groaned. "That's how it works! It's not up to me."

"Huh," Will grunted, noticing the crowd growing on the sidewalk. Among the onlookers were Connie's two former friends, the Chinese girl with the crewcut and nose ring, and the girl with the cobra tattoo. He couldn't tell if she was still recording them.

"Will, come on!" she pleaded. "It'll mean so much to me if you could this. And I'm sorry I was mean to you. You didn't deserve that. You're such a sweet, gentle person. I was totally wrong. I'll be your friend forever if you'll just do this for me. Please!"

Connie sniffed and slid both her arms around Will's shoulders until she had him in a gentle, intimate embrace. Startled, excited, titillated, Will had no defense once he felt the thrill of her skin brushing against his. "Okay!" he said. "I'll do it! I'll do it!"

She made a sweet, tender noise. He didn't know if it was a word or a natural sound to express elation. He embraced her back until she began to sob. "What's wrong?" he asked.

She pulled away. "I'm such a liar, Will. I'm a big fat liar. I don't deserve you as a friend."

"What? Don't talk like that."

"It's true. The real reason . . ."

"What?"

"The real reason why I can't . . . Tomorrow . . . I can't . . ."

"Can't do what? The presentation?"

"I *hate* CRT," she admitted, wiping her eyes with the back of her hand. "It's all spite and lies and jealousy."

"I know. That's why I want nothing to do with it."

"But they're sucking me in, Will!" she said, now almost in a panic. "I feel like I'm losing my soul."

"Your—?"

"They only love me because they think I'm half Indian," she said, no longer bothering to wipe her streaming tears. "But I'm not that smart. I plagiarized most of my essay, Will, and they don't care. These people are evil! Especially Alterman! They just want some pretty *Indian* girl to be the face of the future. And it's a *scary* future! I hear them talk about it all the time!"

"How is it scary?"

"The things Alterman wants to do to whites and Christians . . . She hates them. She really does! And she tells me all this because she thinks I'm Indian. But I'm not!"

"You're not?"

"I'm as white as you are, Will!" she admitted. "My dad was some stupid German guy, probably a Nazi. He knocked my mom up in a youth hostel when she was backpacking in Europe. Then he disappeared. That's my story. That's the truth."

Her eyes were no longer unsteady. Instead they locked directly onto him, transparent and as blue and beautiful as ever. Will knew at that moment that he would be friends forever with this poor, suffering girl. He would do anything to help her. Tittering noises and swift footsteps caused him to turn. The crowd of onlookers had grown. Will squinted and noticed everyone there except the girl with the cobra tattoo.

Chapter 14

Feeling uncomfortable in his only suit—which he was outgrowing both upwards and outwards—Will went down once again to the Bernice Lefkowitz Memorial Auditorium. Walking along the path, he looked up at the side of the building. The ground was as hilly and bumpy as ever, and all the flagging tape, safety cones, machinery, and mounds of bricks were still there. Had they done any work on the building at all? As he entered the semi-circular plaza with only his blazer to protect him from the cold, he regretted not being able to button up his collar, which exposed his bulbous neck to the slicing breeze.

The heat from inside gave Will some relief, but not as much as he had hoped. Despite being on time—a definite improvement since his August visit—he could barely move amid the crowd milling about in the lobby. Irked that he seemed to be the only man under 40 who had worn a suit, he pulled his backpack off his shoulders and made his way through the bodies, not sure where to go. He hoped he would at least recognize someone, and while he spotted a few people from the Critical Theory Club, he recalled no names and did not feel comfortable approaching anyone. He did notice, however, that whites were a distinct minority. This nettled him. The base tribalism on display was all too apparent. How could these people not know that they were being just as racist as the people they condemn? It occurred to him that perhaps they did know, but did not care.

He peeked into the auditorium and saw the projection booth jutting over the back of the room. Inside, three white university students, all men, were setting up to project the slides and videos for the competition. Each was scruffy but dressed appropriately in collared shirts as they performed crucial, behind-the-scenes work. They were flanked by walls of machines, and moved with urgency without seeming rushed. Will thought of JD, who had once worked in that projection booth—and might do so again if he could manage going to State without a scholarship. The familiarity of seeing these young men, not much older than he but so busily employed, gave Will a touch of comfort. This lasted until someone called out a name he had heard many times before, but not his own.

"Peter!" a woman called. "Peter Dorr!"

Will turned and saw Nadine Alterman pushing toward him through the crowd. Following her was a dark-skinned, full-figured black woman, likely a college student. Nadine wore a gray pleated skirt and lavender blouse, with her hair pulled back tightly in a bun. The girl behind her was a couple inches shorter and wore tight jeans and a black T-shirt bearing the words, "BLACK LIVES MATTER." Staring sullenly at Will with distended, half-closed eyes, her hair hung in artificial curls down one shoulder and not the other.

"Chaunté Robertson told me you're taking over for Connie Craft today," Nadine said hurriedly. "Thank you for that! I'm so sorry she's ill. You'll tell her I said that, won't you? Do you have everything you need?"

Will lifted his backpack to show her. "Yeah, I printed the essay and slides this morning. But Professor Alterman, my name isn't—"

She placed her hand on his arm and cut him off, rapidly scanning the room. "We have to be out of here by two-thirty, which is barely enough time for the videos. The projection booth people will turn the slides for you. La-Vonna will show you where you need to go." She shook Will by the arm and smiled as she stepped away. "And Peter! You're up first!"

Frustrated, Will looked to LaVonna, who gave him the same unwelcome stare as before. "This way," she said, jerking her head to her left.

He stopped her before she could turn around. "Wait!

My name is *not* Pete Dorr. I don't know why Professor Alterman keeps calling me that. I'm Will Askew. Can you
tell her that, please?"

LaVonna's expression hardly changed as she considered this. "Uh-huh. Now, follow me."

She led Will through the thinning crowd and into a
small classroom. The vibe inside captured his attention
almost like a slap in the face. As he hesitated by the doorway, he assembled a silent racial inventory of the 15 high
school students occupying themselves with coffee, pastries, and chitchat. Feeling a twinge of guilt, he questioned
the morality of assessing people by their race. He then
questioned the morality of being the only white male
among four blacks, three Hispanics, and five Asians of various hues who, by their cool, dismissive glances, were likely assessing him by his. The group was about two-thirds
female, but with three out of the four blacks being male.
One of these, the bald one in the orange shirt with the
pinky ring, was almost as tall as Will and was definitely
stronger and in better shape. A football player or a wres-
tler, he gathered. Will counted three white girls, all in revealing clothing and with conspicuous tattoos on their
arms and shoulders. He was several steps inside when he
realized that one of the white girls was actually a boy.

Will tried not to let his apprehension show. Desk
chairs were scattered about, and there were quite a few
available, but he was too on edge to sit. He had just placed
a cardboard cup into the coffee machine in the back of the
room when applause emerged from the auditorium. The
event was about to begin, and a woman—Will could tell
she was black—was delivering opening remarks. He began
to sweat, and his heart raced and fingers tingled as they
usually did when he was under stress. He sighed to help
control his growing anxiety and then stopped when he
noticed the other students noticing him. He took a sip of
coffee and then placed his cup on the table, realizing that

the last thing he needed was another stimulant. He looked for something—anything—to distract him from the dread suspicion that he didn't belong there and was making a terrible mistake by standing in for Connie Craft that afternoon.

He noticed a stapled printout from the Critical Theory Club website on the table next to the coffee machine. It listed the competition's official itinerary, which he had seen before but never read carefully. He picked it up and began scanning. On the final page were photos and brief biographical sketches of all eight judges. JD had been right. Only two were black: Chaunté Robertson and the one male in the group, Benjamin T. Willoughby, Jr., EdD, PhD. The remaining six judges were all white and female. Will didn't understand it. How could white people support critical theory when critical theory was so plainly designed to disadvantage white people? He looked at their names to see if he had heard of any of them. Aside from Nadine Alterman and his freshman history teacher Madeline Johnston, none were familiar: Alicia Cohen, Lydia Silver, Natalie Cantor, and Amanda Rothstein. All white. "Why are we doing this to ourselves?" he asked himself despondently.

"Peter Dorr?" someone called. Will looked up. A black girl, a different one from before, was standing in the open doorway and reading from her cellphone. "Peter Dorr?"

Will grunted in aggravation and dropped the printout. "I think you mean me," he said, as he picked up his backpack. People cleared out of his way as he walked heavily to the door. He gave the girl a testy look upon entering the hall and then felt guilty for it. "My name is not Pete Dorr," he said softly. "It's Will Askew. Please tell Professor Alterman that. Okay?"

The girl was lighter-skinned and slimmer than LaVonna. She had the same artificial curls but perhaps a fraction of her predecessor's activist spirit. On her university sweatshirt, the same "BLACK LIVES MATTER" logo appeared, but on a round enamel pin, tiny but prominent. With more applause coming from the auditorium, she had trouble hearing him. "Who?"

Will shook his head wearily. "Never mind. Where do we need to go?"

"We turn left over there, then left again after that," she said, pointing an intricately manicured fingernail to a pair of doors by the entrance. She didn't seem friendly, but she wasn't hostile, either, which for Will was a great relief. He followed her through the doors, around a corner, and through another door, which led to the auditorium's darkened wing, stage left. "Wait here," she said before turning around and leaving.

The curtain to Will's left and the burgeoning mess of technical equipment to his right made the wing resemble a cramped corridor. He pulled the folder containing Connie's paper from his backpack, and focused on Chaunté Robertson, a tall, broad-shouldered black woman in a burgundy suit, standing centerstage at the podium. She was sharing a personal anecdote from her childhood about a racist white person, a story which she believed held great importance not just for American youth but for youth everywhere. It was the usual patter of platitudes and rhetoric Will had grown accustomed to all semester. He zoned out. It was still all so *boring*. He began pacing, knowing that Connie's 12-page paper contained many of the same platitudes and rhetoric. Many of the same turns of phrase as well. He couldn't wait for this ordeal to end, and comforted himself in knowing that the *real* Connie Craft was nothing like this. The real Connie hated critical theory as much as he did.

"Hey, Doofus."

Will spun around and saw a pale, disheveled version of Connie approaching from the door. He couldn't see her well in the poor lighting, and stepped up to her for a better look. She really *did* look hungover. She wore the same black boots and ripped jeans as the night before, but had swapped her black hoodie for a pink one. She was holding a cardboard cup of coffee and squinting through red-rimmed, bloodshot eyes.

"Hey!" Will said. "Are you all right?"

She touched him on the arm. "I couldn't—" she said, and then cleared her throat.

"Couldn't what?"

"I couldn't *not* come and see you after all you're doing," she said. "Thank you, Will. It means so much to me."

"No problem."

"And listen . . ." she added, now stroking his arm. She pulled closer until he could feel strands of her unkempt hair on his cheek. He could hear her breathe—he could smell her. Being so near to her excited him as much as it had the night before.

"What?"

"If you wanna, y'know, ask me out," she whispered with a coquettish shrug, "I won't say no."

She looked him directly in the eyes, baring to him all the pain and humiliation she had recently experienced. There was no defiant pout or heavy mascara this time. Only those transparent blue eyes which hurt Will so much to see for reasons he could not fathom. He smiled. She smiled. He leaned in, finally about to kiss this wonderful, mysterious girl when sudden applause from the auditorium stopped him. He turned and saw Chaunté Robertson facing him from the podium. "Unfortunately, Connie Craft was not able to attend this afternoon due to illness," she announced. "Reading her essay will be her friend Peter Dorr!"

Will turned back to Connie who seemed as baffled as he was about the confusion of names. She then kissed her fingers and touched his lips, igniting a spark which startled them both. She pressed him gently toward the stage.

"Go," she said.

He turned and lumbered to the podium, confidence surging. From the stage, the Lefkowitz Auditorium didn't seem quite so grand. It was narrower than he had imagined, with maybe only four dozen rows. With its lights off, the dark silver projection booth loomed over the seats in the back. The podium was empty when he reached it, but for the heavy cloud of perfume Chaunté Robertson had left behind. Her high-heeled shoes were still click-clacking stage right when he removed Connie's paper from its folder, took a secretive glance at Connie, and began.

He couldn't do it.

The words on the page were not Connie's. He would have known that even without her confession from the night before. Not only this, but these words were repeating lies—insidious lies he had read many times before in his critical theory books. These were no different from the lies about her race and her drunkenness and the protest in Covington which Will never attended. He did not want her to lie anymore. He was prepared to accept her as she was, faults and all. He looked at the audience and then at Connie, and knew that his feelings for Connie Craft went too deep and were too real for him to do anything other than what he was about to do.

"I think that critical race theory . . ." he began, ". . . is the opposite of the truth. It considers colorblindness to be bad not because colorblindness supports white supremacy, like the books say, but because, uh, when whites are colorblind, blacks can't compete with them so well. And when critical theory says that we have to end white racism, what it's really saying is that we should increase black racism so blacks can gain power at the expense of whites. That's what it's all about. Power. Not truth. Otherwise, they would look at things like IQ, test scores, brain scans, and things like that."

A collective gasp from the audience seemed to lower

the temperature of the auditorium by several degrees, but Will forged ahead regardless.

"When CRT says that whiteness destroys the identity and culture of minorities, what they really want is to destroy the identity and culture of the white majority." Will placed his hand solemnly on his chest and looked out at the audience. "I'm white. I can feel this. I feel non-white people telling me that I am not allowed to have a culture or an identity. And I have to be really careful about what I say, or I'll get called a racist. And then, that's it. I'm done. And that's not fair. That's why—"

Stomping footsteps from stage left caught his attention. Nadine Alterman was swiftly approaching and signaling violently for him to get off the stage. Her eyes flashed hatefully, and her teeth were bared in predatory rage. "Racist! Nazi!" she shrieked. "Get off this stage now!"

Will was stunned less by Nadine's shrill demand than by how her deprecations so closely resembled Connie's from over a month before. These were not insults, he realized. These were curses—as if coming from the mouth of a witch. He was collecting Connie's paper into its folder when Nadine approached and tugged hard on his sleeve as if to yank him offstage herself. Appalled, Will pulled his arm back, but she kept tugging until he whirled his arm out of her grasp.

His elbow collided with something—or someone—behind him, causing an uproar from the audience. Will turned just as Chaunté Robertson, a woman in hardy middle age, collapsed to the floor with her hands over her nose. She screamed and writhed in ostentatious pain as if her nose had been broken. This surprised Will since he was sure he hadn't struck her *that* hard. Fortunately, there was no blood. He winced in empathy as he knelt down to help her.

"I'm sorry!" he said. "It was an accident. I didn't see you. Are you all right?"

An alarmed response from the audience confused him. It was louder than its gasp from a moment before. This time it seemed to be reacting to something that was *about* to happen. He heard footsteps behind him. Heavy footsteps. He stood as the primal sounds from crowd were about to crescendo. He saw Nadine Alterman step away and begin to smile. With barely enough time to turn his body, he saw one of the black male scholarship contestants approaching fast. The big one.

He saw his bald head, then his orange sleeve, and then the sparkle of his pinky ring on his clenched fist. He felt the impact explode on his jaw, and for an instant all that was real was not real. Colors dulled, and darkness flashed. Silence blared inside his vibrating skull as his knees refused to follow their explicit orders to keep his large body standing. A marching band of lizards and bats tramped through his mind as a panda bear beat on a bass drum. Didn't he have a toy like that once as a child?

There was no time to remember. Reality soon reestablished itself as it always does, and darkness became darkness once again.

Part 2

Chapter 15

Forty acres.

Forty acres sounded so impressive on paper when Rose Gabler, her husband Brock, and her two best friends Caroline and Derek Brand purchased Smythe Farm from Derek's Uncle Zack just over five years ago. Rose remembered their hope and optimism when they signed the paperwork, and then dove into renovating and remodeling the large 18th-century Shackleford mansion, which was to be their new home. At the time, she could barely sleep as she contemplated all the possibilities for the No College Club, as they called themselves. Farming, raising livestock, horse breeding, the Smythe Farm equestrian club, which she formed right away almost in a frenzy with the help of her family. These had been dreams of hers since she was a little girl. Thanks mostly to her efforts, the No College Club and their families and guests could live and thrive off the land all year round. Up until that point they had never had more than three guests at a time, and currently had two living in the small dormitories on the Club's campus—Samantha Perkins, a middle-aged divorcée and volunteer, and Matt Houska, a 21-year-old who had been doxed and expelled from his university for engaging in anonymous pro-white activism online.

Brock had built his weight training facility behind the mansion with the same enthusiasm—almost too much enthusiasm, Rose felt, since their projects kept them so often apart. How she longed for him during those busy days! And how overjoyed she was when the completion of the gym and the horse stables brought them back together as if from an unwelcome year-long separation. Rose remembered those days as both exhausting and rewarding, especially since she had given birth to Little Brock mere days after Derek, kneeling on metal roofing sheets over 25 feet in the air, had driven the final screw into their barn's ridge cap.

Despite being such an exuberant father, Brock had lately been focusing on the High Health Wizards, his organization which offered seminars on healthy, drug-free living in rural—and mostly white—areas. Was he giving it too much attention? Rose did not want to begrudge her husband his goals, which he pursued with honest and unrelenting zeal. But if he only knew how much her sense of purpose and belonging—as well as her dizzying, crashing swirls of emotions—depended upon him! Still, she was unbearably proud of her husband. This, more than anything, made their time apart bearable.

Derek's writing career was something she took pride in as well—but this was a *secret* pride. There were very few secrets within the No College Club, but this one she kept even from Brock. Derek was the only person she knew who loved literature as much as she did. If you counted the dense, dusty, non-fiction tomes he liked to devour in the wee hours of the morning, not to mention all the Ancient Greek texts he assigned in his classes, he may have read even more books than she had. But as a writer he had no one to talk to besides Rose. It was only natural that she become his editor. That wasn't the secret. Everyone knew that she proofread all his novels and essays and fundraising letters and some of his longer blog posts as well. Whenever he wasn't training in his mixed martial arts gym or spending time with Caroline or Liam—as they called little William Percival—Derek managed the Club's social media accounts and much of their correspondence. So his writing was important. But for all his brilliance, *Rose felt she improved his writing by editing him.* This was her secret. She would never tell it to *anyone.*

Rose was just as proud of Caroline, who educated herself on the law as well as any attorney, despite not having a college degree. With her natural cleverness, savvy, and poise—not to mention beauty, which Rose openly admired—she had become a wonderful representative of the Club. She appeared almost regularly on news programs, radio shows, and podcasts. She traveled at least once a month. She also managed their money and their small team of attorneys. Progress on her pro-white Civil Liberties League was slow and halting but not surprising, given how well prepared and funded the Club's enemies were. Rose could not believe the extent to which some powerful and well-placed people in her own country would go to prevent whites such as themselves from organizing and doing what was best for their people. But Caroline never allowed anyone to get discouraged. "Despair is a sin," she'd say whenever she caught any of them moping in dark corners or wiping tears in the crooks of their arms.

Currently, Caroline was not at home where she was happiest. She was traveling by car across the Midwest for conferences and retreats—despite being pregnant with her second child—and was expected back the next day. Knowing how much her friend suffered whenever she was away, Rose made it a point to suffer along with her, and to constantly wish for her safe return.

Rose rode up the winding pathway on the back of Maisey, the tough old nag Uncle Zack had given her as a wedding present. She had just come from their three-acre winter garden, where they were planting cabbage, celery, arugula, and kale. She had spent much of the morning loosening the subsoil and adding compost to the new beds where she hoped to plant carrots and lettuce in the spring. This being their fourth winter managing their growing homestead, the chores had become more numerous and no less grueling. She felt the strain in her forearms and wrists as she gingerly gripped the reins. Fortunately, Maisey knew the way to her stable.

The path leveled out into a small, east-facing clearing, where the barn and stables appeared up ahead on the right. These were simple, unpainted, utilitarian structures

which closely resembled the ones on her family's horse
farm back home. The sight of them invigorated her and
reminded her of her family's connection to the land. Between man, beast, plant, and earth, harmony was main-
tained by love and toil, which was its own reward. What
other meaning of life could there be?

Rose stopped in the clearing as she always did before
returning home and washing up and starting her day.
Farm life had somehow made her less accustomed to exact time, and more attuned to cyclical periods informed
by the movement of Earth, Moon, and Sun. More and
more, she thought of seasons rather than months, and of
the growth of the soil and of family and livestock rather
than years. This, she felt, was the natural rhythm of life.
Presently it was the quiet, minutes-long stretch between
early- and late-morning. Ten am? Half past? Somewhere
in there, she imagined. She had been up since dawn, and
always used this time of day to enjoy a respite from the
never-ending work and to give herself a chance to enjoy
her health and painfully accumulated prosperity. The air
was fragrant with life, growth, and decay. The breezes
were too cool and crisp for comfort under her cotton undershirt, flannel blouse, and fleece vest. She looked forward to the comforts of her heated home. She was looking
forward to snuggling with Little Brock as well, who would
turn two in March and was now jabbering nonstop and
clambering all over the house if given free rein. She shiv-
ered in anticipation, suspecting her son would soon have a
brother or sister to play with—but it was still too early to
tell. Rose sighed, taking in the expansive, tree-spiked
horizon and the white, glowing sky above. Beyond all that
was the great ocean, over which her ancestors had traveled centuries ago. Did they ever look back to their place
of origin with the same sense of wonder?

The sight of the empty horse stables made her tremble.
The Smythe Farm Riding club had gotten off to a splendid

start over three years ago with a dozen horses and regular lessons for family members and guests. But then their enemies acted. They spread their anti-white slander. They wrote their anti-white libel. With their deep pockets and iron resolve, they bullied ordinary people to turn against the No College Club. Insurance companies refused to insure them. Banks refused to keep their money. Payment processing companies dropped them. Many local businesses refused to serve them. Keeping so many horses quickly became too expensive, and running an equestrian club too risky. It was a sad day in May of that year when Brock, Caroline, and Derek told Rose of her dream's deferment. All but two of the animals had to be shipped back to her parents' horse farm. Like a mature adult, Rose accepted the imbalanced justice of their decision. The Club's other activities were either more essential for their survival—or less expensive. She understood and felt no bitterness, yet cried for two days anyway.

Rose took a deep, melancholy breath, and moved on, preparing to seize the day as she usually did. Just past the stables, however, something appeared which she knew would make that impossible: the chicken coop. It was a small, elevated structure with a ramp, wire mesh, and a gabled roof which Brock and Derek had hastily put together when they established the farm. Rose pulled on Maisey's reins and came to a halt so she could be certain of what she was seeing. Yes, the sight was as appalling as she feared. The leaking roof had not been repaired, the litter trays had not been emptied, and the feeder had not been replenished. These were all Brock's tasks for the day, and he had assured her the night before that he would complete them in the morning. Once again, he hadn't.

Rose seethed, her mind somehow balancing on a tightrope between irritation and good humor. Could she begrudge Brock his goals now? She didn't want to, but she also didn't want to see the chicken coop in such a neglected state. What clever excuse was her husband going to come up with this time? And what would she say in response? Seconds later, she was galloping toward the gym to find out.

Secluded among loblolly pines several dozen yards behind the Shackleford house, the Club's green-and-gray-painted gym seemed almost camouflaged. It was a long, L-shaped structure with vertical wood paneling. Rose remembered how her brothers had helped construct it years ago. It was the first building they erected on Smythe Farm, and Rose was especially proud of it. She had laid down much of the flooring and some of the gravel path herself. That morning, however, the heavy metal music blaring through the walls made her emotions harder to control. She imagined she could see *through* the building—to Brock having fun as he usually did when he shouldn't be having fun at all. Did he actually expect that she and Samantha would do all the farm's winter chores *by themselves*?

The entrance opened into a short hall lined with flattened cardboard boxes to collect mud from outside. It led past the bathrooms and coat hooks to the weight room directly ahead. Rose knew right away it was empty. To her right was the large workout room, which was lined wall-and-floor with soft wrestling mats of various colors. Along the near wall stood several grappling dummies and freestanding punching bags, all repaired to various degrees with duct tape. A haphazard collection of jump ropes, headgear, MMA gloves, and wrestling shoes cluttered the floor between them. Three independent heating units running at full blast kept the room toastier than Rose would have liked, but she was used to it. The heavy smell of sweat malingered in the air.

Brock was sparring lightly on the far side of the room with Matt, a tall, slender young man with shaggy blond hair and a dull, amorphous tattoo on his left arm, which he was in the process of removing. Having bulked up in his chest, shoulders, and arms since getting married, Brock outweighed Matt by at least 30 pounds, despite being just as tall. His light-brown hair was shaggy as well, and he had lost the boyish plumpness in his face and belly. From a distance, he seemed like a grim, determined athlete. Up close, however, his twinkling eyes and ironic scowl revealed the heart of a prankster. Barefoot and in shin guards, shorts, and soaking-wet T-shirts, the pair exchanged playful blows in step with the harsh rhythm of the music. Most horrifyingly for Rose was how Brock had their toddler son strapped to his chest facing forward in a modified baby carrier, which the child was too big for anyway. Brock was controlling his son's hands as if Little Brock were throwing punches at Matt. All three were laughing heartily at their antics.

Rose called for Brock three times from the edge of the room, but the music was too loud for them to hear. Fuming, she kicked off her mud-caked boots and marched onto the mat, intent on rescuing her son from her husband's clowning and pointedly reminding him of his unperformed tasks on the farm. "Brock!" she barked as she took long strides toward them.

Startled, the men froze and then stepped apart, smiling at the oncoming Rose. Little Brock held up his hands and gurgled for joy. Seeing that Rose was in no playful mood, Matt hurried to his cellphone by the wall and turned off the music.

"Honey!" Brock called, cheerfully pretending that all was well. "What're *you* doing here? Weren't you supposed to be—"

"I was *supposed* to be working all morning on the farm, Brock," Rose said as she unstrapped Little Brock from the baby carrier, "which is what I was doing. You, on the other hand—"

"I'll get to the chicken coop this morning, Rose!" Brock

interrupted, gesturing vigorously. "It's not even ten-thirty!"

"Actually, it's 10:34," Matt said smartly, waving his phone.

Brock spun around and pointed a finger at Matt, grimacing like a comic book villain. "Another word from you, see? And I'll have Little Brock clobber you again!"

"Little Brock is going home to join Liam for lunch and a nap, while I relieve Caroline's mom from baby duty," Rose said as she nuzzled with her delighted toddler. "And *you* are going to take care of the chicken coop like you said you would."

"What about Samantha?" Brock asked.

Rose adjusted Little Brock on her hip, causing him to say, "Woo!"

"Samantha is in the greenhouse getting the seed trays ready. While you've been playing around, she and I have been—"

"Playing around? We've been training, Rose. We just did 25 minutes of takedown drills. And before that we were learning the difference between D'Arce chokes and anaconda chokes."

"Right," Rose said sarcastically. "With a baby strapped to your chest."

"We were taking a break! Matt and I jogged five miles this morning! What we do is physically demanding!"

"And farm work isn't?" Rose asked, trying not to smile.

"I'll tell you what farm work isn't, Rose," Brock said, pointing to his wife's dirty socks. "It isn't sanitary. We need to keep these mats disinfected. You *know* this."

"I took off my boots."

"Yeah, but your socks are soaked with mud and sweat and toenail fungus and God knows what else! Who knows what kind of germs you're bringing in here? Do you want us to get impetigo? Hepatitis? Staph?"

Rose pretended to gag. "Oh, God. Maybe if you hadn't

been playing music so loud you would have heard me calling for you by the door!"

Brock tapped into an invisible cellphone. "Two words for ya, Rose! Send a text!"

Matt chortled as Brock and Rose continued to bicker playfully. He disappeared into a nearby closet and reappeared with a mop and a bucket, by which point Little Brock had ended the argument by pinching Brock's nose and demanding *syrniki*, a sweet Russian pancake made from farmer's cheese. But just as Brock was cheekily asking for some himself, the gym office door swung open. Only one person ever worked in the gym office.

It was Derek. He stepped out onto the mat in gray shorts and a blue T-shirt. Less bulky in his chest than he had been as a high schooler, he seemed to make up for it in his bulging shoulders, biceps, and forearms. He gave the impression of being adept at holding things that were difficult to hold onto or extremely heavy. Only his thin glasses and receding sandy-brown hair set him apart from the young man he had been when he married Caroline over five years ago. He approached the group with a triumphant—and thoroughly pugnacious—smile.

"So guess what I've been doing all morning," he challenged.

"What?" Brock and Rose asked.

"Editing news footage together. You won't believe what just happened."

"What?"

"I think the No College Club has found its next recruit."

Chapter 16

The newscasters projected their grim urgency into Derek's cramped office. Huddling in front of the monitors on a desk cluttered with books, papers, and other items, Derek, Brock, and Matt took in the news story. Only Rose stood apart next to an overstuffed bookshelf, bouncing Little Brock on her hip and trying to follow along.

The coverage was extensive, as were opinions coming from a multitude of sources. It was all the American news establishment could talk about once the story broke. An overweight, pimply-faced young white man in a poorly fitting suit had spoken at a scholarship competition at a Midwestern university. He made a few frank remarks about race, and was assaulted for it. For the next three days, the American news media did everything in its power to ruin his life. As the video played, the No College Club could only watch in horror.

***

"In my 20 years in news media I've never heard anything so racist!" exclaimed one news anchor, a slender white woman with round earrings and medium-length black hair. Stress lines around her eyes and lips clashed with her expertly made-up face.

"This young man is no better than Hitler Youth!" warned an incensed older woman in a thick New York accent. She had short, curly brown hair and wore a glittering necklace over a dark, patterned blouse. Her deeply-lined face and squinting eyes gave her a pinched, pained expression. "He violates all the tenets of the Civil Rights Movement and what it means to be American!"

Five well-dressed, well-preserved middle-aged women, sitting at a large semi-circular table with their laptops and coffee mugs, bickered before green-screen footage of the incident. "*Of course*, the First Amendment shouldn't apply to hate speech!" said the black one. The sides of her head were shaved bald, with the rest of her hair set in intricate braids. A floral-print muumuu enveloped most of her shapeless body. "Why did we have all this progress? Why did we march in Selma? Why did we have the Civil Rights Act and *Brown versus Board* if we're not gonna prosecute people like this?"

"You're saying he should go to prison?" asked a tall, slender white woman in a sleeveless yellow one-piece. Red lipstick matched her manicured fingernails as wavy blonde hair fell past modest earrings. Sharp, discerning eyes belied the youthfulness of her attractive face.

"He assaulted an African-American woman!" bellowed a chubby, round-faced Hispanic woman in a sparkling burgundy blouse. Heavy eye shadow, lipstick and rouge further darkened her bronzed face almost to the point of caricature. "She spent almost an *hour* in the hospital. Why *shouldn't* he go to prison?"

"I don't think he assaulted her," interjected the blonde. "Looking at the footage, it seemed like an accident. The police were correct not to arrest him."

This caused an uproar among the women until the black one pointed a stubby finger at the blonde. "*This* is why conservatives like you are so unpopular, Denise! You defend racists!"

Denise raised her chin in defiance. "Let's be clear. As a conservative, I'm not defending his racism. He should be cancelled for what he said until he learns his lesson. I just think there's enough reasonable doubt regarding assault. But your point is well taken. William Askew is a racist."

"There is no defense for racism," intoned a news anchor from another network, this one a gray-haired white man in dark-rimmed glasses. With his jaw set in righteous indignation, he spoke with thunderous authority. "These were despicable statements made by a despicable human being. And in my opinion, minor or not, he got what was coming to him!"

"My only problem is that Quentin St. James got to punch that kid before I could," opined a gaunt, middle-aged black professor with a goatee and dreadlocks. "Far as I'm concerned, Mr. St. James is a hero."

"I heard he's been offered numerous football scholarships because of this," said the anchor.

"Yes!" responded the black professor. "I pulled strings to get him into U-Penn, where I teach, but it didn't work out. Looks like he's staying close to home. But I'm still happy for the young man."

The montage then cut to Quentin St. James, the student who had assaulted Will. He wore a sweatshirt bearing the colors of a certain Midwestern state university. Sunlight reflected brightly off his brown scalp. "Yeah, like, I didn't have a choice," he explained in a raspy voice. "I saw that dude hit that lady in the face, and I's like, 'Oh, Gawd! M'ah gonna take that? M'ah gonna let some white dude get away with that?' I's, like, 'Hell no!' So I got up and cold cock the cracker!"

On a different program, a pale and fidgety Nadine Alterman in a beige blouse was being interviewed by a black female anchor with short, straightened hair and thick-lidded eyes. Fat bulged in rings around her neck above her blue-and-white checkered blouse. Projected behind them was a school photograph of Will in the same suit he had worn at the scholarship competition. Since the photograph had been taken when he was a sophomore and at least 30 pounds lighter, the suit fit him well. But his pimply face and vacant expression made him the unlikeliest of culprits. Beneath the photograph was his name misspelled in all caps: "WILLAM N. ASKEW." At the bottom of the screen, it read, also in all caps, "WHITE SUPREMACIST STUDENT ASSAULTS AFRICAN AMERICAN EDUCATOR."

"William Askew was always a problem," Nadine asserted as she brushed her hair behind her shoulder. "He deliberately disrupted our first Critical Theory Club meeting. He also lied about attending a protest at a nearby school."

"Really?" the astonished host murmured.

"Later in the semester he came to me and tried to explain that critical race theory justifies segregation and Jim Crow laws—even slavery."

The host gasped. "No!"

"Yes. I told him very patiently that this line of thinking was racist. And he argued with me. He actually argued with me."

"He did not!"

"He even told a friend that he approved of the 1921 Tulsa, Oklahoma race massacre. He said the black victims got what they deserved. He used those very words."

The anchor placed her hand on her chest and leaned back in her chair as if repulsed by this horrific news. "In this day and age!"

Nadine waved her hand, signaling her disgust. "Brainwashed young people—especially *young white men*—are the reason why critical race theory is so critical for the future of our nation. Knowledge of our past is the key to controlling our future. We cannot allow our youth to become radicalized into fascism. This happened in Nazi Germany, and we can't let it happen here. Critical race theory is the key pedagogical bulwark against the repeat of history. We must never forget that!"

The montage then cut to the initial news reporting of the incident. A white male reporter with a collar and tie peeking out from beneath a blue sweater was standing in front of Will's high school, wind rustling his impeccably combed hair. He stated that the school had received numerous bomb threats, and so would be closing for the semester that Tuesday, one day before winter break. It had also shuttered its social media presence and provided an official statement condemning Will and his actions. After a brief investigation, they decided to expel him as well. The reporter went on to say that Will was thought to have used an alias during the scholarship competition, claiming to be a classmate named Peter Dorr. The real Peter Dorr, who refused to be interviewed, claimed to have been traumatized by the impersonation and was considering suing Will for defamation.

Back in the news studio, an East-Asian female anchor in a mauve sheath dress with light brown hair curving down either side of her neck asked, "So, Brian, why use an alias?"

"No one knows in this particular case," responded Brian. "But it is common for far-Right individuals to use pseudonyms to hide their identities."

"I see. And Brian, please explain to our viewers how this William Askew was even allowed in the building if he wasn't participating in the scholarship competition."

"He was reading for another contestant who was sick that morning."

"Right. And we have obtained footage of this friend speaking out about the incident. Her name is Connie Craft, and, as one would expect, she had a lot to say."

The video cut to a press conference which had been held in Will's high school gymnasium. A table draped in school colors occupied center court in front of folded bleachers and several furled flags. The school's principal and superintendent—both older white men in sharp, stylish suits—sat at either end. Between them sat Connie in a white blouse, her face tanned with makeup and her hair styled into a Dutch braid. She was reading carefully from a prepared statement and only occasionally looked up at the cameras. An audience of several dozen students sat on the floor directly before her.

"I am a high school senior of Native American ancestry," she began. "I am interested in studying political science, gender studies, and critical race theory. I've known William Askew casually for two years. He was never a friend. In fact, he sexually harassed me in biology class when we were sophomores. A few months ago we thought about doing research together as applicants for the Jaylin Parker Critical Race Scholar Award. But he backed out, citing racist reasons against African and Native Americans. There were many witnesses to his racist diatribe on the afternoon of Monday, November sixth in which he approved of the 1921 Tulsa Race Massacre—or pogrom, as some would call it—the centenary of which was just two years ago."

Connie sniffed, her composure beginning to crumble. She took her eyes off her statement and looked into the crowd. "I refused to have anything to do with him after that! I swear, I never—I never would condone anything like what he said. As a Native American, I was offended. I really was!"

After taking an unsteady breath, she returned to her statement. "However, as I was unwell the evening before my essay presentation, I asked Will—William—to stand in for me and read my essay. With all the awesome competition from the other presenters, I did not want to jeopardize my narrow chances of winning a scholarship. I had no one else to turn to at such a late hour."

Connie gasped and choked as she wiped tears from her eyes with a wad of tissues. "This was my mistake!" she croaked. "And I'm sorry!" The principal placed his arm around her and whispered comforting words to her as her hands shook in remorse. "I'm sorry to Chaunté Robertson, who was the victim of a deliberate assault. I'm sorry to my friend and mentor Nadine Alterman. I'm sorry to the scholarship committee for embarrassing them, which is why I withdrew my essay from the competition. Finally, I am sorry to the university community for exposing them to the very racism that we're trying to eradicate with critical race theory. Knowledge of our past is the key to controlling our future, and this is why critical race theory is so important. William Askew is a prime example of the evil of white supremacy and how its legacy lingers with us today. I am sorry for what I have done and ask the entire community for forgiveness. Thank you."

Connie finally broke down in tears, shoulders heaving, as the empathetic principal wrapped her up in his arms. The crowd applauded riotously, with numerous students, all female, approaching Connie to offer their compassion and understanding.

The video then cut to a montage of Will's racially diverse classmates denouncing him—and not merely for his supposed racism. A few also complained about his personality quirks, offbeat sense of humor, lingering body odor, and overall social awkwardness. One student in particular caught the attention of the No College Club. He had long brown hair, insolent eyes, and a thin, acne-scarred face. He wore a flannel shirt over a T-shirt promoting an obscure, decades-old motion picture. An off-screen news reporter described him as William Askew's best friend. The caption read, "Jonas Delacroix Craiglow."

"Yeah, I was friends with Will until recently," admitted JD. "He was such a racist, though. It was getting hard to take. He kept bringing up this so-called 'race realism.' Even when I told him I wasn't interested, he wouldn't let it go. He has this annoying habit of always saying, like, socially unacceptable things, you know? It's sad actually. I hope he can—get through all this." JD shook his head, as if in shame, and then slunk away.

***

The screen cut to black, and all present members of the No College Club sighed in unison.

"On the bright side," Brock said, pretending to look dazed, "cleaning out the chicken coop is gonna be a blast compared to this."

"I get shivers every time I see that kid get knocked out," Derek said. "Sucker punching someone like that. Such a cowardly move."

"When did this happen, Derek?" Rose asked, still struggling with Little Brock.

"This past Saturday," Derek said, leaning back in his chair and shaking his head like a tolling bell. "News didn't break till Sunday. And here we are Tuesday morning just learning about it."

"We need to pick up our game keeping track of these things," Brock said.

"This poor kid," Matt said sympathetically. "His life is over."

"Excuse me?" Derek asked sharply.

Mortified, Matt realized his mistake. "I shouldn't have said that. I'm sorry, Derek."

Brock shook Matt affectionately by the shoulder. "That's what we're here for. To bring people back from the dead. You of all people should know."

"Yeah, I practically had a fork in my back when you found me."

Brock and Rose tried to laugh, but the atmosphere was too despondent for humor.

"I'm putting together a compilation video for our socials," Derek explained. "But I just can't get it right."

"What you have looks pretty good," Rose said.

"Thanks. But you should see some of the other videos out there. People are memeing this Askew kid like crazy. They have him going backwards and forwards with music and effects and animation. They say CRT book sales have skyrocketed because of this. He's gone viral, and not in a good way."

"How do you say 'viral' in Ancient Greek?" Brock asked.

Derek chuckled. "Well, 'virus,' as we know it, has a Latin root, meaning poison or venom. I think it stems from the Greek *ιός*."

"Ee-What?"

"Have you tried contacting him, Derek?" Rose asked as Brock pondered Derek's exotic pronunciation.

"Yeah. He has no social media, which is not surprising. What is surprising is that I emailed him using his school's domain, and it bounced. They wasted no time purging him."

A confused Matt looked to the group. "So that's it? We're not gonna reach out to him?"

Derek adjusted his glasses and shrugged, looking at Rose. "Well, we have options."

Rose held up a hand in anticipation. "No, Derek."

"Covington is fairly close to this kid's hometown."

Rose gasped. "I can't believe you're even considering—"

"Why not? It's kind of on her way back home. It'll only add a couple hundred miles—"

"Caroline is eight months pregnant!"

"So?" Brock said. "That gives her a whole month, doesn't it? It won't take her that long to drive—"

Grimacing in anger, Rose took Little Brock's fist and pummeled Brock on the shoulder with it. "A taste of your own medicine, mister!"

"Ow! Ow!" Brock clowned.

"The things you say, Brock! You think it's comfortable driving when you're *that* pregnant?"

"Like I would know!"

"She has to drive nearly 500 miles to get home, and you want to add to that?"

"Well, I don't *want* to—"

"Plus, it's not unheard of for a woman to go into labor a month early!"

"Okay. Point taken," Brock said. "But we gotta do something. This kid's perfect for the No College Club."

"And we should get to him before he does something stupid, like apologize," Derek said. "The least we can do is ask Caroline. She can always say no."

"How do we even know where this kid lives?" Matt asked.

"We know because one news article mentioned that his mother teaches cello from her home. Her website is down, so I perused the internet archives until I found an old version of it, which had her home address."

"How did you find the URL to begin with?"

Derek smiled. "I assumed many of her students were Asian. So I went on social media sites in the kid's hometown and looked for chatrooms with Chinese names. Sure enough, one of them had a website that linked to all the best local music instructors. And she was on it."

"Wow."

"Yeah, and let's just hope that our enemies aren't as resourceful as I am," Derek said. "Because if they are, we'll need to get to Will Askew before they do."

Chapter 17

Caroline finally turned off the highway after having driven over 50 miles since her last rest stop. She was only a short distance southwest of her destination and couldn't wait to get there. She also couldn't help but regret her decision to drive halfway across the country at such a late stage in her pregnancy. While the others were enjoying a mild winter at Smythe Farm down in Virginia, she had to deal with frosty winds, icy roads, and bleak skies all across the Midwest. Not only this, but her left thigh was numb, she needed to pump more breastmilk, and she had to go to the bathroom—again. The baby had also started kicking again that morning.

She thought back upon what a successful week it had been. She'd spoken at the annual conference of a world famous white advocacy group. She'd attended a retreat held by another, lesser-known group. She had been the overnight guest of a famous pro-white blogger and his wife. She had also visited her sister Beth, who was a senior at a nearby university. Now desperately missing her friends and family, she had only one stop left, the Northwest Zion Methodist Church in a town called Covington. A group of No College Club donors led by a man named Fort Beaugaard—Fort was short for Roquefort—had arranged for her to speak to an audience of local high school students. Fort had been so supportive of the No College Cub that she couldn't refuse, despite how the visit would take her nearly a hundred miles out of her way and extend her trip an extra day.

The church featured tall stained-glass windows, a steeple surrounded by ornamental parapets, and a roof equipped with four cross-shaped solar panels. Surrounded by photogenic shrubbery, it occupied most of its small corner lot and left little room for grass on its two visible sides. Caroline pulled into its narrow parking lot, longing for fresh air but bracing for the cold, gusty winds she knew would hit her the moment she opened her car door. She parked and texted Derek to tell him that she had reached the church safely. Looking up, she spotted a bearded figure in a thick beige sweater appearing from the back of the building. This must be Fort, she realized, a person she had met only online up to that point. He waved and motioned for her to park in back. When she reached the back parking lot, she noticed only one other car, and so opted for a handicapped spot. Smiling to herself, she wondered if any police officer would ticket a woman as pregnant as she was for parking in a handicapped spot.

After stepping out, Caroline exchanged warm greetings with Fort, but was distracted by what she saw across the side street: an old, abandoned church, not visible from the main avenue. Its mottled roof appeared warped by age and neglect; its near-windowless front face battered by weather and corroded with moss. Peeling white paint checkered the structure in many places, revealing ancient gray wood underneath. On its side were four tall, gothic arch windows with damaged and often glassless panes. A single chimney, blackened with overuse, starkly divided the two middle windows.

Most poignant for Caroline was the brick belltower above the church. Its bell had fallen from its headstock, with only its rust-colored lip being visible from the belfry opening.

"Ah, the old Northwest Zion Chapel," Fort remarked. "A Covington landmark. Built in 1890, but it fell out of use when I was a kid. But let's go inside. It's cold."

They rushed inside as the heavy glass doors *swooshed* closed behind them. Caroline found herself with Fort and his wife Helen in a lobby at the intersection of three hallways. A giant wooden cross facing them upon the stucco wall. The front hallway led alongside the chapel itself and

was awash in vibrant daylight streaming through the
stained-glass windows. The other two, however, interested
Caroline more since she needed to know quite urgently
which one led to a bathroom. But first she had to allow
herself to be welcomed by her hosts. Fort took off his orange beanie, revealing a mess of thinning red hair which
discharged static electricity across his freckled scalp. A
broad, genuine smile revealed dimples on his bearded
cheeks. Of average height and wiry, he had the body of a
track athlete about 30 years past his prime. He was burst-
ing with vigor as he gripped her hand. Caroline noticed
that both his hands were red with eczema.

"It's so great to finally meet you, Caroline!" he gushed.
"Thank you for coming! I know it's a great sacrifice for
you, but it means so much to us! The No College Club
does wonderful work, and I hope next time we can host all
of you. We've reserved a room called the Sanctuary, which
is just down the hall. We're all set up. The others will arrive any moment, and they can't wait to see you. We *all*
can't wait to see you! This is so exciting!"

Touched by Fort's elaborate welcome, Caroline
laughed gently, knowing that if anyone should be doing
the thanking, it was the No College Club. Fort and Helen
Beaugaard, a childless couple from the Midwest, were
their seventh-biggest donors. They were self-described
"refurbished hippies" who ran two computer repair shops
in Covington. They also never failed to provide the Club
with emergency funds or free service whenever they needed it.

"It's no problem at all!" Caroline responded, now regretting that she had ever regretted coming to Covington.
Such a sweet, warm man; she couldn't wait to get to know
him better.

"This is my wife, Helen," he said, motioning to the
short, square-shouldered woman standing to his right.
Overweight, but still boasting a womanly figure, Helen

possessed carefully combed auburn hair which flowed down one side of her neck and not the other. She wore a patterned wool tunic which stretched to her thighs, jeans, and dark leather ankle boots. Large, out-of-style glasses gave the impression that this woman had a fashion all her own.

"Yes, yes," Helen said with serene confidence. "Fort could not stop talking about you for days, and he *still* cannot stop talking about you. Clearly he fails to understand that after a long drive a woman in your condition will need to use the facilities. They're down the hall behind you, Sweetie, three doors to the right. Take your time."

Caroline mouthed a grateful "thank you" before hurrying off down the hall.

It felt like it had been an hour, but her phone told her she'd taken only 25 minutes. Her head was pounding with nausea, and after three hours on the road, she wanted nothing more than to lie down and sleep. But she didn't have the time. She reminded herself that if all went well with her talk and the roads were free of traffic, she could make it home by midnight. She adjusted the shoulder strap of her satchel as she stepped back into the hall. There were now eight others waiting in the lobby with Fort and Helen. They were either elderly or middle-aged, and were busy shaking off the cold in their thick boots, jackets, and hats. All but one were men. Oddly, they seemed too preoccupied to notice her as she approached.

Caroline felt an inward coldness as she surmised the situation—the young people slated to attend her talk were not going to come after all. She hoped she was wrong, but the mortified looks on the faces of Fort and Helen told her otherwise. Fort then regretfully informed her that they had all backed out at the last minute. No reason had been given.

Caroline accepted the news stoically but felt acute dis-

appointment. Nonetheless, she forced herself to smile and
met her hosts with aplomb. Nearly eight years' experience
as a white dissident had hardened her to all manner of
setback. She also understood that success resulted as
much from a good attitude as from hard work, talent, or
anything else. Sure enough, after introductions and chit
chat, she began enjoying herself. These were good people,
she reminded herself. There was much to be gained in
speaking with them. The hall was ringing with their
laughter minutes later as they made their way to the Sanctuary.

"Fort!" a man called as the church doors *swooshed*
open and closed. "Fort! Stop right there!"

From the way the group grumbled apprehensively,
Caroline sensed that this was an unwelcome intrusion.
She turned and saw three men approaching, their footsteps padding on the carpeted floor. Their apparent leader, the one who had called out to Fort, wore dark slacks,
and a thick, wine-red, cardigan over a white dress shirt. A
weak chin rested on his globular neck as his eyes flashed
nervously. His gray hair was sculpted with product. To the
man's right was a town police officer in his dark blue uniform, with a pistol holstered to his hip. He was middle-
aged, red-cheeked, and about thirty pounds overweight.
Sunglasses rested atop his shiny bald head. Both men had
their teeth set in a scowl, as if dreading what they were
about to do.

Not so the third man. This one was black, and was
shorter and much more slender than the others. He had
such round, insouciant features, that Caroline suspected
he wasn't an American. His jacket, shirt, and tie were different shades of green, while his slacks were a rich lavender. He wore a conspicuous silver cross around his neck,
giving him away as a pastor or minister. He seemed perfectly contented to be there.

Fort stepped up to meet the men. "What's this about,

Pastor?" he asked, addressing the man who had called out to him.

The pastor stopped before Fort, breathing heavily. "You know what this is about."

"No, I don't."

The pastor poked the air in front of Caroline without looking at her. "I know who that is! We can't let someone like *that* speak in the Sanctuary."

Caroline felt the people around her bristle. The men stepped forward in solidarity with Fort and began arguing acrimoniously. She, however, knew better. Whoever this pastor was, he was likely two or three degrees removed from the shadowy authority which banned her from speaking that morning. There was no point in arguing. The man's mind had been made up already, most likely by unfair or illegal means of persuasion. Caroline forced herself to relax and began counting the seconds until she could start her journey back home.

"We booked the Sanctuary weeks ago, *Kevin*," Fort said insolently. "We always have people come and speak."

"This is different," Kevin responded. "We don't promote hate or exclusion at this church."

"The No College Club does not promote hate and exclusion."

"Yes, they do."

"Have you read any of their works?" Fort challenged. "Have you listened to any of their talks?"

"I have not."

"Then how do you know they promote hate and exclusion?"

"I bet you hadn't even heard of 'em till today," one of the men added.

Kevin waved his hand like a karate chop. "It doesn't matter! I know what they stand for now! And it is everything this church has stood against since its inception."

"What would you know about that?" Fort asked.

"You've only been here ten years. Helen and I, and many of us, have been here our whole lives."

"Fort—"

"Three of my great-grandparents helped found this church. One of them constructed the old chapel across the street, which served our community for nearly a century—"

"Fort, that has—"

"The *historic* chapel you refuse to renovate and would rather sell over our objections!"

"Fort! That has nothing to do—"

"It has *everything* to do with it! We grew up in this church. We *are* this church!" Fort tilted his head. "Or maybe not," he continued ominously. "Maybe we should find another one."

The others concurred with Fort in a cacophony of dissent, which Kevin struggled to suppress by raising his hands. But it was the black pastor who ultimately silenced them.

"It is no matter," he said in a stolid African accent. "We will replace you."

Hearing this made Caroline's stomach turn in loathing. She quickly mastered her emotions, but also understood that this was no idle threat. With the millions of illegal immigrants streaming into her country every year, it would only be a matter of time before these non-white invaders could replace—literally replace—whites anywhere they wished. The people around her seemed to understand this as well. Their enthusiasm plummeted into silence.

"All because of a talk," Fort argued bravely. "All because we wish to exercise our First Amendment rights."

Again, Kevin pointed at Caroline without looking at her. "She is a racist!"

"She is not!" Fort responded indignantly.

"She most certainly is!"

Fort was about to respond when Helen stepped defiantly in front of her husband and confronted Kevin, arms crossed. "So what if she is?"

The people behind her gasped. Fort began gently reprimanding his wife, but a hard look from her silenced him.

"Well, that proves it then!" Kevin said triumphantly.

Undeterred, Helen blinked her eyes slowly, once. "As racist as she may be, Kevin, she'll never be as racist as you," she said with unshakable tranquility. She gestured to the black man standing by his side. "Non-whites like your friend here organize by race all the time, and with the full approval of our politicians. But when whites do it, you crack down. And you have the nerve to call *us* racist? No," she said, wagging her finger and smiling sweetly. "*You're* the racist. You are anti-white. You're a hypocrite, a bully, and a worthless human being."

Such a consummate insult left everyone speechless. Fort looked to his feet, shaking his head—not agreeing, but not wishing to argue, either. Even the black pastor looked at Kevin uncertainly. But Kevin met Helen's smile with one of his own. He seemed almost *relieved*, as if he could finally speak freely as well.

"I'm not worthless," he said, pulling an envelope from his jacket pocket. "I'm protecting my church. This morning, one of the impressionable *children* you were planning to brainwash informed his parents of your plan. They notified the North American Anti-Racism Council, which sent us an email about an hour ago assuring us that if this woman speaks on church property, we won't have a church at all."

A simultaneous exhalation followed by more silence. This indeed was the trump card. There could be no answer. Fort was no longer shaking his head; Helen was no longer smiling. Caroline knew it was time to act.

"May I see that letter please?" she asked, forcing Kevin to look at her for the first time. He said nothing; neither fulfilling nor refusing her request. The lawyer she could never be began to assert herself in her mind. "As a man of God," she continued. "I assume you believe that all people have inalienable rights, including the right to be informed of accusations leveled against them—and to be confronted with evidence. Or do you wish to overturn the Sixth Amendment as well?"

Kevin took a deep, deliberate breath, not wanting to engage in a legal discussion with this seemingly well-informed stranger. Nodding almost imperceptibly, he removed the printout from its envelope and handed it to Caroline. She took a photo of it with her cellphone, and handed it back.

"Thank you," she said tersely.

"You're welcome," Kevin responded. "Now leave."

When no one moved, the police officer stood tall as if to remind Caroline that she was now an interloper and would face arrest if she continued to linger. Unintimidated, she adjusted the shoulder strap of her satchel and marched forward—as if to walk *through* the officer—daring him to obstruct the path of a pregnant woman. He didn't. He stepped aside. Moments later, she heard the *swoosh* of the church doors as she pushed them open.

It had warmed up outside, and was less windy—but the sky was no less overcast and bleak. She looked longingly to the old chapel across the street, imagining how picturesque it would appear if repaired. Shaking her head, she walked to her car feeling the Beaugaards and the others exiting the church behind her.

She noticed something under her windshield wiper, and then stopped, causing Fort to nearly bump into her from behind. A parking ticket! Swiping the notice, she enjoyed a hearty laugh with her new friends. She reminded herself to check the law in that state to see if pregnant women in their third trimester were allowed to park in handicapped spots. If so, she would challenge it.

Their goodbyes were heartfelt, their embraces warm and prolonged. She exchanged contact information with everyone. As uncomfortable and homesick as she was, she was sad that her all-too-brief time in Covington was about to end. She felt the cold spark of a tear on her cheek when Helen took her in her arms for a final good-bye. "If I had a daughter, she'd be your age," she said with a sad, implacable smile.

Caroline climbed into her car and was about to begin the final 500-mile stretch of her journey when her cellphone beeped. It was a text from Derek. It was about a boy named Will Askew who lived only 63 miles from Covington. He desperately needed her help.

Chapter 18

Will felt the textured paper rub against his fingers. He had received letters before—but never one that read *"CERTIFIED MAIL"* in a green stripe across the envelope. It all seemed so *official*; was he now old enough to receive official correspondence? He had *heard* of certified mail, of course, despite not knowing what it was. So the idea that William Askew—who was turning 18 that very day—had actually received a certified letter was not beyond the realm of possibility.

But the *words* printed on the paper certainly were. He read them repeatedly. The more he understood, the less he could believe.

Dear Mr. Askew:

We, Brandford and Bryce, Inc., are a law firm in Evansville, Indiana representing Peter M. Dorr in connection with highly publicized incidents in which you impersonated and defamed Mr. Dorr at the Jaylin Parker Critical Race Scholar Award presentations on December 16, 2023.

We have evidence proving that your impersonation of Mr. Dorr in which you made several racist and prejudicial statements, as well as allegedly assaulted a respected African American activist and educator, has caused irreparable harm to his reputation and social standing.

We hope to resolve his matter amicably. Please instruct your attorney to contact us at the above address so we can commence discussion of mediation. If we do not receive communication from you within two weeks, we will have no alternative but to file a lawsuit against you. In the event of a lawsuit, our client intends to seek redress to the fullest extent permitted by law including, but not limited to, legal services costs, court costs, and accrued interest.

Sitting on his bed, Will let the letter fall to the floor between his feet. Who could expect him to respond to something like this? Who could expect him to respond to *anything* that was happening to him? This was just another incredible moment in a long string of incredible moments, which he feared would change his life forever.

***

He remembered nothing when he awoke on the auditorium stage that past Saturday. He felt no pain, only a strange floating sensation as if he were adrift at sea. He had no idea where he was. Was it morning? Was it time for school? Did he remember to do his homework? Did he remember to get dressed? He heard nothing. And then he heard everything. Triumphant yelling and stamping. He felt every vibration on the wooden stage. With effort, he sat up, disoriented, trying to make sense of what was happening. Why were the lights so bright? Why was he in a suit and tie? Why did his jaw feel funny? Who were these people, and why was everyone looking at him?

Connie!

Suddenly, everything came back to him. Still seated, he turned and looked for her, but he spun around too quickly, causing his head to throb. He remembered how close he had come to kissing her. Did she really mean what she had said? Did she really want him to ask her out? In spite of his sudden headache he kept looking for her, but could not find her. He did, however, see Nadine Alterman at the edge of the stage in urgent conference with Chaunté Robertson and a hulking, bald-headed black man in an orange shirt. Will couldn't hear her over the din, but she was explaining something to them in emphatic detail, gesturing manically. Both women looked at him sharply. These were unwelcome glares to be sure, but the fierce, brutish look from the man made his heart skip. Will recognized him and remembered everything: the footsteps, the pinky ring, the punch, the lizard-bat-panda marching band—everything.

Security arrived, then the paramedics, and then the police. The police questioned him along with the others. They made no arrests. Mysteriously, Connie Craft was nowhere to be found. Had she even been there at all?

Will's parents met him in the hospital. He had suffered a concussion, but fortunately his jaw had not been broken. The doctor prescribed an icepack, acetaminophen, and lots of rest. On the ride home, his parents pressed him with questions, but he didn't tell them everything. It didn't matter. The news broke in the local media that evening. It broke in the national media the following day. One report even mentioned the racial discrimination complaints filed against Andrew at the library. Within 24 hours the story was everywhere on social media. The videos of Will inadvertently striking Chaunté Robertson and getting knocked out with a single punch went viral. So did his ad-libbed speech in which he identified as white and challenged critical race theory.

"When whites are colorblind, blacks can't compete with them so well."

Will had said this—and news anchors and pundits everywhere made sure to remind the world of it as often as possible. He received notice of his expulsion from high school that very evening, just as he finally recognized that JD and Connie were not returning his calls or texts. By Sunday night, Andrew had stopped talking to him. He had been fired from the museum that morning and spent most of the day either arguing with Melissa or on the phone with his attorney. Melissa, who had been in hysterics all day, received numerous emails from parents of students notifying her that they no longer required her services. She was too emotionally distraught to speak coherently with Will, even though she tried several times. By Monday morning, 20 of her 22 students had left her, including all nine white ones. At three o'clock that afternoon, a small group of black-clad protestors stood on the street outside their home, holding placards which condemned Will and Andrew Askew as racists. One of them spraypainted obscenities on their mailbox before the police arrived and dispersed them without making any arrests.

After this, Andrew became openly hostile to Will, and once even threatened him with violence.

The household remained in crisis on Tuesday, the day Will received that certified letter. It was his birthday, although no one celebrated it. Melissa spent most of the day on her phone in the master bedroom with the door locked. By dinner time, Will was famished. He was in the kitchen helping himself to leftovers when his father appeared with a grim look and a large envelope under his arm.

"It's not even five, and you're already eating dinner?" Andrew said, lips curled antagonistically.

Will dropped his fork with a loud clang and stood. He would go hungry for the rest of the evening before catching any more abuse from his father. "Fine! I'm overweight. I won't eat!"

He was about to walk past his father when Andrew pointed to the table. "Sit down."

Surprised by the command, Will didn't move. Andrew repeated it, and still Will did not move.

"*Sit down!*" Andrew barked.

His father's anger and the veins bulging from his neck made Will comply. He found Andrew's unshaven face and slovenly appearance in an old sweatshirt and jeans unnerving. His father was the cleanest-cut person he knew—

and now suddenly he wasn't. "I thought you said you didn't want to talk to me," Will said.

"This time I have no choice," Andrew said as he slapped the envelope onto the table.

"What's this?"

"Your eviction notice."

"What?"

"Happy birthday."

Will was too shocked to respond. He felt the familiar nervous tingle in his fingers and pounding in his chest. After all that had happened, he thought nothing more could surprise him. But this did. It may have been the worst surprise of them all. "You're kicking me out?" he asked.

"Yep. You're 18. I am under no obligation to keep you under my roof."

"Mom's okay with this?"

"Your mother can't even function right now, Will. You ruined her career. You ruined *my* career. I can't get work anywhere except at a grocery store or a construction site. Our friends aren't even talking to us. All because you broke our rule: *No racist talk!*"

"I was only telling the truth, Dad."

Andrew was about to respond in a rage, but controlled himself. He took a deep, unsteady breath, and placed his finger on the envelope. "You have 30 days to vacate, after which, you'll be considered an interloper and I will call the police. You are forbidden to enter the main living quarters of the house. You must stay in the basement and enter and exit through the basement door. You already have a sink, bathroom, microwave, cabinets, and mini-fridge downstairs, and it is incumbent upon you to keep everything clean and stocked. Since your phone is paid for, you can keep it, but as of tomorrow you're off our calling plan. You can keep your automobile since it's in your name, but our insurance will cover you only till the end of March.

Our health insurance will cover you another six months. After that, you're on your own. Any questions?"

Fighting the urge to panic, Will rummaged his mind for a suitable response, but none came. His stomach began to tighten, and he felt pain in his chest as well. He had known loneliness in his life, but never *this*—never the horrifying prospect of being literally alone in the world. Could anyone survive if he were truly and completely alone?

Looking up, he saw his mother in the kitchen doorway, tears streaming onto her flower-patterned pajama top. Her hair was awry and her face red with grief. Her arms were clutched tightly around her stomach. Will wanted to cry the moment he saw her. "Mom!" he called.

She ran over to him and embraced him at the kitchen table. Whatever she was trying to say was lost amidst her sobs. Will had never seen his mother so distraught before. With her in his arms, he felt less alone—but her anguish was making him fear the future even more. Eventually, her sobs receded, and he could understand what she was saying. She was trying to get him to do something.

"We can still fix this, Will," she pleaded desperately, taking his hands in hers. "It's not too late."

"What are you talking about?"

"That's enough," Andrew said, gently pulling on his wife's arm.

"No, Andrew!" Melissa shouted, brushing his hand away. "You said you wouldn't do this until we tried everything!"

"He's not gonna go for it, Melissa! And even if he does, there's no guarantee it'll work!"

"Not gonna go for what?" Will asked suspiciously.

Melissa reached for her purse on the nearby counter and pulled out a business card, which she handed to Will. "Just consider it, Will," she entreated.

Will studied the card. It belonged to a psychiatrist specializing in adolescent psychiatry. Her name was Judith L. Abramoff. There was a photo of a pretty middle-aged woman with short brown hair, a wide jaw, and slender neck. She struck Will as an underweight version of Nadine Alterman. He dropped the card, repelled by the very sight of her.

"A friend of mine from conservatory recommends her, Will," Melissa entreated. "Many of her clients are young people who—suffer from extremism."

"I'm not an extremist, Mom."

Andrew stepped back and slapped his thigh. "See? I told you!"

"Will!" Melissa shrieked, shaking him by the wrists. "She can help you! You need help!"

"You're saying I'm crazy?"

"No! You're just lost. You're going down the wrong path."

"Mom, no," Will said firmly, breaking free from her grasp. He was scared of the future, but for some reason he was *more* frightened of this strange woman smiling at him from that card. "Thank you, but no. I'm not crazy. I don't need help. And I didn't do anything wrong!"

Melissa backed away in horror. "How could you say you that? After all that's happened?"

"*I to-old you!*" Andrew sang sarcastically.

That his father could actually carry a tune made his remark all the more obnoxious for Will. Ignoring him, he stood up from the table. "Do you really wanna help me, Mom?"

"Yes!"

"Then don't kick me out of the house."

Melissa turned away from Will as if too ashamed to face him. She pressed both hands against her mouth as tears began to stream. "It's your father," she whispered. "I can't say no to him. I'm sorry!"

Will looked to Andrew, nodding vindictively. "You

would do this to your own son."

Andrew shot a discreet look at Melissa. "Do you wanna tell him? Or shall I?"

"What? No!"

Will looked rapidly from one parent to the other. "What's going on?"

"He's gotta know some time," Andrew said.

"Gotta know what!"

"Please, Andrew. Not yet. He's too young!"

"Too young for what?"

"He's 18. I'm telling him now."

"Tell me what?"

Andrew faced Will, folded his arms, and said, "I'm not your father."

Melissa gasped and rushed over to comfort Will as he responded in shock the news.

"What?"

"That's right," Andrew said in a businesslike tone. "I met your mother when she was pregnant with you back when we lived in Boston. Her boyfriend played for the Boston Pops Orchestra just like your mom. Then she discovered he was some closet Nazi who commented on white supremacist websites under a pseudonym. That's when she split up with him and fell in with me. And when they found out about it, they fired him—as they should have—and saw to it that he would never work again as a musician. *But they did the same thing to your mother.* That's why we moved all the way out here. That's why she's teaching snot-nosed little Asian kids the cello rather than playing in a prestigious orchestra herself!"

"Andrew, it's not like that!" Melissa bawled.

Andrew shot her a mean, angry look. "I tell the truth!" He then stabbed a finger in Will's face. "And I promised her, out of the goodness of my heart, that I would adopt you and raise you as my own. Why do you think we're so strict about no racism in the house, Will? Why do you think I gave you such a hard time? Because I'm such a bad person? No! It's because we didn't want history to repeat itself. We saw you in all innocence saying stupid racist things and having stupid racist friends, and we tried to stop you from turning into a stupid, racist, hate-filled loser like your dad!"

Will staggered backward until his shoulders hit the wall. Right away, he knew all of it was true. It was like that day at Uncle Gus's house when everything had crystalized for him all at once. *Everything* made sense now. His feelings of awkwardness and alienation at home. His father's eavesdropping and bullying. Both his parents' trying to turn him into something he wasn't. Relieved and frightened at the same time, Will realized that he was *nothing* like Andrew. He never was.

The doorbell rang. Their faces blanched in fear. Was it more protestors? Were they returning to harass or vandalize—or worse? Andrew refused to own a gun, so at that moment they were not only vulnerable but defenseless against anyone determined to do them harm. Secretly Will wished the person at the door was Connie or JD or someone, anyone, who could take him away from all of this. Could such a person actually exist?

Andrew cautiously opened the door to reveal a cheerful Mrs. Wu with her grandson Edison standing beside his cello. Will noticed that Mrs. Wu looked different from before. Had she visited a hair salon? Had she put on makeup? Her clothes were less drab as well: a teal chiffon blouse, beige slacks, and a sparkly black belt. She seemed especially enthused to be there.

"Mrs. Wu, I'm sorry, but today's lesson is canceled," Melissa explained. "I should have emailed you. We'll deduct it from your tuition."

Mrs. Wu nodded amiably and then did something she had never done before—she spoke without being prompted. What emerged at first was her typical hodgepodge of accented English. Will paid close attention however when she began addressing him directly.

"Weer! I see you on *terrivizh!*" she exclaimed, and then took pains to pronounce the word correctly. "Television! I saw Weer on television. I so solly! Merissa! So hard for you! The radies! The mothers ! They say, 'Don't go Merissa Askoo. She raysis! Her son raysis!' And I say, 'No! She good teacher. She teach my grandson! He improve! Much better than Chinese teacher! We still go to her!' And they say, 'What about the son?' And I say . . . *He tell the truth!*"

Her cheeks now red with passion, Mrs. Wu raised a finger and emphasized this last point with every ounce of her five-foot-tall body.

"In China, where I from, everyone same! Here, everyone different. The white, the brack, the Mex. Different lace. Different people. I don't rike the brack. I don't rike the Mex. They fight. They take from you. In skoo they push Edison. Why you push rittle boy? He just want to study, be musician or doctor. Why push rittle boy? But *you* understand. *Weer* understand. Thank you! Thank you for understand!"

For several moments Will, Andrew, and Melissa gaped in open-jawed shock at what they had just heard. Mrs. Wu was beginning to realize that something was awry when Andrew stepped forward and said, "I'm sorry, but we don't allow racist talk in this house."

He then slammed the door rudely in her face.

Chapter 19

Will hadn't performed a pushup since seventh grade and had no idea how many he could still do. He had seen his father—or stepfather, rather—execute them countless times during his morning exercises. How hard could it be? He remembered being able to do eight of them as a freshman when he was 40 pounds lighter. Could he still do that many?

He started, but the strain in his chest and arms tempted him to bend at the waist and finagle the motion. He kept his back straight anyway as he pressed upwards until his trembling arms locked. Sweat popped from his armpits as his heart raced and breath hissed. He knew he didn't have another repetition in him because for the next one he would have to go back down and then up again. It didn't seem fair. He lowered himself without collapsing, but the trip back up proved futile. His chest lacked the strength, and his lower back strained carrying the weight of his prodigious belly. The moment his torso began to sag, he gave up and collapsed upon his bedroom carpet.

He turned over and didn't move, feeling the pain in his chest. He had hoped he'd achieve at least some satisfaction in causing his own pain, rather than having so many things out of his control do it for him. But he was too disappointed to find solace in that. Not even two pushups! Good job, *Willrus*.

He was numb to everything that had happened. It was all so catastrophic and had transpired so quickly. He understood it was real, and that one day very soon he would have to deal with it all alone. A terrifying prospect. But until then he would have to keep the pain at bay somehow, and berating his fat, flabby self for not executing two pushups seemed like just the thing. He didn't even try a sit up. Never in his life had he managed one of those.

The doorbell rang. It couldn't have been another cello

student since his mother had already sent out a mass email, closing her business indefinitely. Plus, it was ten in the morning on a Wednesday. Melissa never took students that early. The night before, the Askews had overcome some of their anxiety when a handful neighbors appeared at their door and offered their support and understanding. They also promised to keep an eye out for protestors looking to cause trouble. This was a great relief, although Will understood they were doing it more for his parents' sake than for his.

So who could it be? Through his open door, he heard his stepfather conversing with a woman. Was she a solicitor? She was awfully insistent for a solicitor. He could hear Andrew beginning to lose his patience. And did the woman actually mention Will's name?

She did it again! Whoever she was, she was there to see him! Will performed the very first sit up of his life without realizing it as he bounded to his feet. He clambered up the stairs and raced through the hall, hoping his heavy footsteps would warn Andrew and their mystery guest of his impending arrival. He stopped short when he saw an irritated Andrew holding the front door open for a blonde woman in a beige wool coat. She wore a blue scarf, tight black leggings, and brown leather boots. Sunglasses perched upon her white winter hat. Will could see her breath condense in the cold and noticed her reddish nose and blue eyes. It wasn't until he felt the frigid wind blast through the doorway that he noticed she was pregnant. Very pregnant.

It was at that moment when Will remembered that he was in a T-shirt and boxers.

Andrew, fresh from a run in a gray-and-black tracksuit, glared at Will and then turned back to Caroline. "I'm sorry, tell me your name again, please."

"I'm Caroline Brand of the Civil Liberties League."

"And why do you want to talk to Will?"

"Like I said, we are a non-profit public interest law firm that—"

"—represents racists?" Andrew interrupted hotly. "Is that what you do? I can't imagine why anyone would arrive at my doorstep wanting to legally represent this boy after what he did. Do you represent Nazis and fascists, too?"

Caroline adjusted her large satchel across her shoulder. It seemed heavy. "We offer legal services to all Americans when their Constitutional rights are violated—which happens often these days with cancel culture and government overreach. We do however specialize in the interests of the legacy American population, which includes most of the white majority."

Andrew smiled sarcastically. "I knew it! You're a white supremacist. You're the reason why we have these problems to begin with."

"Dad, I want to talk to her," Will said, stepping forward.

"You are Will, I presume?" Caroline asked.

"Yeah. Yes."

"Well, she's not coming through this door."

"Dad, come on. It's cold out."

"No."

"I'll take her straight to the basement."

Andrew was about to respond in his usual unrestrained manner but then clamped his mouth shut and spoke through his teeth. *"She is not coming through this door!"*

"Mr. Askew," Caroline said, now beginning to shiver in the cold, "we've done some research on you as well. We can help you fight those discrimination claims made against you at the library. Same with your unfair dismissal from the museum. You of all people should understand the need for what we do."

A barely perceptible gasp came from Andrew as his mouth fell open in disbelief. He slowly shook his head and said, "Never!"

Frustrated, Will let his hands drop to his sides. "Can you at least let the lady in so I can talk to her, Da—?" Will caught himself as he was about to call Andrew "Dad."

Andrew rolled his eyes, growing tired of the conversation. "Whatever! It's your life, Will," he said petulantly. He then pointed at Caroline without looking at her. "But *she* doesn't come through here. She goes in and out through the basement door."

Will nodded in relief. "Fine. Miss Brand, our basement door is in the back of the—"

"Excuse me, Mr. Askew," Caroline interrupted, leveling tired, steely eyes at Andrew. "Do you have a paved walkway around your house?" Disconcerted, Andrew said nothing. "And did you apply de-icer to it? It's very cold and icy out, and I nearly slipped twice walking to your doorstep. In my condition, if I slip and fall walking to your basement door because you didn't properly maintain a safe walking environment on your property in violation of at least two ordinances in your municipality, you will be opening yourself up to a lawsuit. Now, may I come in please? I'll take up a half hour of your son's time."

Andrew met Caroline with a steely look of his own, but after a moment, puffed out a lungful of air and opened the door for her like a butler.

Will led Caroline to his bedroom and started putting on whatever clothes he had lying around: a green and white striped sweater and plaid pajama bottoms with a rip in the seat he was hoping she wouldn't notice. "How did you—how did you do that?" he asked. "I've never seen anyone boss my—my—*him*—around like that—around here!"

Caroline placed her satchel on the floor by the door and removed her coat. "Most people are not on a war footing," she said.

"What?" Will asked, popping his head through the

neck of his sweater.

"Most people just want to be with their families, or make money, or have fun," she explained. "They want to live their lives, you know? But when you use the law like a weapon—like in a war—you can take people's lives away."

"Oh."

"When faced with the possibility of having to defend themselves in court and having their names and photographs all over the news and internet, most people will do whatever it takes not to let that happen. Honestly, I have no idea what the ordinances are in your town. But since your dad is not an attorney, I gambled that he didn't either."

"You were bluffing?"

"Yes," Caroline admitted. "But what I assumed your dad *did* know is that in a lawsuit, it doesn't matter if you're innocent. It's the process that's the punishment."

"I've never thought of it like that."

"Most people haven't. But it's what our enemies do to us all the time."

"Who are our enemies?" Will asked, faintly disturbed having to reconcile such cold, cynical words with this strange, beautiful woman standing so close to him in his own bedroom.

Caroline hesitated. "They're so powerful I'll need to get to know you better before discussing them. May I sit down?"

Will gestured to his desk chair while taking a seat on his bed.

"I said I represent the Civil Liberties League," Caroline began as she rummaged through her satchel. "But I also represent the No College Club."

"I've heard of the No College Club!"

"We saw the news reports about you and have decided you might make a good fit."

"What do you mean?" Will asked with growing alarm

as Caroline removed textbook after textbook from her satchel, placing them on his bed: *Emergency Medicine Basics, An Ancient Greek Primer, The Law and You,* and *Introduction to Agriculture.*

"We have a campus and dormitories in Virgina," she said. "If you pass our online examinations on these topics, as well as others on reading comprehension and mathematics, then we can offer you a spot. You'll live rent-free with us as long as you'd like, but you'll have to follow the rules, keep up with classes, and do your share of work. These books are yours to keep."

"Thank you," Will said as he leafed through the book about agriculture. "I take it you have a farm."

"Yes. You will also be required to do PT."

"PT?"

"Physical training. Like jogging, weights, calisthenics."

Will shrunk back, thinking about his one-and-a-half pushups from moments before. He shrunk back even further as Caroline produced from her satchel a small piece of plywood and a bathroom scale.

"We have a mixed-martial arts gym as well," she continued. "But full contact sparring is optional. Step on the scale, please."

"What?" Will asked, staring at the device. He hadn't stepped on a scale in a month and a half and could only imagine how heavy he'd gotten since his split with Connie in November. "Why?"

"To measure your BMI."

"What's BMI?"

"Body Mass Index. Weight divided by height squared. It tells whether a person is underweight, normal, or . . . overweight."

"But why do you—"

"Because we work our guests very hard. An obese person would be an insurance risk."

"Wouldn't want that," Will said sarcastically.

"We also don't want to endanger you, Will. I'm sorry for being blunt, but it's the world we live in, and it's hard sometimes to separate—" Caroline sniffed, and Will noticed that her eyes were beginning to water. "Do you have a tissue?" she asked, jaw beginning to tremble.

"Yeah, sure," he said as he jumped to his feet and handed her a box of tissues from his bookshelf. "You all right?"

"Yeah," she said, dabbing her eyes and regaining her composure.

"You know, Miss Brand, you're not exactly doing a good job selling the No College Club," he said, grinning mischievously.

Caroline laughed. "I'm a Mrs. And call me Caroline."

"Okay."

"And considering your situation, Will, I don't think I have to sell anything. What we offer beats the alternative."

Will nodded glumly.

"You should step on the scale now. We don't have much time."

Resigning himself to this latest trial, Will did as he was told. The display read 292 pounds, up a depressing 14 since August. He sighed and stepped off.

"Okay, we'll subtract two pounds for your clothing. How tall are you?"

"Six-three."

"Stand up tall."

He obeyed.

"Taller. Stand tall."

He stood erect like a soldier. She stood and squinted as she considered his true height. "You're six-four."

He looked at her quizzically as she tapped numbers into her phone's calculator. "I guess I'm still growing," he said, but then noticed Caroline suddenly frown. "What's wrong?"

"Your BMI is 35.2. Our limit for recruits is 32. And for a

man your age to stay with us, it can't go higher than 30."

"So I have to lose weight?" he asked, a touch flattered that she had referred to him as a man.

"Yes," she said, tapping more numbers into her phone. "Can you get down to 263?"

He looked vacantly across the room. "Uhh . . ."

"We won't give you your entrance exams for at least two months, so you'll have time."

He looked at her sharply. "Actually, I won't have time."

"Why not?"

"Because my dad—" Will winced, realizing his mistake. "—is evicting me now that I'm 18. I have 30 days to vacate. Or, 29 now."

"Why is he—?" she began and then stopped herself, knowing the answer before she could finish asking the question.

"Yeah, he even gave me an eviction notice."

Caroline's eyes narrowed shrewdly. "Can I see it?"

"Sure." He retrieved it from his desk and handed it to her.

"He had an attorney write this up," she said as she pored over the document.

"Yeah. And I don't know if I can lose 29 pounds in 29 days."

"27 pounds. You know, Will, you can fight this."

"Really?"

"Yes. Did you sign a lease?"

"No."

"Then how do you know what your rights are?"

"Uhh . . ."

"You could inform your father that you'll need another two or three months to prepare for your departure. Because you don't have a lease, you were never informed of the terms by which you had to abide while living here. Some leases stipulate a 90-day notice for landlords to change terms."

"But it's his house."

"I know that. But by contesting this document, you'll force him to possibly defend himself in court. He'll have to spend the time and the money—and risk the exposure— all to kick you out in 30 days. Remember, the process is the punishment. It might be less painful for him to let you stay another three months than to fight you."

Will nodded. "Knowing him, he'd fight me. Even in court."

"Okay. You know your father better than I do." She tapped the eviction notice. "But he is now on a war footing with you, which means you have the right to be on a war footing back."

He bit his lip apprehensively. "Can you help me with another lawsuit? A classmate is suing me for supposedly impersonating him. And I wasn't. It's ridiculous."

"We noticed there was some confusion with your name. But yes. If we accept you, you'll receive free legal services—Oh!" Caroline suddenly bent forward, biting her lip in pain. She reached frantically for the chair behind her and then eased into it, trying to control her breathing.

"Everything okay?"

"Yeah. The baby's kicking again. O-oh, this has been a difficult pregnancy. Ah! Okay, she's calming down now."

"When are you due?"

"Three-and-a-half weeks."

Will nodded, imagining JD joking tactlessly about the baby arriving early and making a mess on his carpet. He still could not believe that his best friend was no longer his friend.

"We can help you, Will," she went on. "Your rights have been violated. All those media people who called you a white supremacist or accused you of assault . . . that Al-terman woman, all of them. By speculating about you without proof, they ruined your reputation and rendered you unemployable. They've done you real harm. This is defamation, and you have a right to sue them for it. For millions."

"I do?"

"Yes. You have rights."

Will chuckled wearily.

"What's so funny?"

"As a white person, I just assumed I didn't have any rights."

Caroline looked askance at him until she understood he was being serious. "Please don't think that way," she said urgently. "Promise me you'll never think that way again."

He nodded, startled by her sudden intensity. "Okay, I promise."

Caroline cleared her throat. "I'll see if we can administer the exams early—in four weeks. I'll also see if we can bend the BMI rule for you a little. But we'll need a commitment from you now. I have the forms right here. Are you interested?"

Will closed his eyes and ran his fingers through his hair. In some ways, the future this woman was offering was even more terrifying than the one he'd been forced to contemplate over the past few days. But at least with the No College Club, he wouldn't have to face it alone.

"Will, are you interested?" Caroline repeated.

He looked closely at her, feeling both grateful and privileged to be in the presence of this striking woman. Her confidence and her worries, he felt, were slowly becoming his as well. "How could I not be?" he asked, breaking into a smile.

Chapter 20

After walking Caroline to her car and seeing her off, Will spotted his mother sitting on their porch swing, watching him and holding a large steaming mug of coffee in her lap. She wore paint-splattered jeans and a white turtleneck under a purple fleece vest, which caught her uncombed hair as it fell in many directions. She must have stepped out of the house while he and Caroline were saying goodbye.

"Where's You-Know-Who?" he asked, stepping onto the porch and gesturing to Andrew's empty parking spot in the driveway. He was hoping to keep it calm and casual and was encouraged when he saw that Melissa didn't seem as agitated as she had been the night before. He rolled his shoulders in comfort, grateful that the day was finally beginning to warm up.

"He decided that he could not be in the same house as 'that woman' and left," Melissa said. "Don't know where."

They both nodded, not wanting to comment on Andrew's overblown reaction to their recent guest.

"So you're a racist now," she said after taking a sip.

Will squirmed rather than answer.

"Well, are you?"

"No! How can you even ask me that?"

"We did a web search for her organization while she was here," she responded emotionlessly. "This No College Club is a front for white supremacists, Will. Are you aware of that?"

Will collected his thoughts before answering. "I don't think that's what they're about, Mom."

"The North American Anti-Racism Council has a hate page dedicated to them. I've read their quotes. I've seen their interviews. All the major news networks say the same thing about them."

Will looked sharply at his mother. "But Mom, the media spins things. They take things out of context."

She took another sip. "One of them, I think this woman's husband, openly supports white nationalism. How is that media spin?"

"I don't know. Maybe there's more to it than that, just like there was more to it with me. You saw how the news networks treated me. Everything they said was lies. I got knocked out, remember? I got hit from behind. Yet *I'm* the one the media thinks should be arrested for assault."

"I'm sorry that happened, and I agree it was unfair."

"Then how can you trust those people?"

"Who am I supposed to trust?"

"I guess you can start with Caroline Brand herself when she says that all she wants to do is protect white people when our rights get—"

"I am not interested in anything that woman has to say," she said. "There's a pot of coffee in the kitchen if you—"

"Mom, you're not even giving her a chance," he said, noticing a strange serenity about her. In the past, Melissa would nearly panic whenever someone even came close to violating racial taboos. Now, she seemed almost bored. "Did you at least go to the No College Club website to see what they themselves had to say?"

Still she ignored him, and stared out into the street with her mug by her chin—not telling him to go away, not telling him to stay.

"I get it, Mom," Will went on. "You don't want history to repeat itself. You don't want me to end up like *him*. You're trying to protect me. I appreciate that. But it's kinda late in the day for protection, isn't it? The whole world knows about me, and nobody else besides the No College Club and Mrs. Wu wants to have anything to do with me. What's left to protect?"

"You could apologize," she answered. "If you're going to refuse counseling, the least you could do is apologize."

"To who?"

"I guess you could start with your parents. For destroying our lives."

"I already said I was sorry that happened."

"That's not the same as apologizing, Will."

He shook his head and looked away.

"See?" she said. "By not admitting you did anything wrong, you're signaling that you really are a racist."

It was Will's turn to keep quiet as he walked to the far end of the porch and back.

"Are you?" she asked.

He considered the question for a moment. "You mean, do I think some races are superior to others? I don't know. I haven't studied it. JD seems to think so, despite what he said in that interview. His Uncle Gus seems to think so. I've only read a little bit of what he gave me, so I'm not really qualified to speak about it. I'm surprised everybody all of a sudden thinks I am."

"It's not about being qualified, Will. It's about being a decent, moral human being."

"What's so decent and moral about giving rights and privileges to one race and not another? That's basically what critical race theory is about."

"Oh, come on."

"Seriously, Mom. If the CRT people were interested in decency and morality, they'd want equality for all. They would want colorblindness. *I* want colorblindness, but they don't! Nadine Alterman told me so. The three books I read on the subject told me so. If there is one thing I *am* qualified to talk about, it's critical race theory. And that's the one thing nobody wants to hear me talk about!"

"Don't you want to get your life back, Will?" she asked weakly.

"What kind of life did I have to begin with if everyone's gonna ditch me as soon as the going gets tough? Including you. Why are you ditching me, Mom?"

Melissa shifted her weight on the swing and then stabilized it with her feet when it began to move. "You know I'm not ditching you."

"Then tear up that eviction notice sitting on my desk."

She sniffed, but didn't seem about to cry. "We went over this. Yes, I will tear it up and you can stay with us indefinitely, but you'll have to agree to counseling. I can't do any more than that. I owe too much to your father."

"Which one?" he asked pointedly.

She glared at him and then sipped from her coffee. "I would fight for you, Will. I really would, despite everything—if I didn't think what you're doing is wrong."

"It doesn't feel wrong."

"I know it is. I know from personal experience it is. Take my word for it please."

"*Your* experience? I thought you said you broke up with my father as soon as you found out about him."

"Yes, he left his laptop open when he went for a jog. I came home moments later and saw it. I moved out that night." She tried to take another sip and realized that her mug was empty.

"Okay, so how is it *your* experience?"

"Because I lost my job at the symphony and couldn't find work after that."

"But that doesn't follow. It's not like you can blame *him* for what they did to you."

Again, she ignored him by looking out onto the street. He did as well. Winter had taken the leaves off the trees and dulled the grass, and the white, cloudy sky seemed weighed down with streaks of gray, which resembled ghostly cables. But the well-kept, two-story homes of his suburban neighborhood remained handsome and inviting. The people across the street had recently redesigned theirs, swapping out old gray siding for beige stucco with brown highlights on the doors and windows. Will suddenly had a sense of what he was going to miss if he were to join the No College Club in Virginia. He felt a stab of sadness, one that he was fully prepared to live with for the rest of his life. Two cars drove past; otherwise, the only neighborhood he had ever known was empty and peaceful.

She stood. "I'm going to get some more coffee. Want some?"

He got between her and the front door. "We need to talk about this," he said.

Age had creased his mother's face around her nose and mouth, and the skin beneath her eyes retained some of the redness from the past few days. He knew she was as lovely as ever, despite this.

"Oh, you've gotten so big," she said as she straightened his sweater. "And tall."

"Big and tall, that's me. Can we sit together on the swing? It'll take our weight, won't it?"

"I think so," she said, giving him a guarded smile as they sat down together. Will was hoping she would hold his hand, but she didn't. "It was weird, I admit," she said. "Getting fired like that."

"What happened?"

Melissa shrugged melodramatically. "I broke up with him. I needed a place to stay because our apartment was in his name. And since I couldn't afford a hotel, I crashed at my friend Gal's place."

"Gal?"

"Yes, Gal. That's her name. She's a violist. Still is. Such a talent, too."

A sinking cynicism struck Will as he looked away—an unwelcome feeling he'd been experiencing a lot lately. "And you told her everything."

She nodded. "I was distraught. I was 22, alone in the big city. She was my best friend. Of course, I blabbed to her."

"And then she told the symphony."

"Well, she *said* she didn't."

"Uh-huh," he said skeptically.

"I don't know what happened, but, three days later he was fired. It was kind of a big deal at the time. It even made the local headlines. 'Boston Pops Fires Nazi Musician,' or something like that. He played the tuba. He was the only one they had. It took them weeks to replace him. The story's probably still on the internet. They showed his photograph, his address, everything."

"Looks like history does repeat itself," Will said, as he began searching on his phone. "They didn't do the same to you, did they?"

"No. Thank goodness. They just called me up and fired me, like, a week later."

"Did they give a reason?"

"The director was 'displeased with my performance.' That's all I could get out of them. And I knew it wasn't true because they had recently promoted me to first cello. I tried to appeal, but I couldn't get past Irving's secretary."

"Irving?"

"Irving Kline, the director. He recently retired."

"Oh."

"But I realized something was really wrong when I couldn't find work anywhere else in the city. And not anywhere in New England, not New York City, Albany, Buffalo." She raised the mug to her mouth before remembering that it was empty. "You know, your grandfather was still alive back then, and, sick as he was, he offered to pay for a lawsuit for wrongful firing. I didn't tell him everything, but when I finally told his lawyer, he advised me strongly not to file suit. Because if I did—"

Will looked up from his phone. "Let me guess. The orchestra would put you in the news as well."

"Yep."

"The process is the punishment."

"That's right."

"Speaking of which . . ." he said, holding up his phone to show the news story documenting his father's downfall. "I found it."

Most of the sites Will had found reported only the bare facts and were no longer than three paragraphs. They all said the same thing. Istvan Bіró, a Hungarian national who was the principal tuba player for the Boston Pops Orchestra, was found to have posted racist comments on various "white supremacist" chatrooms under the pseudonym "Van Yarborough." Curiously, these sources did not reprint any of his actual comments. If they offered any photograph at all, it was the Boston Pops' stock photo of a smiling Istvan in a tuxedo posing with his instrument. Will saw the resemblance immediately—in the man's round race, his bright, open eyes, and in the clear heft in his chest and shoulders. Will had an inkling of something he had lacked his entire life. An unfamiliar melancholy made him fidget, causing the swing to move and the chains to creak above them.

One website, however, dedicated full coverage to the incident, complete with sensationalist headline: "POPS SACKS ÜBER TUBIST." This one, which was dated March 27th, 2005, included interviews with the Orchestra president and two conductors, each of whom expressed shock and dismay that one of their principal musicians could do such a thing. The president in particular voiced her profuse regret and promised to redouble the Orchestra's efforts to diversify itself. Generic Anglo-Saxon names such as Sally Henson, Peter Morgan, and Alexander Terrell prevented Will from gleaning the races of the people interviewed—except in the case of an assistant associate director named David Williams, Jr. and a recently hired second violinist named Cathy Crane, whose photos revealed that they were both black. They expressed vindictive anger at Istvan, frustration with the Boston Pops for hiring him in the first place, and a general dissatisfaction with the "racial atmosphere" of the Orchestra.

Unlike the other articles, this one reprinted some of the comments that Biró had made online. These included referring to Muslim immigrants in Europe as "invaders," linking recent grooming gang scandals in England to the Islamic religion, and admiring how the Christian King Béla IV of Hungary had fortified his kingdom against the Mongol hordes in the 13th century. The article included an additional photograph—a candid one—of Biró exiting the concert hall moments after being fired. The image was grainy, and it had been taken from across the street where the photographer must have been waiting for Biró to appear. It revealed little of Istvan's facial features, but his hung head and slumped shoulders vividly captured his bewilderment. In relation to the tuba case he was carrying in his left hand, he seemed like a very big man, just like his son.

"That's him," Melissa said. "We used to call him Van."

"What happened to him?"

She shrugged. "Don't know. I don't think he even knows you exist, Will. I didn't realize I was pregnant until almost a month after this all happened. And by that point he disappeared. I guess he went back to Hungary."

"Did you try to find him?"

"Not very hard. I'm sorry."

"Why not?"

"I was terrified. I was alone, unemployed, and pregnant. And I had broken up with him. I had very little money. Few friends. Gal eventually stopped talking to me. Plus, your grandfather was sick. He'd be dead in a year. If it weren't for your father—I mean, Andrew—I don't know what I would have done. He was the Orchestra librarian, recently divorced, and I knew he liked me. We got along really well. And when I told him how they fired me, he resigned in protest, just like that. For me."

"Wow."

"We weren't even dating, Will," she said assertively. "And after I found out that I was pregnant, he proposed. We passed you off as his, and since we never told our families about Van, nobody was the wiser."

"You were going to tell me eventually, weren't you?"

Melissa sighed. "Eventually, yes. But I just want you to understand why I can't push back too hard against my husband over this. I owe him too much."

Will nodded. "I get it, Mom. And I'm sorry I said you were ditching me."

"It's okay," she said, stroking his hair.

"But—"

"But what?"

"When you say you know from personal experience that I am doing the wrong thing. I don't think that's true."

"Why not?"

"Because what my father said and did . . . was separate from what the Orchestra did to you."

"No, it wasn't."

"My father could have been right or wrong," Will reasoned, "but that didn't give the Orchestra the right to ruin *your* life. You were completely innocent, Mom."

"You and I both know that it doesn't matter if you're innocent."

"It *should* matter, though," he insisted. "This is why I'm not apologizing. I could be right or wrong, but what *they're* doing to me is unjust, just like what they did to you was unjust, and probably to my father too. It makes me wonder who the *real* enemy is."

Melissa closed her eyes tightly for a moment. She patted Will on the knee and stood. "I can't talk about this anymore," she whispered.

"Okay."

She walked toward the front door and then turned to face him, now on the verge of tears. "But no matter what happens, I hope we'll still keep in touch," she said. "I'll send you money and care packages. Maybe I'll even visit if you'll have me." She then rushed back inside before Will could respond.

He fought the urge to follow her inside and embrace her and tell her that everything was going to be all right. He *would* do that. He promised himself that he would. She was his mother, and he loved her dearly, and that would never change. But he wanted to search for something on his phone first. He wanted to know something urgently. It was the Hungarian equivalent of the name William. He found it on his first try:

Vilmos.

Chapter 21

This kid! What am I gonna do with this kid?

Derek Brand had never encountered a more pathetic excuse for an athlete than Will Askew. Sure, he was *nice*. He liked him. Everybody liked him. And after all he had gone through—and was still going through—how could anybody *not* like him? Admire him, even. He was always so cheery and pleasant. He had such a great attitude about his classes and chores. And no matter how hard Derek pushed him on the mat or on their daily runs, the kid always seemed so darned happy to be there. So happy, in fact, that Derek could actually feel relaxed in his presence, which for him did not happen often.

He also knew that if it had been him who'd been maligned like that in front of the whole world—and kicked out of his own home by his own parents—he'd be spitting fire every day of his life. Derek had never quite understood the concept of dueling until he met Will Askew. Afterwards, he imagined himself challenging the kid's loudmouth fake of a father to a duel right there on the wrestling mat. *Black belt in taekwondo—whatever. Let's see how your spinning reverse side kick and your fancy blue pajamas stand up against a double leg takedown and an elbow to the bridge of the nose, which I've drilled, like, seventeen thousand times by now. You won't be posing for pictures and kicking at cameras after I get through with you.*

But this kid, Derek soon discovered, had some deep reservoir of durability which didn't even seem human. He was slow, fat, uncoordinated, and had all the balance of a potato. He couldn't even run one mile without gassing out like a flat tire—even Rose when she was five months pregnant could outdistance him. But one thing he could do was take it. *Oh, boy, could he!* Once when they were sparring, Derek accidentally popped him in the face with a left hook. Since Derek was a converted southpaw, his left hook was his money punch. He threw it hard, too. And what? Nothing. Derek had knocked *Brock* down with that punch. But this kid? He just took it. Didn't whine or call time or anything. He just kept trying to fight.

That was the thing about Will—even after four months with the No College Club he was still *trying* but never *doing*. He would *try* to fight, but was too nice to sit down on his punches or kick anything with bad intentions. He would *try* to keep up with his classes, but always slowed things down with his never-ending need for remedial attention. He would *try* to do calisthenics, but ten pushups was just a bridge too far for him. Three whole sit-ups was his current record, and Derek didn't have the heart to ask him to even try a pull-up. Yes, Will had trimmed down, but he still tipped the scales around 250, which was couch-potato weight and a few pounds over his No College Club limit. Why couldn't he trim the fat? Did he think they'd make an exception for him forever?

The only positive thing Derek could say about Will Askew—aside from somehow raising everybody's morale, including, surprisingly, his own—was that he was turning into a competent farmhand. And, to be fair, Rose had been giving him solid Bs and B-plusses in Agriculture Studies—which was much more than could be said about his performance in Ancient Greek.

One morning, after another 20-minute walkathon mile, Derek was trying for the umpteenth time to teach Will how to throw a head kick. The kid's flexibility wasn't terrible, so being able to augment his fighting arsenal with some leg attacks shouldn't have been too much trouble. But as with almost everything else with this lunkhead, it was. Brock was lifting weights with Matt and another recruit named Tyler, so Derek and Will had the wrestling room to themselves with only the takedown dummies to keep them company. Derek wore a plain gray T-shirt and blue shorts, while Will had on light sweatpants, boxing headgear, and a green, sweat-soaked, extra-large T-shirt with the initials "HHW" emblazoned on it. This had been Brock's attempt at a logo for his High Health Wizards a couple years before, which never caught on. Caroline and Rose berated him at the time for wasting money on merchandise that few had use for—except for Will, who grabbed as much apparel as he could as soon he moved in. It was lost on no one that "HHW" could have also stood for "Heavy-Heavy-Weight."

Derek placed his hands on Will's shoulders to initiate a break in the action. "Will, you need to keep your head off the center line," he exhorted. "You're just asking to be hit!"

"I know! I know!" the kid answered.

"When that punk took a swing at you, you weren't prepared for it, so of course he nailed you."

"Right. You get knocked out by the punch you don't see coming."

"So always know where your opponent is and keep your head on either side of the center line so that never happens again."

"Got it."

"All right," Derek said, stepping forward and throwing a slow, roundhouse right. "What do you do when a man comes at you like this?"

"You grapple," Will said, reaching for Derek's legs. "You take him down."

"Yes, but what if you have to fight on your feet?"

Will stepped back and shifted awkwardly into a fighting stance. "Slip outside. Shoulder roll. Chin tucked. Hands up. Jab! Cross!" he said, throwing punches. "Then kick behind the cross!" Will pulled his kick to Derek's head at the last moment, but he didn't need to. It had been slow enough for Derek to dodge with nearly a second to spare.

"Not bad," Derek said unenthusiastically. "But the most important thing is distance. Touch him, just to keep him away from you. Pop! Right in the face. Pop! Give him something to think about. Make it so he can't even see you. Pop! He's bound to get tired sooner or later. And when you see his shoulders shift for a punch, throw a straight right down the middle. Pop!" Derek landed a couple of light, harmless blows to demonstrate and then glided expertly to his left. "This'll give you space and time to get set. *Then* throw your one-two. *Then* the kick behind it."

"Okay."

"Try again."

Derek started with his overhand right, and Will responded with the same techniques, but compared to Derek's fluid movements, his appeared labored and rudimentary. When it was over, Will lowered his hands to his sides.

"Keep your hands *up!*" Derek commanded, firing a quick left hook to Will's jaw and stopping before it could make contact. "In a fight, you're always in danger. Be aware!"

"But I thought—"

"Don't think!" Derek interrupted. "You're not gonna have time to think. That's why we drill. If you try to think in a real fight, you're dead!"

"Are you coaching him or lecturing him, Derek?" Rose asked. Both turned and saw Rose, plump in her sixth month of pregnancy, holding hands with Little Liam and Little Brock in matching overalls as they toddled into the wrestling room. She wore green pregnancy shorts and a beige V-neck T-shirt. Beside her, Caroline was removing her flannel pajama top to adjust to the heat, causing her long, blonde hair to splay in all directions. Underneath she wore one of Derek's old heavy metal T-shirts, which hung down almost past her denim shorts. All four of them were barefoot.

"Same thing, Rose," Derek said with a smile as the women approached. "You know me."

"I'm taking notes," Will said, tapping his temple. "Up here."

Derek kissed Caroline on the forehead. "Where's Heather?"

"My mom has her."

"Is she eating?"

"It's a struggle, but yes. She was crashed when I left." Caroline looked to Will. "We have news for you, Will."

"Good news?" Will asked.

Caroline smiled. "Mostly. First, Judge Li finally dismissed Peter Dorr's suit against you. It's unlikely they'll appeal."

"That *is* good news."

"Yes, and even better, Judge Stinson has allowed the discovery process to proceed in our defamation lawsuits against the media corporations. We knew he would. This just makes it official."

Will took a deep breath. "Okay. It's getting real."

"And about your father," Caroline continued delicately. "What we—"

Heavy footsteps interrupted her as Brock came barreling in from the weight room in a tank top and shorts, muscles glistening. "Got your text, Rose! Are we finally gonna tell Will about his dad?" he blurted. He stopped short and looked at Will. "Oh, hey, Will! Nice shirt."

Rose rolled her eyes in aggravation. "Brock! 'Tact' is spelled T-A-C-T. Look it up in the dictionary."

"You coulda told me he was here, Rose. Matt, Tyler, and I've been doing dumbbell rows for the last half hour. How was I supposed to know?"

"Maybe you would have known if you weren't such a dumbbell yourself."

Brock smirked. "Come on, Rose. That joke was low-hanging fruit. Do better."

Snickering, Rose picked up Little Brock and handed him to his father. "Here. Maybe your son will beat some sense into you."

"Enough, you guys," Caroline said, smiling despite herself. "So, Will, we finally got in touch with a person who was in Boston when your father lost his job."

"Yeah? What did he say?"

"He thinks he met him at a revisionist history event the year before. He described him as a tall, bearded Hungarian guy, and remembered recognizing him from the news reports. Your father was dating a friend of his before he met your mom. But this friend is no longer in the movement and she wouldn't talk to us."

"Oh, no."

"But she did give our contact an old phone number and address in Hungary where your father might have moved to."

"Really?" Will asked excitedly as he folded his arms close to his chest.

"Yes. We reached out to him, but so far nothing. But we'll keep trying."

"We know a few people in Hungary, Will," Derek added. "When we put the word out—"

"Oh, don't go out of your way for my sake."

Rose gave Will a maternal, scolding look. "*Of course, we will. This is important.*"

"And how many six-and-a-half-foot-tall tuba players are there in Hungary, anyway?" Brock asked as his son tried to yank clumps of hair from his scalp. "He shouldn't be too hard to find." He pried the boy loose and handed him back to his mother.

"Unless he doesn't want to be found," Derek pointed out.

"Derek, don't say that," Rose admonished.

"But it's possible. Will, your father doesn't even know about you, right?"

Will nodded sadly.

"So, there's nothing stopping him if all he wanted to do

was disappear."

Will looked away from all of them. "I appreciate what you guys are doing. But you really don't have to—"

"Yes, we do, Will," Caroline insisted. "This is what we're here for. It's no trouble at all."

The rest of the No College Club quickly seconded this, which made Will blush. He took a moment before deciding what to say. "Derek, do you mind if I hit the showers?"

"Not at all," Derek said, privately regretting that their session was being cut short. There was still so much this kid needed to learn.

"And Rose, do you mind if I ask Samantha to trade shifts with me this afternoon? I'd like to take the rest of the day off, if that's okay. The tomato crop was in pretty good shape the last I left it. I can clean the stables for her tomorrow morning, no problem."

"Sure, Will," Rose said. "Take all the time you need."

"Thanks," he said with a dejected smile as he headed toward the men's locker room.

After Will disappeared, Caroline and Rose glared at Derek, while Brock bent over and guffawed. "And they say *I* lack tact!" he said.

"What?" Derek objected. "I told him the truth!"

"But it's how you said it, Derek," Rose said. "This is a sensitive topic for him."

"Yeah, and the way you always ride him," Brock added. "I don't know . . ."

Derek put his hands on his hips. "What's that supposed to mean?"

"It means we think you're being a little too harsh on him," Caroline said.

"We?"

"Yes, 'we,'" Rose said.

Derek stepped back, realizing he was outnumbered. "I only want what's best for him. That's why I push him so hard!"

"We know," Rose said. "But maybe you're pushing him past his natural pace."

"Yeah. You were yelling at him again this morning because he took a break during our run," Brock added. "I mean, this isn't the army."

"I don't know. He keeps saying his ankle hurts," Derek argued, "but I never see him limp."

"So?"

"I know. That shouldn't matter."

"Derek, even my mom has noticed," Caroline added.

Derek hung his head. "All right, I was out of line. I'm sorry. But ya gotta understand—that footage of Will getting knocked out *haunts* me. I can't get it out of my head. It's *apocalyptic*."

"What do you mean?" Caroline asked.

Derek looked about the room as his mind shifted into high gear. He always felt as if he could see forever whenever mind shifted into high gear. "It's like this kid is a symbol. It's perfect. He's a symbol for white people."

Brock slapped his forehead. "Not this again!"

"Seriously! He's the chipper, undermotivated avatar of the degenerate, enervated remains of the Faustian European spirit!"

"Rose! Make him stop!"

"No! It's perfect!" Derek raved, gesturing wildly. "We all know, as white people, that a big catastrophe is coming our way, and we're not ready for it. We're oblivious. We think everything is going to be just fine! And when it comes, we're gonna get blindsided, just like Will was!"

As Derek began to raise his voice and pepper his rant with profanity, Rose handed Little Brock back to her husband, and then shook Derek by the shoulders. "Derek! Will is not a character in one of your novels! He's a human being!"

"But—"

"Yeah, and screaming in his face until he does five sit-ups won't exactly give us an edge during Ragnarök," Brock added as his son tugged at his eyebrows.

"But—"

"And he's not so chipper. Matt says he gets depressed from time to time."

"But—"

"No 'buts', Derek," Rose said. "You have to lay off!"

Derek looked from Rose to Brock and back again, trying not to smile. "Caroline!" he whined playfully. "Brock and Rose are ganging up on me!"

Caroline stepped up to him and kissed him smartly on the lips. "I can't help you, my love."

"Because you agree with them?"

She stepped away to collect Little Liam who was about to trip over a wrestling dummy. "I do," she said.

Derek held up his hands. "Okay, I give up! I'll put him back on the beginner PT schedule. That oughta ease things up for him."

"Now you're talkin'," Brock said.

"But he still needs to lose weight."

"Yes," Rose said. "But at his pace. We know he's doing his best."

"Okay, fine," Derek said. "I really like the kid, and I didn't realize he was so unhappy here. I'm feeling pretty bad about this. I got a bunch of things I have to take care of in the office. After that, I'll head over to his dorm to apologize and let him know how things are gonna change."

Brock patted him on the shoulder. "I'm sure it'll go fine."

***

Three hours later, Derek strolled over to the dormitories behind the gym, but there was no sign of Will. No one had seen him, despite his car still being parked in the lot. He wasn't answering his phone, and neither Rose, Samantha, nor Matt had seen him on the farm. Caroline's mother Joan hadn't seen him in the house either. The group was about to panic when Caroline received a call from one of the No College Club's local allies. Will had just been spotted entering an ice cream parlor in the center of the nearby town of Sedgewick. He must have walked the three miles by himself or taken a cab.

While guests were not forbidden to enter Sedgewick, they were forbidden from doing so alone and without notifying the No College Club ahead of time. This rule was in place due to the unpopularity of the Club among certain segments of the population. An incident occurring outside Smythe Farm could become a public relations disaster for the Club, and might even result in a trip to the hospital or worse.

Derek sprinted into the house to grab his wallet and keys, and insisted on being the one to bring Will back. *This kid!* he thought to himself as he sped out of the driveway in his black pickup truck. *Now I know why he's not losing weight!*

Chapter 22

The town of Sedgewick, Virginia had made a big impression on Derek when the No College Club established itself four-and-a-half years before. Its well-kept downtown, with its quaint storefronts, local businesses, high-steepled churches, and historical monuments, made the town resemble a time capsule from early in the previous century—something which filled Derek with wonder.

After meeting some of the townsfolk and noting the town's peculiar isolation among hills seemingly at the foot of the Appalachian Mountains, he wrote an alternate-reality short story based on Sedgewick in which a stranger discovers that despite all appearances, the entire town is in fact the grounds of a mysterious hospital. Many years earlier, there had been a plague which affected some people critically and others only mildly. After several years in which the doctors had difficulty managing the disease, the nurses revolted and took charge of the facility, banishing all doctors and abolishing the formal practice of medicine. In its place, they stressed kindness and empathy and implemented various holistic healing methods. Without trained physicians, however, all of the seriously ill patients died of the disease, a fact the nurses kept secret from the other patients. They soon realized that in order to maintain their roles as caregivers they needed to find a way to prevent the surviving patients from ever getting better. Their solution was a miracle drug which hindered the healing process while inducing a burst of euphoria in the patient—but which was lethal in one out of 50 cases.

Enthralled by the drug and unaware of its dangers, the townspeople eventually formed a secretive cult around this cabal of nurses and grew increasingly suspicious of outsiders. To question the nurses' authority or even to attempt to leave the town became a treasonable offense and could result in the death penalty. The townspeople had also grown so accustomed to their persistent illness that they had quite forgotten what it felt like to be healthy.

In the story, the stranger falls in love with a hospital denizen, a beautiful girl, who is asking all the right questions and suspecting there is a better world outside the borders of her blighted town. Together, they learn the town's dark history and plot their escape. But can they avoid the wrath of the nurses? Do they dare tell the people of Sedgewick the truth?

***

Derek knew the ice cream parlor their ally had mentioned—a regional chain which also served coffee, artisanal pastries, and imported candies. It was a popular spot, especially for college students and young families. A half-block from the town's main avenue, it shared a parking lot with a florist and a hardware store. Derek found it full despite not yet being dinner time. He had to parallel park three blocks away along the main avenue—difficult in his large pickup—and then hustle nearly a quarter mile in the warm, humid air. He remembered to put on his baseball cap and sunglasses to help avoid being recognized. He wore the expensive navy-blue polo shirt which Caroline had gotten him for his birthday, but also the same army-surplus shorts, keychain, and work boots he'd always worn. On their page dedicated to the No College Club, the North American Anti-Racism Council website included a recent photograph of him wearing these very items. As he loped across the street toward the ice cream parlor, he was hoping nobody would make the connection.

The brightness inside the restaurant caused Derek's eyes to adjust even though it wasn't dark outside. The place was also cold, with air conditioning rattling through the vents. It resembled a classic American diner with vinyl booths, Formica bar, swivel barstools, and black-and-white checkered floor. Posters featuring 20th-century movies and pop stars decorated the walls, yet a modern pop song streamed from the speakers mounted on the ceiling. Over a prominent banjo, thumping bass, and drum machine, a deep-voiced black woman sang a country/hip-hop fusion number abounding with inapt urban slang and profanity. Derek recognized the song for what it was, and shuddered in revulsion. He wondered moodily if anyone else was as sensitive to these things as he was.

Fortunately, the song soon ended. Once another song followed—this one entirely synthetic, superficial, and harmless—Derek took off his sunglasses and plunged into the crowded parlor in search of Will.

Moments later he spotted him in a striped shirt and shorts seated at the bar. He was chatting with a pretty, waifish blonde girl who was scooping ice cream behind the counter. Before him was a massive sundae, which he had only partially consumed. The girl didn't seem to be waiting on Will, but the way she smiled and laughed when they interacted indicated that something was going on between them. Derek looked carefully to be sure. *The kid has actually found a girlfriend.* He smiled in admiration despite knowing how this would gravely complicate what he had come there to do.

Both became aware of him at once. The girl finished scooping and scuttled away as Will swiveled to face him. "Hey, Derek," he muttered sheepishly.

Derek got close to Will, not wanting to be overheard. He had much to say—about discipline, rules, and the overall purpose of the No College Club. He felt another humorless lecture welling up inside of him, but then stopped short. "I owe you an apology," he said. "I've been too hard on you. We're putting you back on beginner PT."

"It's okay, really," Will said.

"There's no point in pushing you past your limits."

"Oh, you're not—"

"Yeah, we are. I mean *I* am. And I'm sorry for that."

Will sighed deeply, not knowing what to say. "I'm sorry, too. It's just that—" He snaked his eyes to his left, noticing the blonde girl walk past them from behind the counter. "I don't know—It's just . . . I don't know."

"And I'm sorry if I was insensitive this morning about your dad," Derek said, putting his hand on Will's shoulder. "It was not intentional, I promise."

Will nodded gratefully and was about to respond when someone abruptly stepped up to them. It was a middle-aged man of average height, with a paunch, balding head, and flabby neck. He wore a white, ice cream-stained apron over a brown T-shirt bearing the parlor's partially-obscured logo. The restaurant manager, obviously. His lips were tight with indignation. He looked to Derek, and with an arm bristling with tattoos, pointed to the door. "You have to leave now," he commanded with a feminine lilt in his voice.

Derek knew an enemy when he saw one. He also knew the futility of challenging such a person on his home turf in front of at least two dozen strangers, who could become hostile witnesses at any moment. Yes, his civil rights were being violated, but by causing a scene he would be depriving the No College Club of the ability to control its own narrative. Any video of a public altercation would soon reach the news media, which would then use it to slander the Club further—and it wouldn't matter who was right or wrong. Will knew this as well, and was sliding off his stool before Derek could even look at him. They were already walking briskly toward the exit when the manager decided to make a scene of his own.

"I know who you are!" he announced self-righteously. "You are the No College Club! I've seen pictures of you on the internet! You are racists! You are homophobic and transphobic and anti-Semitic and Islamophobic and *atrocious* human beings! I hope you both *die!*"

Everyone in the restaurant suddenly stopped and

stared at Derek and Will. As luck would have it, the synthetic, superficial pop song which had been playing ended at that moment as well, shrouding the restaurant in a mortifying lull of silence and air conditioning. This afforded Derek a moment to size up his tormentor as a man, such as he was. With a growing sneer, he quickly surmised he was soft and spoiled, and would have his mind greatly expanded by a punch in the face. Only a person completely unaccustomed to violence could speak so violently.

A gasp and a crash destroyed the silence. The girl with whom Will had been flirting had dropped a large bowl of ice cream. Her hands trembled on either side of her face as she looked to Will in horror. "You didn't tell me!" she bawled. "Why didn't you tell me?" Wide-eyed and frantic, she looked to her co-workers, three girls—one white, one East Asian, and one whose ethnicity Derek couldn't pinpoint. "I didn't know!" she pleaded. "I never would have gone out with him that one time if I knew!"

Will hung his head and let out a moan that only Derek could hear. Derek caught a glimpse of the anguish on his face. Startled by this sudden transformation, he wondered how he could ever have called this young man chipper. Forgetting all about the manager, who was now sputtering furiously and spicing his ongoing rant with profanity and unimaginative insults, Derek spun Will around by the shoulders and led him outside. The humidity felt like a warm embrace, a sudden relief from the ice-bath air in the restaurant. But Derek knew the relief wouldn't last. Soon, the oppressive outside air would make them sweat clean through their clothing.

"I'm parked a quarter a mile away. Let's run for it," he said as they bounded across the street.

"Okay!"

"And don't make me yell at you again. Go! Go! Go!"

***

The Shackleford mansion was humming with household activity, which through the door of her bedroom sounded to Rose like happiness. *How could anyone be happy at a time like this?* She had worked five hours on the farm that day—a marvel for a woman as pregnant as she was—and was still feeling it in her shoulders, forearms, and back. *Especially* her back. She had also played another exhausting game of hide-and-seek with Liam and Little Brock. There were so many places to hide in their home that they hadn't yet found them all. Then after the scare of Will's disappearance and reappearance in Sedgewick, how could life return to normal so quickly? She knew it had to—but still!

Caroline was in her office on a conference call with the Club's attorneys. Tyler was outside tending to crops. The boys were taking a late nap. *The sweeties played so well together, they deserved it.* Samantha and Joan were in the kitchen minding Heather and preparing dinner, the delicious smells of which were making Rose hungry. But what was Brock doing? Playing video games with Matt in his office! *Of course that's what he was doing!* It was some obnoxious shooter game, too. The bangs and crashes could be heard throughout the house. *At a time like this!*

Rose had just washed her hands, arms, and face and was about to upbraid Brock yet again over his blithe lack of interest in all the important things he should be interested in when Derek finally texted the group. He and Will were on their way home.

She hadn't fathomed how exhausted she was until she collapsed into her easy chair to enjoy her relief. Derek and Will were coming home. Everything was as it should be once again. Suddenly, she didn't want to move or do anything. She didn't even turn off the reading light, which was shining in her eyes. She just felt her body shut down little by little until her chin fell onto her chest in a blissful doze.

She awoke with a gasp, heart racing. *Omigod! Is something wrong? Am I still dreaming? Is it morning? How long was I out?* Through the window she could see it was still daytime. The house was still buzzing with sound, and dinner smelled almost ready. Nothing else seemed to have changed—yet she sensed that something was terribly wrong! She struggled out of her easy chair without disturbing the baby inside of her. The unpleasant tingling in her leg had returned, and she endured a few anxious thoughts of the upcoming delivery while she waited for the sensation to go away. After finding her phone by the foot of the bed, she realized she'd slept for almost 20 minutes. *Derek and Will should be home by now. Where are they? Why didn't they come to the house for dinner?* Running to the window, she saw Derek's truck in the lot and concluded that they must be in Will's dorm.

Rose suddenly entertained unwelcome thoughts of all the things Derek could be saying to Will at that moment. In a flash, she found her shoes by the door, and was hurrying down the hall.

What the No College Club called the dormitories were really just three small off-grid, single-slope, one-room cabins, each equipped with two twin beds, two desks, two dressers, an air-conditioning unit, and a direct-vent propane heater. They stood side-by-side at the end of the parking lot. 20 yards of stone-paved walkway separated them from the gym, where guests accessed bathrooms and showers. Whenever walking past them, Rose often reflected on how hard her brothers had worked to construct them in less than two months. Yet this time she kept her eyes focused on Will's dorm, which was furthest from the gym. She could only imagine the things Derek was saying to him. Soon, though, she didn't have to. She could hear him well enough through the walls.

"You gotta take this seriously, Will! I mean, what are we doin' here? What's the point of life if you're not going to give it your all? Have you been giving it your all, Will? Is sneaking out and eating ice cream giving it your all? You've already broken enough rules for us to expel you. You know that, don't you? We've done it before to others. Why shouldn't we do it to you? What makes you so special?"

Rose's crisp, determined footsteps must have been audible from inside because Derek had stopped haranguing Will by the time she reached the door. Opening it, she saw Will seated at the foot of his bed, hunching forward. His dazed, hopeless expression made her heart burst with sympathy. Derek had been standing over him, and took a step back as she entered the room. She folded her arms, awaiting an explanation.

"He was breaking the rules, Rose," Derek said. "And not for the first time."

"Maybe he has good reasons," she responded.

"All rule breakers think they have good reasons."

"All rule breakers aren't Will, though."

"Guys, I can go home," Will said, his voice husky and raw. "It's okay. Maybe I'm not a good fit here."

"You're not going anywhere!" Rose snapped. "You're family. You're staying. And that's all there is to it."

"Yeah, dude," Derek added. "Why do you think I'm giving you all this extra attention?"

"But you're right, Derek," Will said. "I screwed up. This is my fault. I feel terrible putting you all through this."

"Shush!" Rose commanded, raising a finger at Will like a schoolmarm. She then looked to Derek. "Can you leave us, please?" Despite wording it as a question, it was anything but. Derek understood and reluctantly complied, but not without giving Will a warm pat on the back on his way out.

Placing her hand on his shoulder, Rose kept her eyes fixed on Will until he looked back at her.

"What?" he asked.

"Let it out," she said.

He swallowed hard. "Let what out?"

"*Let. It. Out.*"

He sniffed and looked away, clamping his mouth shut as if forcing himself not to speak.

She leaned over and whispered in his ear. "It's okay, Will. You're home now. Let it out."

Will looked back at Rose and was about to respond when his face began to melt into an expression of exhaustion and despair. He blinked hard and shook his head almost like a tremor as his bloodshot eyes finally overflowed with tears. When the sobbing began, there was no stopping it. He fell into her arms and released all the grief, anguish, and loneliness he had ever felt—and had never stopped feeling.

"It's okay," she whispered. "Let it all out."

Chapter 23

Brock leaned back in the collapsible rocking chair he brought with him everywhere he went. It supposedly had a weight limit of 250 pounds, which he jokingly took to mean that he couldn't travel anywhere for the No College Club unless he stayed south of a deuce and a half. Anyway, who would take him seriously as the President, Chief Executive Officer, and Dictator-for-Life of the High Health Wizards if he stepped in front of audiences looking like he was addicted to French fries, deep dish pizza, and mayonnaise? Not that he could eat any of those things. Fortunately, before he left Virginia two weeks earlier he was tipping the scales at a cool 229. That afternoon, however, just as he was about to slurp down his second 20-ounce, 640-calorie mango-and-banana coconut milk protein smoothie of the day, he estimated that his bloated carcass would veer past 235 if you put him on a scale then and there.

It was bad enough he had acid reflux—or, to be specific, gastroesophageal reflux disease (AKA GERD for the uninitiated). When he had recently turned 29 he discovered the hard way after drinking a glass of milk that he was also lactose intolerant. Who could have seen *that* coming? And those pills designed to help you digest dairy? Might as well be candy for Brock—not that he could eat candy, either, especially the chocolate kind. He couldn't get a break. So it was either consume what he knew his body could handle throughout the day and *not* leer jealously at Will, Fort, Helen, and the others as they feasted like lords over their debauched and voluptuous dinners while he forced down his fennel, arugula, and avocado salads with brown rice, quinoa, couscous, or whatever other high-fiber, low-acid collations Rose insisted he eat—or simply not join them for dinner at all. But that would have been exceedingly bad form. The No College

Club had a job to do in Covington, which was to help renovate the recently-purchased old Northwest Zion chapel.
Although the construction company owned by Rose's
brothers had been contracted to do the work, Brock was
the first banana of the bunch as far as the No College Club
was concerned. He had to be everywhere all at once—or
guess who Rose, Derek, and Caroline would take turns
flogging if anything took a whirl on the old goat rodeo on
his watch? And it's not like Rose ever needed an excuse to
shy away from a good, old-fashioned flogging, anyway.

As Brock was about to take a well-deserved prandial
hiatus after eight hours on the construction site, he noticed a small gathering of pastors exiting the church across
the street. *Churches competing with each other like fast
food restaurants*—there was a joke in there somewhere,
and he vowed to dig up a zinger and lay it on the Club
back home when they least expected it. The paunchy,
gray-haired one in black slacks and a beige blazer was ne-
gotiating intensely with the tall one in the tan suit—and
seemed to be coming in second. Brock squinted to get a
load of the others: a short, slender black man in a royal-
blue jacket with a crucifix hanging from his neck and a
thickset, short-haired white woman in a dark-green cas-
sock, black stole, and white sneakers. The more Brock
squinted at the tall one, the more he suspected he was an
attorney rather than a pastor.

After a moment, the paunchy pastor threw up his
hands and stormed off into the parking lot. Brock wondered if the rainbow flags flying all over the church and
the "Refugees Welcome!" banner hanging over its front
doors had wormed their way into their conversation. As
the pastor approached his car, he noticed the work being
done on the old chapel. He hesitated and then began
striding purposefully across the street like a bully going
the extra mile for his lunch money.

Brock took a big slurp of his smoothie and nudged a

napping Fort, who was seated next to him in a beach chair. "This the guy?" he asked.

Fort stirred and cleared his throat. "Hmm? Yeah. Kevin. A piece of work."

"He's the one who booted Caroline three years ago with that letter from the NAARC?"

"Yep."

"Well, your prediction came true. Here he comes."

"A week early by my estimate. Once they brought in that female pastor, I figured he'd be canceled soon enough. Helen and I know his history. It's a bit sordid."

"Did that lady-pastor have anything to do with all the Technicolor clown makeup I'm seeing over there?"

"Probably. It's all she talks about on social media."

"What do you think he wants from us?"

Fort chuckled. "A job?"

"Well, he's gotta talk to Will, then. He's paying for all of this, the lucky duck."

"Yeah, I was surprised how quickly the TV networks settled with him," Fort said, sitting up in anticipation of Kevin's arrival.

"I was there during the settlement negotiations," Brock said. "Will got a good deal. Maybe he could have held out longer or gone to trial and ended up with more. His defamation case was really strong."

"Yeah, but who wants to drag all that out, you know?"

Fort stood as Kevin stepped carefully across the dusty construction site, and past the temporary fencing, wheelbarrows, sawhorses, ladders, and other equipment left by Rose's brothers, who had recently gone to the stone fabricator to pick up the marble slab for the chapel altar. Fort wore a faded orange polo shirt over green gym shorts, and blue-and-white striped athletic socks under his work boots. Brock shook his head mirthfully, wondering if it was laundry day in the Beaugaard household.

"By the looks of it, I'll probably need to talk to him

alone," Fort said, looking to Brock.

Taking the hint, Brock stood and pointed with his thumb to the chapel behind him. "All right. I'll check on Will and the guys." Heading toward the chapel, he could hear Fort and Kevin bicker even as he slurped his smoothie.

Once out of earshot, he stopped and gazed up at the chapel beneath the calm blue sky of late spring. What a difference three weeks had made! The roof had been repaired, the wood siding had been replaced in spots, and the entire structure painted a medium brown. Brilliant stained glass lit up the windows, and the thin and partially crumbling chimney had been removed. But the crowning achievement had been replacing the cracked, rotting headstock in the belltower with a brand new replica and then hanging the century-old bell from it. That thing was a half-ton beast if it was a pound, Brock remembered. Since they couldn't afford a crane, six burly men, including Brock and Will, had to clear out the tower and raise the old bronze instrument three feet straight up until it could be fastened to its new headstock. Brock had felt the wind ripping menacingly through his shirt in the wide-open belltower, an unsubtle reminder that a 50-foot plummet awaited anyone who might lose his balance while handling that heavy, bulky object. It was one of the most frightening yet exciting things he had ever done.

The endeavor turned out to be entirely symbolic, however. The noise ordinances in Covington prohibited bells of that size from ever being rung. Caroline checked; there was no way around it. Not wanting to call unnecessary attention to itself, the Club simply secured the bell's clapper to its lip to ensure its regrettable silence. Brock smiled sullenly at such a bittersweet accomplishment.

Inside the chapel, Brock found Will at work with a pair of local guys Fort and Helen had recruited. These were near-homeless ex-drug abusers in dingy T-shirts and jeans who were in desperate need of redemption. They were some of the first people to join Fort's new church after he had been ordained that winter—and they worked like dogs. Not only that, they took instruction well—especially from Will, who seemed to be growing into a natural leader. At that moment, he was sanding the beams for the altar, which Brock had helped dry fit earlier that day. One of the guys, Jesse, was sweeping up between the pews, while the other, Cayden, was hauling unused lumber out the back door. Both were of average height, wore short hair and goatees, and were rakishly thin. They looked alike, but telling them apart was easy since Jesse had tattoos on his face but not his neck, and Cayden had tattoos on his neck but not his face. They both smoked like fiends.

Will stopped sanding and looked up at Brock through his goggles, in good spirits as usual. "Hey, Brock!"

"Need me for anything?" Brock asked after taking another slurp from his smoothie.

"I'm good!" Will responded. "We should be ready for the final assembly tomorrow. After that, we're pretty much done."

Brock squinted at Will for a moment just to remind himself that it was really him. The kid had changed so much since the No College Club took him in over three years ago. He had grown another inch and lost over 30 pounds. Derek had finally prevailed in their morning runs, getting him to clock in a perfectly decent 11-minute mile. Last he checked, the kid was doing three sets of ten sit ups every day. Will was also improving in the weight room, having benched his own weight for the first time earlier that year. He had solid grades in all his subjects and excelled most in Rose's agricultural courses. But Brock was struck most by Will's confidence and assertiveness. When he knew he was right, he was never afraid to push back—not against him, Derek, Caroline, or even Rose.

Brock nodded, grateful that the No College Club now

had a true fifth member and not merely a guest in Will. Of all the others who had come around the time he did—Matt, Tyler, and Samantha—he was the only one who stayed. After the windfall from his lawsuits, he could have left the Club and pretty much done whatever he wanted. But no. He stayed on and invested a sizeable portion of his settlement back into the Club. This effectively bankrolled Fort and Helen's church and allowed Rose to bring horses back to Smythe Farm—something for which she and Brock were tremendously grateful. Most importantly, it helped pay for the attorney services and information technology maintenance which helped keep the Club in the fight against its murderer's row of well-funded enemies. Brock was nominally the first banana in Covington, but he could easily see Will assuming that role in future outings. And that was fine with him.

Upon stepping out of the chapel and seeing Fort still squabbling with Kevin, a wickedly brilliant idea occurred to Brock. With Fort indisposed, Rose's brothers not yet back from the fabricator, Helen still out getting dinner, and Will busy constructing the altar, that left little old Brock all alone to enjoy himself some little old me time! And what better way to kill a precious half hour than sitting in front of his laptop playing video games?

Brock smiled like a kid about to skip school as he darted around the chapel and entered through the side entrance. It opened into a small kitchen, which led to a room behind the pulpit called the sacristy. On the first day, Rose's brothers had set up a couple folding tables and claimed it as their *ad hoc* office. But with no one around and with the chapel Wi-Fi chugging out a pristine signal, Brock pulled his laptop from his backpack in the corner of the room, and sat down to play a shooter game he'd been enjoying a lot lately.

But the game required online teammates and opponents. While waiting for others to join, Brock noticed a news item appear on his sidebar. Some female politician whose face he recognized was going to speak that evening at the local state university less than an hour away. He clicked the link and saw a stock photo of a beaming brunette with a pretty smile and a long nose. Brock stared at her with one eye and then the other as he decided whether she was attractive. He could usually adjudicate these matters in seconds, but this woman ran out the clock. Her eyes seemed sweet under her arching eyebrows, but with her splotchy skin and man-jaw, he didn't know what to think.

The headline read "NADINE ALTERMAN TO AN-NOUNCE CONGRESSIONAL BID AT STATE" and jogged unpleasant memories of Will's early days with the Club after he had been humiliated before pretty much the entire world. This Alterman woman had been one of the people shoveling dirt on his grave, and he wasn't even dead yet. Brock felt his chest tighten in anger as he read the story. An undergraduate political group called Critical Justice was co-sponsoring the event. A photo showed another woman, this one younger and with a shock of wavy black hair, standing behind Alterman while she was giving a talk. Cute, if not for the politics, Brock thought. She looked familiar as well, and was not named in the caption or in the article—but appeared in no less than three photos with Alterman. Brock suspected that if anyone knew who this woman was, it would be Will. He'd probably be interested in this story, anyway.

Will popped his head into the sacristy as soon as he got Brock's text. He read the article without much comment and denied knowing who the second brunette was—although they both learned that she was also a member of the university's Indigenous-American student organization, another co-sponsor of the event. Will didn't seem terribly interested, even though it was taking place in the same auditorium where that black kid had sucker-punched him. If Brock remembered correctly, this was also where Will had first met Nadine Alterman when he joined the Critical Theory Club in high school. Will thanked Brock for showing him the article and left pretty quickly, anxious to get back to work. Brock took this as a sign that the kid was finally moving on with his life. Good for him.

Before Brock could start his game, Little Brock and Liam initiated a video call on his laptop. At five years old, the boys were becoming real terrors around the house when it came to stealing cellphones. Brock was thrilled to take the call, of course, and was soon talking kiddie gossip with them, which had both boys in stitches. He forgot all about his video game and his smoothie, which was growing less appetizing the closer it got to room temperature. He sniffed it, made a face in disgust for the benefit of the laughing children, and threw it in the trash.

Fort stepped into the sacristy, looking concerned, which prompted Brock to say good-bye to the boys and end the call.

"Have you seen Will?" Fort asked. "Helen has dinner. Rose's brothers are back as well."

"He was just here. Ya can't find him?"

"No. We looked everywhere. When was he here?"

Brock checked the time on his laptop. "Oh God! It's been over a half hour."

Fort seemed perplexed. "Well, your car's still here. And he's not answering his phone."

Brock stood in alarm. He could hear Jesse, Cayden, and Helen calling for Will outside. "He's not? Where could he have gone?"

"I don't know. It's not like Will to just walk off like that."

"Wait! He did something like that once, years ago."

"Did he leave a note, or—" Fort clapped his hands with realization. "Maybe he texted you!"

Brock swore loudly as he pulled his cellphone from its holster. But to his horror, it was dead. The two then searched frantically for a charger in the cluttered sacristy. After finding one in Fort's satchel, they had to wait one nervewracking minute for the phone to switch on. During this time, Helen, Jesse, Cayden, and Rose's brothers appeared, wondering what was going on. In front of the entire crew, Brock turned on his phone and read aloud Will's cryptic text:

"Brock, I have something I need 2do. Taking cab. Don't call pls. Hopefully see you at Fort and Helen's 2nite."

Everyone stared at each other, dumbfounded, until the ringtone on Brock's phone crashed the silence. It was a call from Caroline. Brock's heart sank. She couldn't have called at a worse time. But why was she was even calling him at all? She almost *never* called him. Their one-on-one communication remained almost exclusively within the Club's group chat. Regardless of this—and whatever Caroline wanted to tell him—Brock knew that in the next few moments he would have to painfully admit that Will Askew, the No College Club's star recruit and benefactor, has disappeared into thin air on his watch. *On his watch!*

Welcome back to Brock Gabler's famous goat rodeo! May the flogging begin!

Chapter 24

Will went down to the Bernice Lefkowitz Memorial Auditorium for what he hoped would be the final time. Again, he was forced to walk past orange flagging tape, piles of bricks, safety cones, and dormant machinery. After three years, the building which housed the auditorium was still under construction—or *de*-construction, as Will remembered. Yes, he understood the joke now, and could identify all the equipment on the construction site: a front-loader, a backhoe, a winch machine, aluminum scaffolding. He could go on.

Stepping into the semicircular plaza, he realized that the building's architects had missed an opportunity. The plaza could easily have been fashioned in the style of an ancient Greek amphitheater, with steps doubling as seats and a stage in the center instead of metal benches and tables. The auditorium's front doors were almost buried in shadow below a long, top-heavy metal cladding facade, which reminded Will of an angry unibrow holding up a shock of unkempt hair. He hadn't considered how ugly the building was until that moment—the result of having studied Ancient Greek architecture with that taskmaster Derek. Will had never felt terribly comfortable in Derek's presence back home, but whenever he was out in the world, he couldn't help but adopt Derek's perspective on things—and heed his many lessons. Will knew that turning off his phone and shielding the No College Club from what he was about to do had been the right decision. He laughed to himself, realizing that the one time he sincerely did not want to visit the Lefkowitz Auditorium was the one time he had shown up early. Over an hour early.

The patient crowd of students waiting by the doors was about half white—similar to Will's high school except with more piercings and tattoos. From their conversations, he surmised that most were sympathetic to Nadine

Alterman but were not as well informed about her as he was. He was gratified to read on the flyer that the event was open to the public, and so took his place in line with only about 20 students ahead of him. He had left the chapel in Covington so quickly that he hadn't had time to change out of his work clothes—cargo shorts, boots, and a long-sleeve T-shirt—and so stood like a dusty behemoth among his would-be peers. With the construction site so close by, he felt he fit in better than they did. This allowed him to enjoy the languid spring breezes and the hazy sun slipping behind the leafy trees surrounding the university's gothic stone buildings. Despite it all, he knew it remained a wonderful world.

He felt the familiar tightness in his gut as his stomach rumbled. He hadn't eaten since lunch, and it was now past six. He was tempted to find a vending machine or gift shop where he could purchase a snack, but didn't want to lose his place in line. Regardless, he wasn't seriously tempted. Living the farm life for so long had weaned him off processed, mass-marketed foods, which were invariably filled with high-fructose corn syrup, trans fats, preservatives, and other useless things his body no longer craved. This, as well as running two miles each morning (thank you, Derek!), had contributed to his drastic weight loss, which now made him appear almost normal.

Was something still a little *off* about Will Askew? At a clean-cut six-foot, five inches and 220 pounds, he suspected not—but it wasn't for him to say. He had promised himself to abandon his stepfather's last name and assume a new one. But which one? His mother's? His *father's*? His father's full name was Istvan Biró, with Biró meaning "judge" in Hungarian. Having still not discovered the man's whereabouts, Will could not decide.

During the hour-long wait, there had been no sign of Nadine Alterman or Connie Craft, who Will estimated must be a junior by now. In spite of what she had done to him, he still thought about her occasionally and wondered how she was doing. That evening, would he encounter the real Connie Craft, the first girl—and so far the only girl— he had ever loved? Or the weak, corrupted, manipulative thing who let callous and self-serving people define who she was? Either way, he had to stop her. If she wanted to live a lie, that was her business. But he could not allow her to promote the political career of this Alterman woman. Nadine Alterman was the enemy, he knew, and a formidable one at that. He hoped that Connie had not turned into one as well.

When the doors opened, Will claimed a seat near the stage and then headed for the bathrooms, once again noticing the darkened projection booth jutting over the back of the auditorium. Moments later, as he shuffled back through the buzzing crowd, he kept an eye out for Connie, but could not spot her. Was she even going to be there? Being so tall, he had a good view, and so scanned every corner of the room as he walked slowly back to his seat. He knew he was taking the risk of being recognized, given his high-profile fall from grace years earlier. Fortunately, the passage of time and 70 pounds had made a significant difference in his appearance. No one seemed to recognize him.

Will returned to his seat and tried unsuccessfully to relax and not think about what he was about to do. But with Connie arriving soon, his mind was hopping on hot coals considering all the possibilities. After another ten minutes, four women, including Nadine and Connie, finally appeared onstage. He leaned forward to get a clearer look while the audience applauded. Alterman, in a green jacket, white blouse, and black skirt stepped confidently in front of the other women. She hadn't changed at all, he noted, but Connie certainly had. She had slimmed down, and like him had continued growing. She was nearly as tall as Nadine. She wore a teal cardigan long-sleeved sweater over a light patterned blouse and blue slacks. Will was struck by how grownup she looked as she beamed broadly and waved to people she knew in the crowd. The only thing that hadn't changed about her, it seemed, was her hair, which was as black, wavy, and lovely as ever. Waiting for them were four sofa chairs with small tables between them, upon which sat glasses and pitchers of water. After the ladies got comfortable in their seats and the applause died down, Connie began to speak.

"Welcome, everyone! Welcome, all!" she announced. Her voice was deeper and more confident than he remembered it. Could a mere three years have made such a difference? Or was this just another affectation? "On behalf of Critical Justice, the Indigenous Peoples Student Alliance, the Black Student Union, and the LGBTQ-plus community, we would like to welcome you to this once-in-a-lifetime opportunity to meet with a great force of change in American politics, Nadine Alterman, our next representative in the United States House of Representatives!"

Will stood amid the tumultuous applause. Others were standing as well, but he was the only one who had stepped out into an aisle. He couldn't bear listening to another word of what he knew were outrageous lies coming from a person he once cared about. "Connie!" he shouted. "Connie! Don't do this! I'm begging you, don't do this!"

The women onstage peered into the crowd, trying to assess the disturbance. They were unclear of what was happening and what to do about it, with one woman grasping the armrests of her chair as if about to bolt for safety. The crowd began to hiss and murmur as this six-and-a-half-foot-tall heckler continued to harangue one of their speakers.

"Connie, you know this is wrong!" Will went on, ignoring the two female students attempting to usher him to the door. "I know your secret! You are not who you say you are! Leave this stage now or I'll tell everyone the truth about you!"

As the speakers stood and Nadine Alterman called for security, Connie finally recognized him. "*Will*?" she cried in disbelief.

"Connie, this is wrong!" he repeated urgently, pointing to Nadine. "It's immoral and dishonest for you to promote this woman who you yourself said was evil!"

A sharp gasp from the crowd was followed by one from Connie. "Omigod!" she whispered, now hopping about and tugging on Nadine's sleeve. "We have to call security now!"

As Nadine called again for security and began apologizing to the crowd, Will easily freed himself from the two students trying to eject him and looked to the projection booth. "Okay, I warned you!" he said. As if on cue, the lights dimmed as a giant movie screen descended behind the stage. Video was already being projecting on it. The speakers' microphones cut off and were replaced by the video's soundtrack. Onscreen, two teenaged kids, a girl and a boy, were kneeling on a gravel driveway beside a dented sedan covered in bumper stickers. The inebriated girl had just gotten sick, and the boy was comforting her. She was asking him to do something.

"Please, Will? My mom and, like, all my friends, are expecting me to get this scholarship! Alterman herself told me I'm a shoo-in!"

"Wait, what?" the boy said.

The girl sat up as the camera zoomed in on her face. Despite the tears and the redness, it was impossible not to notice that this was a young Connie Craft, the very woman onstage who was watching along in horror. "Nadine told me in secret that they already picked the three winners. Me and two people of color from Covington. All we have left are our presentations."

"You mean the scholarship competition is rigged?" the

boy asked, incredulous.

By its groans and exclamations, Will could tell the audience was catching on. A few people even looked back at him to check his resemblance to the boy in the video. Fortunately most were still watching the video itself, or Connie as she melted down onstage. "Turn it off!" she pleaded, now in hysterics, "Someone please *turn it off!*"

Onscreen, the pair continued their intimate talk as the audience began to grow impatient. Will looked apprehensively to the projection booth from which he could hear loud banging. It seemed people were trying to break into it.

The crowd hushed as the conversation between Connie and Will took an unexpected turn.

"I *hate* CRT," young Connie admitted, wiping her eyes. "It's all spite and lies and jealousy."

"I know. That's why I want nothing to do with it," the boy responded.

"But they're sucking me in, Will! I feel like I'm losing my soul."

"Your—?"

"They only love me because they think I'm half Indian. But I'm not that smart. I plagiarized most of my essay, Will, and they don't care. These people are evil! Especially Alterman! They just want some pretty *Indian* girl to be the face of the future. And it's a *scary* future! I hear them talk about it all the time!"

"How is it scary?"

"The things Alterman wants to do to whites and Christians . . . She hates them. She really does! And she tells me all this because she thinks I'm Indian. But I'm not!"

At this, Connie yelped in despair and fled the stage amid a torrent of tears. Nadine was too mortified by what was unfolding onscreen to stop her.

"I'm as white as you are, Will!" young Connie admitted to the gasps of the crowd. "My dad was some stupid German guy, probably a Nazi. He knocked my mom up in a youth hostel when she was backpacking in Europe. Then he disappeared. That's my story. That's the truth."

The footage then cut to the image of a menacing pink-and-black cobra, the logo of a popular internet video streaming channel. Speaking beside it was the channel's creator, a chubby white man with round eyes, a feminine demeanor, and unnaturally orange hair. The tattoo on his neck perfectly matched his channel's logo. "How about that, Cobra Tat!" he exclaimed, "Documenting the decline of America, one wasted college student at a time. Smack the bell and give a like, or click the link below to sub-scribe!"

As the crowd voiced its frustration, a disconcerted Nadine attempted to restore calm. But it was too late. The audience was no longer interested in anything she had to say, and began its disorganized push to the exits—all this as campus security finally arrived and began rooting through the crush in search of Will. Amid the confusion, he was nowhere to be found.

***

Will worried that his heavy footsteps up the stairs might be heard by campus security. His boots were big—size 15—and it was difficult to do anything discreetly with them. He was entering the older section of the building, the university's Film and Television Studies Department, which was undergoing construction outside. The floors were uncarpeted and grungy, the classroom doors were scratched and battered, and the lighting a bright yet sickly yellow.

He turned a corner and stopped short, spotting the person he was looking for.

"My God, Will! Is that you?"

JD stepped into the hall from a classroom with a back-pack over his shoulders. He wore sneakers, tan shorts, and a black T-shirt with a skeleton-faced, bunny-eared monster on the front. He had gained some weight in his belly, as well as some solid muscle in his arms and shoulders. His eyes were as insolent as ever, but his thin face was neither acne-scarred nor scruffy. Above his lips, however, was something entirely new—a thin, wispy mustache. Tied into a tight ball above his head was a manbun.

"JD!" Will exclaimed as he ran up to his friend.

"You must have grown, like, three inches!" JD said.

"And you grew a mustache!"

"And you lost weight!"

"And is that a manbun?"

Together they said, "*Dude!*" as they exchanged hugs.

"We'd better go," JD said. "They're gonna be looking for us!"

"Us? You mean me."

"No. Me, too. I'll probably get expelled for this."

"What?"

"I'm a film major, Will. I practically live in this building. I'm one of three people on campus who has keys to the projection booth. It won't take much deductive reasoning to figure out who locked the doors when that video started playing."

"JD, I'm sorry! I had no idea—"

"Oh, please," JD said as they rushed down the hall toward the stairs. "I'm the one who should be apologizing. I'm sorry for what I did to you!"

"It's okay."

"Will, my mom and the school put me under so much pressure. You have no idea."

"JD, it's fine."

"My mom couldn't afford to send me here. You know that right? But she was so desperate for me to denounce you, Will, that she promised to send me here if I did. She even got a second mortgage on—"

"Really. It's okay."

They stopped by the stairwell door at the end of the hall. "But now that I'm *in* college, I realized that you were right all along!" JD said, grasping Will's shirt. "The people here are insane! They are left-wing, group-thinking mid-wits who have completely taken over the university. They don't tolerate dissent, and they don't like white people. And, Will, I swear to God, the students are worse than the professors!"

"I'm aware of that," Will admitted sadly as they burst through the door and began descending the stairs.

"So, when you texted me, boy, was I ready to help! You think the No College Club has room for a dashingly hand-some audio-visual technician who still intends to be the greatest filmmaker ever?"

"Absolutely. How's Uncle Gus?"

"Hanging in there. I'm working my way through his li-brary. For 40 years the guy was a rock star dissident and never told anyone!"

"We should visit him again."

"I would love that!"

"And how did you find the video of me and Connie? Was my description helpful?"

"Of Cobra Tat? Yeah. His channel is famous. It took me 15 minutes to find your video. The guy graduated a couple years ago. He's working as a scriptwriter in Hollywood now. I just didn't know that he was a she."

"I didn't know that she was a he."

"Sign of the times, baby," JD said as they reached the first floor and burst through the door to the construction site. "Sign of the times."

Before them was what Will had seen only at a distance up to that point—the piles of bricks, the safety cones, the traffic drums, the machinery, the orange flagging tape. It was getting darker, but was still bright enough for him to notice the uneven ground all around them. But the one thing he hadn't noticed before was a chain-link fence surrounding the site. "How are we gonna get out of here?" he asked.

"We'll have to climb," JD said.

Will pointed to an opening in the fence to their right. "Look!"

JD swore triumphantly. "We're gonna get you out of here yet! I'm parked at the library, which is in that direction. Come on!"

They were about to pass through the fence when Will spotted a group of people standing behind the building, as if to avoid notice. Looking closer, he realized that in the center of the group and staring directly back at him was Connie Craft.

Chapter 25

"Ah, yeah. No, Will. No," JD warned, waving his hands. "Bad idea."

"I just wanna talk with her," Will said.

"Look what happened last time! No!"

"But she needs help, JD!"

"Help? She's beyond help! If you're looking for a redemption arc on this chick, we're *way* past that expiration date, buddy!"

"How do you know that?"

"She's in charge of, like, three different left-wing organizations in school, Will. She's infamous!"

"But I doxed her."

"So?"

"I could have ruined her life," Will argued, now stepping toward Connie. "I gotta apologize."

JD pushed back against Will's massive body until his sneakers slid in the dirt. "Apologize? Trust me on this one, Will. You are the *last* person on the planet who should be apologizing to anyone!"

"Oh, come on. That's not true," Will said, gently trying to push past his diminutive friend. "I think I really hurt her back there."

"Will! I can't believe you're doing this!" JD exclaimed, now growing desperate and pointing to the fence opening. "Freedom is that way! I can see my car from here. If we run, we make it in 30 seconds! We'll be home free!"

"But I feel bad. I gotta talk to her."

"They're gonna arrest you!" JD cried, now in full panic.

"I know. I know," Will said, now finally getting past his friend. "But I need to make things right with Connie. That's more important."

"Dude!" JD cried helplessly.

Will ignored him and approached Connie, who was surrounded by four women, all of whom were giving him withering stares. He didn't look at any of them, focusing only on Connie. She backed away from him, looking hurt and vulnerable. He could see it in her transparent blue eyes. If anything, she had grown more beautiful and more bewitching since he'd last seen her.

"Connie, I'm sorry it had to be this way," he began. "I didn't mean to hurt you, and I hope you can recover from this. I just want you to know there's no hard feelings, and if there is anything I can do for you, to help you—uh . . ."

Stepping to within a couple feet of her, Will began to notice how much she had changed. He remembered her face being rounder, more baby-like. Her eyes were harder than before, with that defiant pout now seeming more like a sneer. And the way her body was shifting told him that she was about to throw a kick at him. He had seen it many times in the gym and was well prepared to deflect it before her foot had even left the ground. It was a groin strike. A cheap shot. He swatted her leg aside and stepped back, realizing how wrong he had been about her. Again, he should have listened to JD. There was no saving this girl, Will realized. She was gone.

Her eyes narrowed in rage as she charged at him, screaming insults and profanities. As her flailing punches landed harmlessly on his arms and shoulders, he defended himself while making sure not to hurt her. He caught her right wrist and then her left forearm and was about to push her away when he heard footsteps behind him. Heavy footsteps.

"Uh, Will?" JD said, sounding worried.

Will noticed Connie's four friends stepping back. Connie broke free from him and backed off as well. He had barely enough time to turn before he could see what was coming. He couldn't believe it. It was happening again! He saw the bald brown head, then the shirtsleeve, then the clenched fist, then the pinky ring. This time, however, he knew to keep his head off the center line. He knew how to slip punches and use his footwork. He knew how to react and then to act. But was this the same guy as before? It *couldn't* be!

The punch ricocheted off Will's shoulder and landed squarely against his temple. It rang his cranium like a bell. Just like three years earlier, reality confused itself with unreality. Colors washed out, darkness flashed brilliantly, and silence blared as Will struggled with his wayward legs to keep his tall body upright. Again, a marching band of lizards and bats and panda bears paraded through his mind.

As captivating as all this was, he had experienced it before. He knew the following act was oblivion, and was determined never to go there again. He slipped the next two punches without realizing it. His hands were up protecting his face even though he couldn't remember putting them there. Will was having difficulty moving on the uneven ground, and this afforded his attacker the freedom to whale on his arms and shoulders with hard, wide shots. Unlike Connie's blows, these hurt. Coming so hard and fast from such a big, powerful man, they had deadly intent.

"Get him, Quentin!" Connie screamed. "Get him!"

So it *was* the same guy, Will realized. He remembered that this Quentin St. James person had accepted a football scholarship at State, where they were right now—so it made sense that he would be on campus. But what was he doing behind the film school building? Did he know Connie? Were they part of the same political groups? Were they currently in a relationship?

Fortunately for Will, Quentin switched tactics and began to grapple. This gave Will time to recover from the blow he had absorbed and to finally respond in earnest. He sprawled his long body against Quentin's takedown attempt, snapped Quentin's head down, and spun around behind him as he had drilled so many times before. After this, he achieved wrist control and drove his man face first into the dirt. Quentin made an energetic attempt to throw Will off of him, but Will's balance and timing was too sound. As with the bandana-wearing gunman on Uncle Gus's driveway, Will forced Quentin flat to the ground every time he got to his knees.

Will had the stamina to keep this up for another several minutes, which, given the wheezing he was beginning to hear from Quentin, would most likely be sufficient time for the police to arrive. Connie, however, introduced an unwelcome wrinkle into this plan when she leapt on top of Will and started pulling his hair and pummeling the back of his head, all while letting loose with her usual litany of insults and profanities. She may have lost weight, but she was still a tall girl, and had a lot of pent-up bad intentions, apparently. Will did his best to avoid her blows, but many were landing. This was making it difficult for him to control the raging football player beneath him, who was beginning to get his second wind. She was also repeatedly calling Quentin by name, which settled the question in Will's mind of whether they were in a relationship.

"Don't worry, Will!" JD screamed. "I'm comin'!"

Will didn't know what his friend had in mind until he felt him land on top of Connie. For several moments, the four of them struggled, grunted, punched, and flailed in what could only be described as a wriggling battle royal dogpile with legs. In the middle of the tottering melee, Will detected that a crowd was forming around them, taunting them and egging them on. No doubt all of this would soon go viral, Will thought—if hadn't already. But where was campus security? Where were the police?

"Ya know, Will?" JD shouted. "I get the feeling we look pretty ridiculous right about now!"

"Yeah, ya think?" Will answered.

Quentin St. James finally decided to end matters once

and for all. Perhaps he was growing tired of having all these white people laying on him like babbling blankets. With tremendous effort, he lurched one way, then the other, and then the other until all came toppling down. Will was relieved. This stupid confrontation was finally over. But as he got to his feet, he discovered that it wasn't over at all. Quentin St. James, with fists clenched and teeth bared, would see to it that it be over only when he said it was.

Quentin threw a roundhouse right, which Will saw coming. Will rolled his shoulders and tucked his chin, and slipped it to the outside, just as Derek had taught him. He then stepped back, assumed a fighting stance, and fed a pair of sharp left jabs into Quentin's face. Pop! Pop! This put some distance between them, and every time his man tried to bridge the gap—Pop! Pop! Every time he lunged in with a punch—Pop! Pop! Will kept his head off the center line and kept moving laterally, making himself difficult to hit cleanly. Pop! Pop! He dearly wished not to turn this into a slugfest in which either he or his opponent would risk serious injury.

Despite his skilled efforts, however, the uneven ground, the piles of bricks, and his heavy work boots were making this game he was playing especially dangerous. It was tiring him out as well. Even worse, he was running out of space on the construction site. Quentin was slowly bullying him toward the building where he would have little room to move and less to escape.

Behind Quentin, Will saw that things weren't faring any better for JD. His hands were clasped from behind around Connie's waist as she reached around to grab his manbun. Together they spun like a whirling dervish as Connie tried to punch him in the head and JD tried to keep his face hidden between her shoulder blades. Ridiculous didn't even begin to describe what Will was seeing.

Another near-miss from Quentin redirected his attention to where it needed to be and convinced him to end this altercation then and there, one way or the other. With only inches separating him from the building's steps, Will waited for Quentin to move his shoulders, signaling that he was about take another swing, and then rudely interrupted him with a spear of a right hand down the middle. He threw it hard, with all the force his arm, hips, and legs could muster. Pop! This stood his surprised opponent straight up, with his hands dangling vulnerably at his sides. Without thinking, Will stepped in and threw his one-two, his left-right combination, with both blows landing. This stunned Quentin further and forced him back a step—still with his hands dangerously low. This gave Will plenty of target from which to choose. He threw his kick behind the right as hard as he could, just as Derek had taught him. He threw it to the head.

Quentin St. James never saw it coming. Will's shin collided with the left side of his jaw, momentarily disfiguring his face as spit, blood, and sweat flew in all directions. Quentin was unconscious before he even began falling—and when he did, he folded in half almost like a jackknife and landed face-first in the dirt.

At that exact moment, Connie had finally freed herself from JD's grasp. After spinning him around while keeping a tight grip on his manbun, she wound up and punched him straight in the face, sending him on an ungainly, off-balance swerve toward the fence. Seeing his friend's distress, Will ran over to help him, but this distraction caused him to get hit by the one blow he did not see coming that evening. It wasn't a punch, though. He understood this important distinction at the very last moment. It was a strong, violent shove. And Connie gave it all she had. With a pile of bricks close by, the force of her shove caused him to trip over a large one which was embedded in the dirt. This sent him reeling toward the fence in the direction of JD, who was lying on his back. Being a foot taller and nearly a hundred pounds heavier than his di-minutive friend, Will did not want to crash into him, and so spun away and landed awkwardly on his right ankle.

Even with three years of training in wrestling and mar-tial arts, Will did not think to roll his body to remove the pressure on his ankle as he struck the ground. No one could ever have accused him of being nimble. His ankle snapped under his considerable weight—crack!—and the rest of him flopped gracelessly against the planet like flopping bodies always do.

The Willrus strikes again!

He knew instantly what had happened. And the pain! He felt pain like he had never felt pain before. There was nothing to insulate him from it as it shot like electric ra-zors through his entire body—his perfectly normal and healthy body. He groaned through gritted teeth and streaming tears until he realized that he was laughing. He was actually laughing.

He tried to sit up, but JD crawled over and gently kept him down. "Don't look at it, dude," he said. "Don't look at it."

"Is it bad?"

"Oh, yeah. I think you invented a new angle in geome-try. The cops are here, by the way. They're calling an am-bulance."

"About time," Will said, noticing his friend's swollen black eye. "You all right?"

"Of course, I am, you doofus. Why are you laughing?"

"Because it hurts, JD! It really hurts!"

"That bad, huh?"

"Yeah," Will laughed. "That bad."

Chapter 26

The police had handcuffed Will's wrist to a bed in the recovery room of the university hospital. Sky-blue curtains separated the beds in the long, uncarpeted, brightly lit room. Fortunately, the x-ray had revealed a simple fracture, but considering Will's size and weight, and the fact that this was his ankle's second break, the emergency room physician had opted for a cast rather than a walking boot. Shortly after it was applied it was already itching underneath. But at least by that point the pain had whittled itself down to a thin, unpleasant tingle. Will had laughed at the pain, yes, but he didn't miss it when it was gone.

The police officer who had arrested him was waiting in the hall outside. As soon as Will received medical clearance from the physician, he would be taken to the police station, where he would be officially charged with disturbing the peace—just like all the other participants in the fighting—and jailed until he could appear before a judge for his bail hearing. Maybe then he would call the No College Club and tell them what had happened. With video of the incident going viral and appearing on newscasts that evening, however, he had a feeling that they already knew.

From the other patients in the emergency room who were watching on their cellphones, Will gathered that he had pulled off something of a public relations coup. The news coverage seemed less slanted this time, and more focused on the sensation of the same event essentially happening twice—but with opposite outcomes. While it was recalled that Will was the racist high school student who had said blasphemous things about black people three years earlier, this time the news commentators could not ignore the ample video evidence proving that he had been attacked four times by two people—twice from behind—and was merely defending himself throughout.

They also grudgingly admired Will's fighting technique as well as that peach of a head kick which laid out Quentin St. James. One newscaster had even commented approvingly on his dramatic weight loss. This made Will chuckle cynically to himself. *Everybody loves a winner.*

As he waited in his hospital bed for his release, Will had no doubt he would be exonerated. The issue was entirely black and white—regardless of the pun—and had just about resolved itself when Quentin St. James came to after a minute and was perfectly responsive to the paramedics. Most rewardingly for Will, the exposure was proving harmful to Nadine Alterman and her political ambitions. The Cobra Tat video had received nearly two million views so far that evening. It was being reported that Nadine's campaign was attempting damage control while pointedly avoiding questions about their candidate's alleged hatred for whites and Christians. Despite their obvious sympathies for Nadine, several newscasters were already claiming that this incident was placing her campaign for the US House of Representatives in dire jeopardy. Predictably, Alterman herself was unavailable for comment.

Since Will had spent most of his time after the fight either on his back or on a wheeled stretcher, he never had the chance to see Connie Craft being led away in handcuffs, crying and begging shamelessly for leniency. JD had found it funny, but Will could only sadly shake his head. He couldn't help it. He still felt sorry for the poor girl. She was the first person to ever make him feel like a complete human being. It was a debt he felt he could never repay. And like him, she had never known her true father. Will wondered about all the ways this could damage a person from the inside.

As for JD, he apologized once again and promised to be his friend forever, just as he had done on that fateful night when this adventure began over three years before. He was embracing Will and spilling tears on his shirt when the police pulled him away. Will cried a little himself, insulated from neither the dreadful circumstances they were sharing, nor the thrill of having the best friend he ever had back in his life once again.

Despite the room's brightness, and the constant footsteps of the sneakered nurses, and the loud hum of the air conditioning and the muffled bleeps and blips of electronic equipment, Will gradually grew drowsy. It was past eleven pm, and he hadn't eaten since noon. He felt his energy deserting him with each breath. So sweet it would be to simply close his eyes. He felt himself nod several times before entering that ambiguous half-space between dreams and the waking life. What was happening? What would his future be like? With so much pain coming his way as a dissident and member of the No College Club—and with nothing to protect himself from it—could he survive? He missed his mother. He missed his childhood. Would there be a day when he'd miss his innocence as well? A day when he would have to sacrifice something true about himself just to keep away the pain? Wasn't there anything that could give him comfort by mooring him to what's firm and constant? He was still so young—was there no one who could link him to the past and guide him to the future?

He heard footsteps. Was this his dream? These weren't sneakers—they were too loud and sharp. Too heavy. This wasn't a nurse. Who was it? Was someone coming here to save him? In life, does it ever work out like that?

"Will?"

A voice. Deep and masculine. One he had never heard before. The inflection curling the end of his name sounded strange as well.

"Will?"

Who is this? Who comes to me?

"Will?"

Why? Why do you come see me?
"Will!"
Why have you waited so long?
"Vilmos."

Will's eyes burst open. With a sudden gasp, he leaned forward in dry-mouthed, heart-bursting fright as his dreams skidded to a halt. Or did they? Who was this person? Breathing more rapidly than he ever thought possible, Will looked up and gazed in awe at this large presence approaching, looming ever so high above him. Was this death? Was this life? Was this a dream?

It was a man. A tall, broad-shouldered man in black jeans, a battered black leather jacket, and a dark-red shirt which was unbuttoned almost halfway down his chest. A full face of stubble lay siege to his well-trimmed beard. His long straight brown hair was combed neatly down to his shoulders. He seemed middled-aged and tired, with bags under his eyes, small flabs of skin protruding from his cheeks, and excess weight around his neck and belly. His reddish, aquiline nose suggested a recent struggle with a cold. Above his left hand was the biggest wristwatch Will had ever seen.

The stranger's eyes were clear and discerning. Will looked into them and saw something he knew, something he had seen many times before whenever he looked in a mirror. He knew this man, he realized. He asked the question anyway, but he knew. He knew.

"Dad?"